BULL CITY BLUES

Ryan McKaig

Sawtooth Valley Publishing
Copyright © 2016 Ryan McKaig
All rights reserved.
ISBN-10: 0692722661
ISBN-13: 9780692722664

DEDICATED TO THE MEMORY OF MARJORIE BRAMAN

CHAPTER ONE

YOU KNOW you've been in the crime business awhile when you can look at gruesome murder scene pictures and eat Krispy Kreme doughnuts at the same time.

We were in Stuart Roth's law office. He was sitting behind his large oak desk and I was sitting in one of the chairs across from him. We had the pictures and the rest of the discovery file spread out on his desk. After awhile, Roth looked up at me like he was waiting for me to say something, so I did.

"She knew him."

"You're sure about that?"

"Definitely."

"How do you know?"

"Strangulation. No forced entry. No 911 call. She's in her bed. She's covered up. Yeah, she knew him."

"What do you think she was strangled with?"

I spread the pictures out on the table and pointed to the red ligature marks on her throat.

"Looks like some sort of a cord to me."

I pointed to her eyes, where you could see the busted capillaries in the corneas and reddish spots of petechiae on the skin above her cheekbones.

Roth got up out of his high backed leather chair and walked over and looked out the window down West Main Street. Outside, the sky was the color of nails and sheets of rain hammered down on the street five floors below. Roth was wearing gray suit pants and a starched white shirt with a red tie. His jacket was folded over the back of his chair. He turned away from the window and looked back at me. He said, "I didn't want to hear that she knew him. I want him to be a stranger. Come back when you've got something better."

"I thought you wanted the truth," I said.

"Not if it incriminates my client, I don't."

"I can't change the facts."

"I thought you said this boy was innocent."

"I still think he is."

Roth walked back and stood over the table and looked at the pictures again. He held his palms out and said, "Well who then?"

"Hell if I know."

I reached down and picked up the box of doughnuts at my feet and put it on top of the pictures, opened the box, reached in for a chocolate glazed doughnut and took a bite of it. Roth pushed the box to the side and, sitting down, studied the pictures.

"The DNA from the semen matches our client?" he asked.

"That's what the lab report says."

"You don't believe it?"

"It's probably right," I said. "They were dating. Why wouldn't the semen match his DNA?"

"You brought me this case," Roth said. "You vouched for this kid. But you haven't given me anything except shit about Mexicans and drugs dealers. I don't mind losing a case, Egan, but I'd rather not do it on TV and look like an asshole."

2

I crossed my legs and picked at the threads coming loose at the bottom of my jeans. I said: "No such thing as bad press, right? Besides, I've known this kid since he was in diapers. Never known him to be violent. At least not outside the ring."

"That's it?" he said. "That's all you got?"

"I've got some interesting stuff on Mexicans and drug dealers too."

Roth leaned back in his chair. He laced his fingers together and put them behind his head and reclined, letting his eyes wander to the ceiling. I sank down in my chair. I had thrown my gray tweed jacket on the couch behind me when I came in and I sat there wearing jeans, cowboy boots, and a black Harley Davidson t-shirt that exposed the bottom of the skull tattoo on my right bicep. I looked down at the Latin inscription under the skull, which said: "I shall never die."

I had a Smith & Wesson .38 caliber snub nose wheelgun in a small holster on the left side of my belt. Most people wore their gun on the same side as their dominant shooting hand, but I was never comfortable drawing and firing from my right side. They say you lose valuable seconds from cross drawing, but I always figured if I didn't have enough time to cross draw in a gun fight, I didn't have enough time period.

"In my business, we only got four cards to play," Roth said. "Four." He put his right hand out with four fingers showing.

"Number one is the guy didn't do it because somebody else did it. Number two is the guy might have done something but not the thing he's charged with. Number three he did it but there's some excuse that lessens his culpability. Maybe he caught his wife banging the plumber and killed both of them before he had a chance to cool off. Number four is he's crazy as a shit house rat. I'm seeing this as a number three, at best."

I took a sip of my coffee. "We're still trying to put it all together," I said.

Roth said, "None of the evidence we've seen so far is any good to us."

"We still don't know what happened that night," I said. "The cops don't either.'

"We know Sheryl Rose is dead. We know she was strangled. We know our client's semen was inside her. We know we don't have anybody else to blame. That's a lot we know, right there."

I nodded. "I didn't say what we know isn't bad."

"Bad?" he said.

"Yeah."

"Bad is when I do a line of coke off a stripper's thigh and then can't get it up and there's some hot naked girl lying there going to waste and I've paid to fuck her," he said. "This is fucking horrible."

"We don't know what we don't know," I said.

"That's it? You find things out for a living and that's what you give me?"

"I give you what I've got when I've got it," I said.

"And you don't buy that it was probably your boy?"

"No, I don't."

"What about this am I missing?" Roth said. "What about the fact that his blood came back positive for Winstrol and elevated levels of testosterone?"

"Boxing's a dirty business," I said. "If the other guys are doing it, Ray'd be stupid not to."

"Look," Roth said. "The way I see it is this. Best case scenario, I'm talking about. She said or did something to set him off. Made him madder than shit. Maybe she was fucking another guy. Maybe she didn't want to see him anymore. Maybe she made fun of him for having a crooked dick. Whatever. He's hopped up on juice, he loses his shit and grabs her by the neck."

"Could have gone down that way," I said.

"Maybe he doesn't realize his own strength or how little pressure and time it takes to kill a woman. Maybe she dies before he comes to his senses. Maybe he panics and runs. Or hell, maybe she's into kinky sex and that's what they were doing and it went too far. The ME's report doesn't say anything about vaginal tearing, so whatever it was, the semen got there consensually."

"Maybe he fucked her and left and then she ordered a pizza and the pizza guy choked her for giving him a shitty tip," I said.

Roth ignored me and got up and started pacing. "A jury might buy that. A killing in the heat of passion gets us down to murder two. Voluntary manslaughter if we get real lucky. An accidental killing gets us all the way to down to involuntary. That's hitting the fucking lottery on these facts. But if we go for an instruction on a lesser included, he's got to take the stand and tell the jury what really happened."

"He still swears he didn't do it," I said.

"You need to reel him in, Egan. If we go for manslaughter, the burden is on us to put on the evidence for it. The only way we do that is through his testimony."

"Maybe somebody else did it and we're looking at it all wrong," I said.

"There's no jury that's going to buy that unless we give them another suspect," Roth said. "Hell, they may even want to fry this kid. I mean, they saw this girl on the news every night. She came into their homes and tucked them into bed. She woke them up in the morning. They felt like they knew her."

"Have they said anything about going for death?" I said.

"No, but they will," Roth said. "This prosecutor always threatens to play the death card. Sometimes it's a little game we play. He shakes his death stick at them and scares them into taking a plea to life without parole. If I don't have any chance of winning, I help him do that. Other times, he does it just to be a dick."

"This isn't a death case and he knows it," I said.

"You try telling him that. There's a bunch of cameras outside his office. The media wants to see a public hanging. He's an elected official. You do the fucking math."

I flipped through the file and skimmed the reports. I said: "This all the discovery?"

"Everything I got so far."

"I'll make a copy of the file and take it home with me."

"Good," he said. "See if you can find something in there that helps us."

"I'll see what I can do."

I took out another doughnut and bit into it. It was covered in powdered sugar and had a strawberry filling that was just revolting.

"Jesus Christ that's terrible," I said.

I put it back in the box and closed the box and pushed it away from me. I reached for my coffee and washed the rancid strawberry taste out of my mouth.

"You got anything good in court today?" I said.

"Got another masturbator at the Dollar General," Roth said.

"What is it about people jacking off at the dollar store?"

"I don't know. But that's where they always go."

I shook my head.

"Perverts are weird," Roth said. "That's what makes them perverts."

Roth put on his coat and straightened his tie. He said, "You got any big plans for the weekend?"

"I got an AA meeting tonight," I said.

"What the hell are you talking about?"

"Mondays and Thursdays," I said. "We meet over at the New Hope Baptist Church."

"You drink all the time," he said. "You were drinking beer at lunch yesterday."

"Yeah, but they have good stories there. It's like a comedy club with crying and hugging."

I remembered my first AA meeting. I assumed it would be an hour of depressing stories and lectures about the dangers of drinking. I was surprised at the amount of laughter. Stupid drunk stories really are the best.

"That's an odd hobby," Roth said.

"I went for real for a little while."

"Didn't work?"

"I decided I'd rather drink than be in a cult."

"Why do you go now?"

"I think the kids call it trolling," I said.

"Do you pick up chips?"

"Oh yeah. Why not?"

"Because it's a lie," he said.

I laughed and thought about telling Roth about the shoebox full of chips I had. They made great poker chips.

"It's just something I do."

"Do you ever share with the group?"

"When they call on me."

"What do you say?"

"Whatever I think up at the time," I said. "Last time I said I was at Myrtle Beach one time and got so drunk that I pretended to be a Scottish golf caddie and used the fake accent to pick up this girl in a bar and took her back to my hotel and got a blow job out of her. In the morning I'd forgot I'd done it and woke up speaking with a southern accent. I said that she called the cops on me but the cops said you couldn't rape somebody with a lie. Everybody laughed at that."

"Do you go after you've been drinking?" Roth said.

"Sometimes I drink while I'm there."

That was a lie. I always drink when I'm there. Vodka and pink lemonade.

"You're a strange person," he said. "You know that?"

"I'm so awesome I should wear a cape," I said.

Roth shook his head and picked up his briefcase.

"I'm a student of human nature," I said. "I like details. Like the dollar store thing. Details tell you a lot about people."

"Do you troll churches too?"

"Hell no."

"Why not?" he said.

I looked at him like he was crazy. "What if God turns out to be a real thing?" I said.

CHAPTER TWO

I TOOK OUT my yellow legal pad and flipped to the page where I'd written "Interesting Shit" at the top. It said: "1) Mexicans getting robbed. 2) Bernard Little."

I sat in front of the computer at Roth's desk. He'd gone to court to deal with the dollar store masturbator. It had stopped raining, but the gray sky become darker, and all I could see outside was the mist. The cars passing on Main Street, the lights of The Pinhook, the old concrete fortress of the courthouse—all were invisible to me. They tolled away quietly in the dead afternoon hours.

I pulled up the Youtube video of Sheryl Rose profiling our client, Ray. I saw her standing in front of the Bull City Boxing Club with a microphone in her hand. She had a petite frame and straight brown hair and a pretty young face. She had this innocence in her eyes. Watching her, I wished I could go back in time to the moment that she sent her resume to the television station, and tell her that Durham kills and eats people like her. She was in her early twenties, about the same age as Ray, and she looked like she enjoyed what she was doing.

"They call him the Bull City Wrecking Ball," she said. The video cut to Ray strafing Curtis Moncrief with left hooks to the body and head. I remembered watching the fight live at Dorton Arena, which is an ancient building on the fairgrounds in Raleigh. It looks like what the Roman Coliseum would have looked like if it was built by Southern bureaucrats in the 1950's and then smashed by an asteroid. It has two sides rising up where the seats are and a collapsed middle reaching all the way down to the stage. In the video, Ray had Moncrief on the ropes and was hitting him at will until the referee pushed his way in and stopped it. Moncrief looked relieved when the referee stepped in between them and stopped him from being hit by more of Ray's thudding left hooks. Watching it live, I remembered the sounds of the punches landing. I remembered Norman Mailer's line about punches sounding like an ax chopping into a wet log. That's what it sounded like.

The video cut to a shot of Ray working the focus mitts with his dad, then cut to a close up of him hitting the speed bag with his hands wrapped in white tape. Sheryl Rose's voice played over the footage. "Ray Marks, Jr., was born right here in Durham and graduated from Hillside High School, where he was a standout on the football field. The son of a former amateur boxer and Durham police detective, Marks is making a name for himself in the world of professional prizefighting." The voiceover dropped off and the video cut to a shot of Ray telling Rose about himself. He was standing in front of the ring and his face was dripping with sweat.

"Fighting is my passion," he said. "It takes lots of hard work and dedication, but it's what I was born to do."

The video cut to shots of Ray lifting weights and doing pushups and jogging through Duke Gardens. "I get up at five, five thirty every morning," he said. "Run five miles. Come back home. Sleep another hour or two. Then I get up and go to the gym. That's when the work really begins."

"What motivates you?" Sheryl Rose said.

"I grew up watching my dad fight. Wanting to be like him. I'm always pushing myself to get better. I want to make a name for myself and represent Durham as best I can in and out of the ring."

The video cut to Sheryl Rose standing back out in the parking lot in front of the gym. "When he's not training or demolishing opponents in the ring, Marks attends Durham Technical Community College part time studying criminal justice," she said. "His teachers describe him as a quiet but conscientious student and say he's a good role model in the classroom. His dream is to be middleweight champion of the world and he's well on his way to getting that coveted shot. His professional record? Eighteen wins and zero losses, with fourteen knockouts. Ten of those knockouts came in the very first round."

It cut back to the anchor desk.

"He sounds like he's doing a good job staying grounded in spite of his growing fame," the anchorman said.

"He is," Sheryl Rose said. "He even admits to being shy in front of the camera. But in the ring, he's a terror to his opponents."

I pulled up the Youtube video of the initial news report of the murder. The anchorman sat behind the desk with a grave expression on his face and a black ribbon on his lapel.

"It is with heavy hearts tonight that we bring you our top story," he said. "Sheryl Rose, who came into your living rooms every night as a reporter for this station, was found dead this morning in her townhouse near the Duke University campus. Police believe she was murdered."

I clicked to another clip. "More tonight on the murder of WRDU's own Sheryl Rose," the anchorman said. The female anchor, who wasn't bad looking, took over. "Police haven't named any suspects in the slaying, which occurred sometime between Thursday night and Friday morning, but WRDU has learned that investigators are focusing their attention on Durham-based professional boxer Raymond Marks, Jr. Sources say the two started dating after Rose did a feature on Marks two months ago. Police haven't released any details about the crime and Marks has not been named a suspect or a person of interest in the case, but Durham Police Chief David Jaggers had this to say today when asked about the case: 'It is one of the most brutal, senseless killings I've seen since I started with this department more than thirty years ago.' Marks's father, Raymond Marks, Sr., was a Durham police detective for eighteen years. Calls to the family's home were not returned and when a reporter knocked on the family's door, no one answered."

I clicked off the video and sat there thinking. I remembered when I was transferred from Vice to Major Crimes. I remembered how much pressure they put on us to solve murders, especially when they had the media on their ass. I remembered how much I hated having to empathize with the killers to understand their motives so that I could interrogate them. A lot of times, I just wanted to beat them to death with my bare hands.

But as a student of human nature, I knew that criminals were just like everybody else and that their crimes repeated the same patterns over and over again. If you followed the patterns, there was usually a certain logic to it and that logic pointed you where you needed to go. There was never much surprise involved. Most criminals were just idiots and garden variety nuisances. They aren't trying to be bad people. They just lack average intelligence and self-control. I always want to tell them to just stop it. That the only good in their efforts is in the entertainment value I get from watching them fail.

Suspects in homicide cases are usually more intelligent than the District Court regulars and most of them aren't inherently evil people. A lot of them are just people who've snapped and done something they can't take back. Most of them end up crying and confessing within a couple of hours. Confessing gives them relief and makes them feel better and it was my job as a homicide detective to coach them there.

Psychopaths are very rare. They never confess. It doesn't matter what evidence you have against them or what you bluff them with. They know the difference between right and wrong and they actually get off on making other people suffer. Some of them are even highly intelligent.

Ray was certainly not a psychopath. I knew him well enough to know that. But he hadn't confessed either. I watched the video of Detective Fields interrogating Ray and what I saw was a confused and terrified kid being manipulated and bullied.

Fields had tried all the tricks. He'd left Ray waiting alone in the interview room while the detectives watched him fidget and squirm.

After two hours, Fields finally came in and started with the compassion and empathy phase. He told Ray he understood how things sometimes got out of hand and that it could happen to anybody. He told him that you could be a good person and make a mistake you didn't mean to make.

"I'm just trying to help you, son," Fields said. "I know you're not evil. I know you feel bad about it. I know you want to tell me what happened. I can see it. I can see it in your eyes." Fields was good at his job.

Ray just sat there and cried and said over and over again that he didn't do anything. Fields stood up and shook his head like a disappointed father and walked out of the room.

He let Ray squirm for another two hours, then came at him with the ticking clock phase. "They got a rush order on the DNA from the crime scene," he said. "They did a rape kit and found semen. If that semen comes back to you, you could be looking at the needle. Once it goes to the DA, there's nothing I can do to help you. You need to tell me the truth. This is your only chance to help yourself."

Usually at this point in the process, the suspect starts to talk and tell you lies. But the lies are helpful because they have details that you can use later to trap the person. Ray kept insisting that he didn't know what happened. Fields got up and left the room again.

After another hour and a half wait, Fields busted into the room and started the bluffing and bullying phase. He slammed a blown-up picture of Sheryl Rose's dead face onto the table in front of Ray and then got right up in Ray's face: "It's truth telling time, mother-fucker," he said. "Look at me, boy."

Ray just looked down and sobbed.

"I know your daddy," Fields said. "All of us do. He's a good man. Can you imagine how he's going to feel when he finds out his only son is nothing but a piece of shit murderer? Can you even fucking imagine what this is going do to your mama? Cause that's the only story they're going to hear, Ray. That's the only story you've given us. You haven't given us one reason to think you feel the slightest bit of remorse for what you did. Sitting here, I don't see nothing but self-pity. We got a name for that, boy: stone cold killer."

Fields tapped his fingers on the table and went in for the kill: "There's a surveillance camera showing the only door to that townhouse."

He studied Ray's reaction. "Didn't know that, did you?" he said. "And ain't but one person went in and came out during the time that girl was killed. And you know who that person was?"

Ray just continued to sob. "I didn't do it," he said. "I swear to fucking God I didn't."

"Videotape don't lie, son. The windows were all locked. From the inside. You got something to tell me now?"

"I want to see my daddy," Ray said.

Fields got up and walked out of the room again. He made sure to leave the picture of Sheryl Rose's dead face on the table in front of Ray. Ray turned away from it and kept sobbing.

I stopped the tape. I didn't need to see anymore. Roth would figure out what was admissible and what wasn't but it didn't really matter. Ray never broke down, never told them anything.

That was unusual. If he was guilty, he would have done what they all did and either confessed or tried to talk his way out of it with some bullshit story. But he didn't do either of those things, which meant that he was either innocent or he had no remorse whatsoever. I knew the kid well enough to know that he had a conscience.

I had read the discovery packet several times. The police report was typical and the forensic report wasn't anything particularly unusual, although it did tell me that other fingerprints were found in the bedroom that police couldn't identify. It also told me that there was no foreign DNA found under Sheryl Rose's fingernails. It was clear she had been strangled, but it didn't look like she'd fought back. A strangulation victim usually left marks on her own neck from trying to pry the killer's hands away or loosen the cord.

The cell phone logs were the most interesting thing. I cross checked the phone numbers and could account for most of them. There were calls to and from the news station, calls to various numbers in a south Florida area code, which I figured were calls to her family and friends, calls to the bank and the utility companies, and calls to various takeout places nearby.

She began calling Ray a few days before she interviewed him. I assumed those calls were to confirm times and places and to get background information. The calls to Ray's number stopped after the interview. Then they started again a little over a week later and when they started again, a pattern began to emerge. She called him every couple of days at first. Then the calls became more frequent. On the day she died, she called Ray early in the morning and twice in the afternoon. He called her at 5:06 that night and that was the last call between them.

But there were other calls that interested me. There was one number in particular. The logs showed the calls going back and forth between Rose's phone and that number all the time. Mornings, afternoons, evenings. Even sometimes late at night. The police would probably tell me it was a friend or relative, but I still wanted to run it down. The calls didn't start until several months before she was killed. Either an old contact had changed cell numbers or she had made a new friend. I wanted to know which one it was. There was nothing about the calls in the police report.

Under "Interesting Shit," I wrote: 3) Didn't confess. 4) She didn't fight back. 5) Mystery caller.

CHAPTER THREE

RODNEY JACKSON was wearing a white shirt with a blue tie and black crocodile boots. He had his tie pulled down and he was wearing his sunglasses on top of his shaved head. He was on his second beer when I sat down across from him.

The Kells was nearly empty but I knew it would fill up as soon as the day shift cops got off work. Jackson was the only detective in Major Crimes who would still talk to me. When they fired me, it was like a high school couple breaking up. Everybody had to choose sides and only one side was paying their salaries. Jackson didn't give a fuck. None of them had to balls to be a dick to him about it, at least not to his face.

I'd been persona non grata in the Durham PD's office for going on six months now after having a major disagreement with the brass over the handling of the investigation of a serial killer named Charles Lee Newsome. He killed young women by stabbing them in the head. He liked doing it. We knew who he was. We knew where he was. We even had an informant who told us all about him. She was a young girl named Sarah Olsen. She was a sixteen year old runaway who had fallen in love with a member of Newsome's crew. His crew cooked meth and sold it through trailer dwelling rednecks in the rural part of the county.

They were all teenagers except for Newsome, who was twenty one years old and their undisputed leader. Sarah heard the others talking about the murders and came to see me. She was a naïve and sweet kid who had grown up with no brothers or sisters. Her father died in a construction accident when she was nine and her mother was a waitress and an alcoholic. She thought she'd found a family with her new boyfriend and his friends, although she was terrified of Charles Lee Newsome. She didn't know that the rest of them were basically the Manson family.

We had enough for an arrest. We even had Newsome on a supermarket surveillance tape walking out of the store thirty seconds after one of the victims left. But the mayor was facing a tough reelection bid and Chief Jaggers wanted more. He wanted an airtight case, complete with accomplice charges against the rest of Newsome's crew. He wanted them all talking about the murders on tape so that they wouldn't have any choice but to plead guilty and testify at Newsome's death penalty trial.

I told him it was too dangerous to put Sarah back in with them, but he insisted on putting a wire on her and sending her back in there to get a confession. He wanted them on tape laughing about the murders. Despite my better judgment, I promised her that she'd be safe. But she was a nervous kid, and she inevitably said and did things that raised their suspicions.

Newsome had her boyfriend lure her to the woods behind a Food Lion grocery store, where she thought she was going to smoke a joint. Newsome was waiting for her there and he stabbed her sixteen times. I was listening on the wire in a nearby car. I sensed that something was off and I radioed the other detectives on standby and said it was time to go in, but Jaggers told me to stand down. I ignored him and got out of the car and ran as fast as I could.

When I got there, I found Newsome standing there laughing. He put his hands up and said, "Go on, arrest me." I shot him in the face.

About twenty feet away, I found Sarah still alive and crawling out of a ditch, blood trailing her like a bridal gown. I gathered her in my arms and felt her body heaving against me. She died in my arms with this helpless look in her eyes, like she didn't want to die but was sorry for inconveniencing me. I watched her as her eyes went from looking at me to looking at nothing.

I still saw her dead eyes staring into mine, night after night, staring at me through the space in my dreams. I wanted to tell her I was sorry but I couldn't tell her anything because she was dead. I was left living with the fact that I'd gambled with her life and lost. I made a promise to myself that I'd never let myself be pushed into compromising my principles or my judgment ever again, and this promise meant the end of my career as a homicide detective with the Durham Police Department.

The chief said he was going to put me in for a commendation. I told him I didn't want any goddamn commendation. He said that she was just a runaway and a meth head and that she would be dead in a year or two anyway and that I shouldn't worry about it. I punched him in the face and knocked him down.

He didn't demand my badge and gun on the spot because he still had an interest in keeping the public in the dark about the whole botched investigation, and without the threat of being fired, I was a loose cannon and potentially dangerous to the mayor's political ambitions and the chief's.

That concern ended when I told the whole story to the Durham Herald and the paper printed it in a front page expose. The mayor was reelected anyway and the chief got a raise. The guys in Major Crimes had laughed when I punched out the chief, but they considered it an act of betrayal when I went to the press. I was fired several hours after the story hit the newsstands. After that, Jackson was my only friend on the force.

"Well if it isn't John Egan, world famous private eye. I heard it doesn't look good for your friend," Jackson said.

"Tell me about it," I said.

"What's Roth say?"

"What do you think?"

"All I know is what he says on TV. Everybody is innocent on TV and we're either incompetent or a bunch of goddamn liars."

"You know that's not what he says in private," I said.

"I figured not," he said. "Roth is a lot of things but stupid ain't one of them. I don't got nothing against him. A lot of the guys do, but not me. We all got our roles to play. If I killed somebody, I'd want him defending me."

"His business isn't any different than ours," I said. "They're all guilty. Most all of them, anyway."

Jackson took a sip of his beer and called out to the bartender: "Hey Mickey, send Michelle over here when she gets a chance." Michelle heard him and finished wiping down the bar and came over.

"Whatever he wants," Jackson said. "Put it on my tab."

"Blue Moon draft," I said.

"Tall one or short one."

"I don't want to make a terrible mistake," I said. "Better make it a tall one."

"Orange or no orange?"

"I don't care."

She left and Jackson put his beer down. "That's a girl beer, you know?"

"I don't care."

"You listen to faggoty music," he said. "You might as well drink a faggoty beer."

"I'm comfortable with who I am," I said.

Jackson yawned and rubbed his eyes. He said, "I got into some shit last night."

"Oh yeah?"

"Yeah," he said. "It was my friend's bachelor party. Guy from college. You don't know him. Anyway, we end up at the strip club and you know how they do at the strip club. This girl named Justice comes over and asks me if I'll buy her a drink."

"Justice?"

"Yeah. I thought that was funny too."

"She asks me what I do and I tell her I'm a cage fighter. She calls bullshit on that and finally somebody tells her I'm a cop. Then she starts coming on to me real hot and heavy. She takes me in the back and really puts it on me."

"Hell yeah," I said.

Strip clubs in Durham aren't like strip clubs in most other cities. For a hundred and fifty bucks, you can get pretty much whatever you want.

"God, before I knew it she was asking me to go home with her," Jackson said. "Now, what's the number one rule of the strip club?"

"Leave the strippers there."

"Exactly. They're like polar bears. They're cute to look at in their natural environment but you don't want to be alone with one."

"You fucked her, didn't you?"

"Man, I was drunk as hell. We'd been drinking since I got off work at noon. I'm talking brown liquor drinking."

"So you went home with her?"

"I did."

"How'd that turn out?"

"She rolled a joint and smoked it right in front of me. I didn't say shit, because what the fuck do I care? I'm murder police. She told me she was naughty and that I should arrest her for breaking the law."

"What'd you do?"

"I don't remember, exactly. But I woke up naked next to her and one of her hands was cuffed to the bedpost."

I took a drink and looked around the bar. It was beginning to fill up with cops who had just finished their shifts and were ready to drink.

"Sounds like a good night."

"She kissed me goodbye and gave me her number, so I guess she liked it, whatever it was."

"Jesus, I've been in a monogamous relationship too long," I said.

"I'm too old to be doing shit like that," he said.

"But you don't regret it, do you?"

Jackson started laughing. "No I do not."

"What happened to your friends?"

"They went to some rave club, I think."

"I hate those places."

"Me too."

The waitress brought my beer and said, "Ain't seen you in a while."

"I been busy being good," I said.

"I know that's some bullshit," she said, and walked back over to the bar. I began drinking my beer. I put it down when I saw two men walking toward our table. I recognized them as Greg Fields and Brian Hampton, two of my former colleagues in Major Crimes. They had been sitting at a table across the room with detectives Mark Jester and Richie Hunter. Neither one of them took a seat.

"The fuck you doing here?" Fields said. "This is a cop bar. Not a bar for people who shit all over cops' work."

Fields was a big guy with an explosive temper. He'd played defensive tackle for East Carolina and was very proud of this fact. He came across as a loud meathead jock right out of central casting. He was especially obnoxious when he was drank. I worked with him in Vice and was happy to get away from him when I transferred to Major Crimes. But I got stuck with him again six months later when he transferred in. Fields was the kind of guy the bosses loved. He took orders and carried them out with enthusiasm. He was a real by-the-book prick.

Hampton wasn't so bad. He was a decent enough guy if you were alone with him, but he had one fatal character flaw: he thought Fields was really, really cool.

I looked up at Fields. He was standing there with his chest out and his hands on his hips.

I said, "I'm glad to see you rocking that detective's shield. I was so happy for you when they got rid of the spelling test."

Jackson started laughing and Fields just got madder. He took a step closer to me.

"You got a big fucking mouth," he said. "You know that?"

"I said the same thing to your sister once," I said. "How's she doing by the way? I never called her again."

"Fuck you, Egan. You think you can cross the street with that ambulance chasing motherfucker and still come in here?"

"Obviously I do," I said. "I'm here, aren't I?"

"Calm down, Fields," Jackson said. "You're drunk."

"What are you doing hanging out with this prick?"

"He's my friend."

"You got shitty taste in friends."

"I don't like being bored," Jackson said. "What can I say?"

Fields looked back at me and said: "You ain't welcome in here, asshole."

"I'm not welcome lots of places," I said. "I don't take it personally."

"The force is better off without pieces of shit like you. I'm not surprised the chief fired your fucking ass."

"I'm surprised he hasn't made you deputy chief yet," I said. I looked at him and then shook my head. "No, I guess a politician like him is smart enough to keep his toadies down in their holes."

Fields stood over me and said, "What did you say?"

"I said, in a manner of speaking, that you are an errand boy for a hack politician. It's a shame I have to spell it out like that for you. A smarter man could have read between the lines."

"Step outside and say that shit to my face, asshole."

I smiled and took a sip of my beer. Jackson stood up and tried to get between us. "We don't need any of that shit here," he said.

"No," Fields said. "This motherfucker comes into my bar talking shit about my work. Saying shit about my sister. You stay out of this, Rodney."

"I'm just trying to help you out here, Greg."

"I don't need no help."

"You're making a mistake."

Fields jerked his thumb toward the door. "Outside, motherfucker. If you got the balls."

I followed Fields and Hampton outside to the parking lot. Jackson followed behind us. I took off my coat and handed it to Jackson. Fields took off his tie and gave it to Hampton. He unbuttoned the top button of his shirt and rolled up his sleeves.

"You really want to do this?" I said.

"What, you pussying out?" he said.

"Just checking."

"It's time somebody did something about you, boy," Fields said.

"One thing you should know," I said. "My mom was half Mexican."

"The fuck's that supposed to mean?"

"It means you're not just representing yourself and the force, but all white people everywhere. So try not to embarrass them."

We began circling each other. Fields put his hands up and I could tell from his stance and the way he held his hands that he'd taken some mixed martial arts classes. He had a striker's pose. I studied his footwork. It was terrible. His feet were always too close together or too far apart. I figured he would be easy to knock down. I put my fists up and my left foot forward and moved my head slightly to the right so that he wouldn't have a straight line of attack on me. A crowd of cops and bar girls had come outside to watch the fight.

I smiled at Fields and said: "Come on. You wanted to swap licks in the mouth. Let's get to it."

Fields came forward and I turned my body to narrow the angle. He lunged at me with a right to the head and I tucked my chin and rolled the punch off my left shoulder. I felt his fist go over the top of my head. I planted my left foot and turned my hips and leveraged all my power into a left hook to his liver. Fields sank to the ground and doubled over in pain. People started laughing.

I stood over him and said, "Take as much time as you need, buddyrow."

Fields struggled to get up and I could tell he was still in pain from the liver shot. He was breathing hard now. He put his hands back up and came at me again, this time with a left hook. I ducked under it, caught his left arm and pulled him toward me, then hit him in the jaw with two quick uppercuts. Then I pushed him back and waited for him to come forward again. When he did, I planted my right foot and hit him in the mouth with a straight right hand. He would have fallen on me if I hadn't moved out of his way. Hampton rushed over to help him.

"My daddy used to always say the fight's over when a man falls forward," somebody said.

Two uniformed cops pulled up to where we were standing and got out of their patrol car. The cop in the passenger's seat had his baton in his right hand. They must have been new because I didn't recognize either of them from Patrol.

"What's going on here?" the cop with the baton said.

"Just cops versus ex-cops," Jackson said. "Don't worry about it. It sorted itself out."

"That's assault on an officer, Sergeant," the patrolman said.

"Not if the officer started it," Jackson said.

"We need to take witness statements," the patrolman said.

"I don't think Greg will want any of this in a report," Jackson said. "It's embarrassing enough as it is."

The patrolman looked around the crowd and saw heads nodding in agreement. He pointed his baton at Fields and said, "He started it?"

Jackson nodded.

The patrolman looked at me and said, "Are you pressing charges?"

"Naw," I said. "I'm good."

CHAPTER FOUR

I BLEW OFF the AA meeting when Jill called and said she wanted to get some dinner. I told her to come by my apartment after work. I stopped off at the grocery store and bought some chicken breasts and couscous and three bottles of red wine. I went home and turned on a Don Giovanni performance from the Met and escaped into the thundering overture.

As a kid of the 80's and early 90's, my musical tastes had once been confined to bands like R.E.M., U2, Smashing Pumpkins, and Jane's Addiction. Later, I learned to appreciate opera. I resisted it at first, even made fun of it, but I eventually came to love Mozart, Beethoven, and Bach.

I learned about Mozart and how he told the priests and the patrons to go fuck themselves then stamped his place in history by creating some of the most stirring music known to man. When I listened to his music, really listened to it, I didn't just hear it, I felt it. It went through me like an earthquake. I felt something moving in my soul. It lifted my heart in ways no music ever had before and I understood now why his music, like all great art, would never die.

Jill loved it too. She had been raised on it. On our second date, she took me to her house and played for me Mozart's Requiem and explained that he had written it, knowing he was knocking on death's door at age 36, as his own funeral dirge. I had heard some of his music before, but I couldn't name any of it. Listening to it, I was lowered to the depths of despair, so low that I could feel the hellfire burning my fingers and my toes. Then the movement changed and I was raised into a state of panic and then lowered, softly, into a state of calm acceptance, as if I was fading out into that darkness myself. And then, at the very end, I could hear the drum, the heartbeat of life returning and triumphing. Of humanity outlasting, transcending, and defeating death, and in that moment, I came to understand love, time, and immortality in ways that I had never previously even imagined.

One night, she took me out into the woods carrying only a backpack and spread a blanket onto the banks of Jordan Lake. We opened a bottle of red wine and sat there and looked at the lake, the waning gibbous moon, and the sky. The black Carolina sky was full of stars. She took out an iPod and a speaker and put on Beethoven's Moonlight Sonata and took a pair of binoculars out of her backpack and showed me what had looked like a smudge in the canopy of the sky. Through the binoculars, I saw something new and astonishing.

"That's the Andromeda Galaxy," she said. "It comes from Greek mythology. Andromeda was the most beautiful creature in the universe and she was left as a sacrifice for a monster."

That didn't surprise me. It fit in with the world I'd seen and I was immediately fascinated. I had seen that before, over and over again. I saw it in the faces of the dead. The pictures of them lying there. Their eyes, dead and full of human longing. Longing for some rescue or salvation. Longing for prayers that had gone unanswered. There were no prayers for justice in their eyes. That prayer had been my guess as to their next thought and it had been my mission and my purpose.

She explained that in the ancient world, people believed that the stars were agents of the gods put there to allow mankind to divine their unknowable will. I often thought back on that night and its magic whenever I found myself mired in the blood soaked streets of Durham, where poor and helpless people died and nobody knew their names and nobody wanted to know.

I MADE a wine sauce from a California table wine and used it to marinate the chicken. It was a new recipe I'd improvised but it tasted good because you could actually taste the red wine in the chicken. I poured the rest of the wine into a glass and took a seat on the couch.

I picked up a book off the coffee table. It was a crime thriller I'd bought at the grocery store. I opened it and started to read.

Jill got there just after seven. I kissed her and poured her some wine and went back to the kitchen to check on the couscous. She followed me into the kitchen and stood there leaning against the door and turning the wine glass around in her hand. She had on jeans and a red tank top under a black leather jacket. Her long black hair, which she usually wore in a ponytail, was loose and reached down past her shoulders. She wasn't yet thirty, but she carried herself like somebody who was older than that. She had a confidence that I found irresistible. She'd graduated from Chapel Hill with a bachelor's in biology and a doctorate in microbiology. She had a good job at one of the big research campuses in Research Triangle Park and she owned a nice little house near the UNC campus in Chapel Hill. She was smart and she knew it. I had no idea what she saw in me. We'd been together for a year now and I wasn't sure what scared me more—losing her or giving her my heart forever. That had always been a thing with me, which is why I was 37 years old with no children and no ex-wives.

"Does it ever cease to amaze you how stupid people are?" she said. "I mean, it's just unbelievable. Sometimes I wonder how they built all these tall buildings."

"Never bet against stupid," I said. "It's like betting against the house at Caesar's."

"But I'm dealing with Ph.D's," she said. "You'd expect a little more from them."

"What happened now?"

"We were talking in the break room and somehow the subject of this nature documentary came up and one of my coworkers, this guy who has a fucking doctorate in biogenetics, asked whether penguins can breathe under water."

"Can they?" I said.

"Oh stop it."

"Seriously. Can they?"

She groaned and walked back into the living room. "How did the human race survive this long?" she said.

"Don't worry," I said. "We'll blow ourselves to smithereens eventually. It probably won't take too much longer."

"How did we build flying machines?" she said. "How did we make it to the fucking moon?"

I brought the plates from the kitchen and put them on the table and then went back for the half-empty bottle of wine. We sat down and started eating the chicken and couscous. "I was going to get some rolls but I forgot," I said.

"I don't care," she said.

"Good."

"They were talking about your boxer friend on the radio," she said.

"Oh yeah?"

"This is a big story."

"Fuck the media," I said.

"How are you and Stuart holding up?"

"We're going through the discovery," I said.

"Anything interesting so far?"

I reluctantly nodded my head.

"One or two things," I said. "There's this mystery number that exchanged a bunch of calls with her. And there's no sign of her fighting back. Plus, Ray didn't confess."

"Maybe he can't face what he did."

"Guys in that situation always confess," I said.

"What about the science?"

"The lab report matches the semen from the rape kit to his DNA. But that's not a surprise. They were dating."

She refilled her wine glass. She said, "Do you just have the report or do you have the underlying data that was used to generate it."

"Just the report," I said.

"You need to get the data."

"I wouldn't know what to do with it."

"You know anything about DNA?"

"No."

"It's more complicated than you think," she said.

"I thought it was open and shut."

"Nothing in science is open and shut."

"What should I be looking for?"

"I don't know," she said. "Different labs use different criteria for confirming matches. With blood or semen, there can be one contributor or multiple contributors and it's not always easy to tell. It gets tricky because you're looking for certain markers and scientists might disagree about what's a marker and what's just background noise in the test. You could show the data to my friend Ellen. She could tell you if there's anything they overlooked."

I took a bite of my chicken and nodded. "I'll tell Roth to get it," I said.

She shook her head and started laughing. "Penguins breathing underwater," she said. "Christ, you do know ostriches can't fly around like blue jays, don't you?"

"All I know is they make good boots," I said.

She smiled.

"Any breakthroughs at the lab today?" I said.

"Yeah, we cured genital warts."

"It's about fucking time," I said.

AFTER DINNER, Jill said, "Let's put these dishes up and watch a movie."

"Any movie in particular?"

"I don't care," she said. "I've been on an Alfred Hitchcock binge lately."

"Any favorites?"

"I like the one where Joseph Cotton plays a serial killer."

"Yeah," I said. "That's a good one. Been awhile since I saw it."

We did the dishes and sat down next to each other on the couch. She had taken her jacket off and her tight red shirt really showed off her breasts. She was flipping through the channels and stopped on The Shawshank Redemption.

"I could watch this movie a million times," she said.

"Everybody could," I said. "That's why it's on so much."

We sat there and watched it until the end, when Andy makes his withdrawal from the bank and Warden Norton blows his brains out. I had my arm around her. She put her wine glass down on the coffee table and we started to kiss. I put my hand on her hip and slowly worked it upward until I was holding her breast and we sat there kissing each other.

"You want to go into the bedroom?" she said.

I just nodded and stood up and picked her up with me. She wrapped her legs around my waist and I carried her into the bedroom and put her down on the bed. I took off my shirt and jeans. She took off her pants and pulled her shirt up over her head. She sat up on the bed wearing just a black bra and matching panties.

"You are way overdressed for the occasion," I said.

"Come here, you," she said.

I crawled over the bed to her and she gathered me up in the covers. Later, we lay there next to each other in the dark.

Finally, she said, "You really believe that kid is innocent?"

"Yes," I said. "The evidence doesn't look like it, but I think he is."

"I don't understand your work," she said. "In my work, we make objective observations, make logical assumptions from those observations, and then test the assumptions. I've never had a gut feeling about any of it."

"What I do isn't that different."

"Then why do you think he's innocent?"

"It doesn't feel right."

"See?" she said. "That's what I mean. That's a gut feeling."

"It's just too goddamn convenient and it doesn't make any sense," I said. "The kid I know is more concerned about his next fight than any girl."

"She wasn't just any girl."

"No, I guess not. But I saw him in that interrogation room with Fields. Guilty people don't act like he did."

"How do guilty people act?"

"If the crime was planned, they tell you some bullshit story they've rehearsed. If it was a crime of passion, they're usually dying to confess because they feel so bad about it."

"What are you going to do if he turns out to be guilty?"

"Live with it, I guess. I've had to live with stuff before."

"I know," she said. "And you're not very good at it."

"What's that supposed to mean?"

"It just means I'm worried about you, that's all," she said.

"I'll be okay."

"You always say that. And don't take this the wrong way, because I like you. I really, really like you."

"I really like you too."

"But I can't go down that road with you again. The darkness. The depression. The guilt. I can't do it."

"I understand," I said.

"You know I'm not here for your money, because you don't have any," she said. "And I loved you enough to stay with you when you lost your job and spent six months drunk and depressed. We rode that out together. I'm here now and we're in a good place. I don't want to lose what we've got."

I took a deep breath and exhaled slowly. "I don't want to lose it either," I said.

She put the palm of her hand on my cheek and leaned in close to me. "I think there's some part of you that still thinks you can save her," she said. "I think sometimes you still live in that place. You can't let go of it and you can't forgive yourself."

"I don't deserve forgiveness," I said. "And she's not alive to give it to me even if I did deserve it."

She looked me in the eyes and said, "It wasn't your fault."

"I promised her she'd be safe."

"You did everything you could."

"No I didn't."

"It wasn't your decision. You weren't the one in charge."

"No. But I'm the one who promised her."

"You got justice for her and you sure as hell got your revenge on your bosses."

I broke away from her and looked at the ceiling. I looked at the fan blades turning slowly above me. "I wanted to rub their noses in it and I did," I said. "And now I'm stuck tailing cheating husbands and assholes who lie to insurance companies. I was only put on this earth with one talent, and it's something I can never use again. I'll never be a cop again. Not anywhere. A police chief will tolerate you being late or drinking too much or even skimming from drug dealers. What he won't tolerate is you being disloyal."

She reached over and put her arms around me. She said, "You made your decision. You did what you thought was right. People always say it's hard to do the right thing, but it's not. What's hard is living with the consequences after you do the right thing."

She kissed me on the lips for a long time and then she got out of bed and started putting her clothes back on. I said, "Where are you going?"

"I need to get home," she said. "Louie is outside and I haven't fed him yet."

Louie was her cat. Being a microbiologist, she named him after Louie Pasteur, the guy who invented penicillin or something. I always associated that name with the scene in Blazing Saddles where the two guys are talking in the saloon and one of them is going on and on about the amazing scientific breakthroughs being made in France by Louie Pasteur and the other guy pushes him aside and yells, "Fuck that shit! Here comes Mongo!" So I always called the cat Mongo, but never in front of her.

"Wish you would stay," I said.

"I'll call you tomorrow," she said.

I followed her to the door and watched as she got into her car and pulled away. I knew I wouldn't be able to sleep, so I went back into the bedroom and poured another glass of wine. I thought about my situation. I felt something for Jill that I'd never felt before. I confirmed it for myself every time we made love. When I looked into her eyes, because that's where love is communicated, through the eyes. But I had also made a promise to my friend, and that promise involved saving the life of his son. I had made promises to two people who were indispensable to me and now I had put myself in a position where I might have to break one of those promises in order to keep the other. This thought was terrifying to me and so I finished the glass of wine and, to quiet those feelings, I poured myself another one.

CHAPTER FIVE

T HE OTHER PROMISE I had made was to Ray Marks, Sr., who everybody called Big Ray. When Little Ray was arrested, his father called me on the phone and could barely put two sentences together. The agony in his voice made his words jerk and break off. Finally, he just said, "Can you come?"

I met him in the parking lot of the police station. Neither of us needed directions. We'd spent years bringing junkies and thieves and killers to that same station. We always went out drinking afterward, until the day we both quit drinking together. We kept hanging out, but instead of spending time in bars we spent time in AA meeting rooms listening to drunkalogues and telling our own. Eventually, I couldn't take it anymore. When I started drinking again, Big Ray and I slowly drifted apart.

The 12 Steps worked for him. He acknowledged his problem and his powerlessness over that problem. He surrendered to his Higher Power. He made a fearless and searching moral inventory, and he worked hard to make amends. He had a lot of them. I admitted nothing, surrendered to nothing, inventoried nothing, and made no amends for anything I'd ever done.

Big Ray turned me onto the Delta blues. In our patrol car, he made me listen to Ma Rainey, Blind Lemon Jefferson, B.B. King. He told me the story of Robert Johnson and how he met the Devil at the crossroads and traded his soul for the ability to play the blues like no man had ever played the blues.

We used to have arguments about it. I told him that opera told you all you needed to know about human nature. I told him that Mozart was to music what Shakespeare was to literature. He told me that the Delta blues told you all you needed to know about the soul and about human suffering.

Big Ray also took me to places I'd never been and would never have gone to on my own. Places like Smokey's Roadhouse, which was an old speakeasy where the blacks in Durham gathered to drink what the government called non-tax paid liquor. I called it moonshine. The blacks at Smokey's called it splo. There, in the dark plywood cave, the blacks who still lived their lives on the poverty-laced fringes of Durham would drink their splo and listen on an old jukebox to the songs that told the story of their people—the blues that had evolved from slave songs and embedded itself into the darker part of the Southern soul. They were songs of pain, oppression, loss, struggle, and the courage to fight through it all to live to fight another day.

As a white man, I got some strange looks from the regulars at Smokey's, but since I was with Big Ray, who everybody knew as a former boxer turned hardass cop who nonetheless maintained an affinity for his less-accomplished brothers and sisters, nobody dared to fuck with me.

Our trips to Smokey's reaffirmed something I had long known instinctively—that to be an effective crime-solver, you had to live among the criminals. You had to understand them, to see the world through their eyes. Many of the regulars there were involved in the drug trade at the retail street level, and many of them were involved in small time theft and robbery.

Big Ray knew who they were and what they did, but he never arrested any of them, because he knew that they knew all about who the harder guys were. And when the serious shit went down, when there was a murder or a violent robbery or a rape, those same people became sources who trusted Big Ray and would talk to him.

To people on the outside of the crime business, criminals are all just criminals. But people who really understand the crime business understand that a small time thief or fence has the same innate sense of justice that everyone has. They don't like cruelty either, and while they aren't the type to pick up the phone and call CrimeStoppers, they never minded privately telling Big Ray what they knew. They did so without fear of retribution, because they knew Big Ray would keep their confidence. They also knew that when Big Ray was done with a murderer or a rapist or any other sort of violent bully, the bully wouldn't be in any condition to come back and do them any harm. To the small time criminals just trying to get by, Smokey's was a plywood sanctuary hidden among the pine branches in a dirt lot at the end of an unpaved road off Highway 98. To Big Ray, it was a wiretap on the criminal confession booth.

BIG RAY was waiting for me in front of the station. He looked about like he did the last time I saw him. He was in good shape and didn't have a trace of a gut like so many middle aged men did. He had been a tough cop, even a mean one. I'd seen him beat criminals he didn't like and then charge them with resisting arrest, just to cover his ass when they screamed about police brutality.

His eyes were red and his face was slicked with tears. We shook hands. "He got a lawyer yet?" I said.

He shook his head. "They let me talk to him," he said. "I told him to keep his mouth shut."

"I've been doing some private eye work for Stuart Roth," I said. "You want me to take the case to him?"

Big Ray nodded. "Thanks," he said.

"What are they saying so far?"

"Same thing they always say."

"He's a good kid," I said. "I can't believe he'd be involved in something like this."

"I need your help," he said.

"You got it," I said. "Anything you need."

Big Ray wiped the tears from his face and stared off into space. He finally looked back at me. I saw something I'd never seen in his eyes before: fear.

"Maybe this is God's way of paying me back for all the bad things I did when I was young. The sins of the father," he said.

"No," I said. "No. It's not. This is just a fucking tragedy that your boy is getting swept up in. We'll get it sorted out."

"You remember that boy who killed that hooker over in Few Gardens?" he said.

"Yeah," I said. "That was a bad one."

"You remember his confession?"

"I remember it," I said. I remembered that Big Ray had written out the confession for the kid and the kid had signed it with broken fingers.

"You lied to Internal Affairs about it."

"I didn't want him getting off just because you broke his eye socket," I said. "I didn't want you going to jail in his place either."

He nodded.

"He was guilty," I said. "What we did there was justice. I never lost one minute of sleep over it."

"I did," Big Ray said. "And now they got my boy in there."

I could see the muscles in his jaw tighten up and I looked down at his hands. He was balling them up into fists. "Any of those detectives lays a hand on him. . .," he said.

"They won't touch him," I said. "No way they're that stupid."

Later that night, I spoke to Ray in his cell. He was sitting on the ground sobbing. All he kept saying was that he didn't do it. The next morning I called Roth. He'd seen the news stories the night before and agreed to take the case if I promised to help him with it.

I HAD NOTHING to go on but Ray's denials and the news reports, so I decided to hit the streets to see what the criminals were saying. It was early August and we were in the middle of one of our typical summer cycles with 100-degree heat for more than a week. The streets smelled like decaying roadkill and you couldn't be outside for more than a few seconds before you started sweating. I was wearing jeans and a light, olive colored jacket. I'd have rather been shirtless, but I didn't want the criminals to see the gun on my hip.

It was a little after noon when I found Kenny Rogers playing pool in the Wooden Nickel. I didn't know if he was named after the country and western singer or if his parents were just retards. I guessed it was probably both. All I knew was that he was a reliable snitch.

Kenny still had his long hair and beard, and both of them looked like they needed to be wrung out like a wet towel. He was starting to go bald and it occurred to me that being bald on top and simultaneously sporting a mullet made for a pretty ridiculous look.

The Wooden Nickel was a true dive bar. It had one pool table with torn felt and a Budweiser light hanging over it, a lighted Pabst Blue Ribbon sign on the far wall, an old dart board, and some old country music posters tacked onto the wall behind the bar. It was one of the last places you'd go in your drinking career. Nobody in there had gone to college, but all of them had gone to prison.

When Kenny saw me he nodded and kept playing his game. He was hustling some Mexican guy in a sleeveless work shirt with gold chains and earrings and tattoos on both arms. I went to the bar and ordered two Budweisers and waited for him to finish. He came over when he was done and I gave him one of the beers and we went to a quiet table where we could talk.

"Ain't seen you in forever, boss man," he said.

"I'm in the ministry now," I said.

"Shit, man. That's the best damn hustle anybody ever come up with. You ain't even got to pay no taxes on it."

"What you been up to?" I said. "A little breaking? A little entering?"

"Naw, boss man. I don't do that shit no more."

"I've heard you say that before."

"I mighta said it, but my mind won't right then."

"And it is now?"

"Damn straight it is. I got me a good job, man. I climb TV towers now."

"Good place to case houses, I guess."

"I'm tellin you for real. Got me a good girl, man. I ain't like I used to be."

"I quit drinking and I'm a homosexual now," I said.

"Man, you don't never believe me, do you?"

"You entertain me, Kenny. I put up with a lot from people who entertain me."

"What brings you down here, boss man?" he said. "You lookin for somebody I know?"

"Just came by to see how you were doing."

"That's bullshit, man. I ain't never seen you when you didn't want somethin."

I nodded because that was true and then took a drink of my beer.

"When did you get out last?"

"July of last year."

"Where were you this time?"

"They had me down in Johnston County at a green clothes camp."

"How was it?"

"It was all right."

"You on post release supervision?"

"Naw, man. I ain't got a PO or nothin."

"What are you hearing these days from your friends?"

"About what?"

"About anything?"

Kenny pulled on his beard and straightened it out. "Nothin, man," he said. "Just the usual shit, you know?"

"Like what?"

"Some of them houses over in Forest Hills might be missin a big screen or two."

"Anything else?"

"Only motherfucker makin any real money is Bernard, man."

"Bernard Little?"

"Yeah. He goes by Freedom now."

"I remember when he was just a kid doing hand to hands over on Alston Street," I said.

"He rollin like a motherfucker now, man," Kenny said. "Them police lockin motherfuckers up like shit but he still doin his thing, man."

"Who are they fucking with?"

"You remember Elrico?"

"Yeah."

"They popped his ass good, man. Him and his boys. They takin their case federal. He was Bernard's main competition. Motherfucker's got like a. . . what you call it? That game, you know?"

"Monopoly?"

"Yeah," he said. "That motherfucker's got a monopoly."

I looked at my watch. It was two o'clock.

Kenny leaned on his pool stick and said, "They fuckin with them Mexicans like shit, man. Jackin them motherfuckers left and right."

"Who's doing it?"

"Those boys you used to run with."

"Vice?"

"Naw, man," he said. "Them murder cops. I know that boy Fields is always over there with that other boy. What's his name?"

"Hampton?"

"Yeah, him. They ride around plainclothes in that Tahoe actin like they Bernard hisself. Takin motherfuckers down, man. And what they gonna do about it? They can't say shit less they want to back to Mexico."

"It's that bad, huh?"

"I'm tellin you, man. I'm glad I ain't no Mexican. It's open fuckin season on them mo-fuckers. But I say good riddance. They shouldn't be here in the first place, you know?"

"What's Bernard's story these days?"

"He just rockin and rollin, man. Things been pretty quiet. I ain't heard of no bodies or nothin."

"How about your old line of work?"

"Same old, same old, man."

"Who's fencing stuff these days?" I said.

"There's this boy has a pawn shop down there on 98 right when you get out of town. He got two doors, you know? Front door, they make a copy of your driver's license. Back door, they don't ask no questions. You know how them places is. Front door, you lucky if you get thirty cents on the dollar. Back door, you lucky if you get ten. That's the rumor, anyway. You know, I ain't know nothin about that shit myself."

"You been following the news about that TV reporter's murder?"

"It's all the fuck they talkin about on TV today, man."

"You hear any talk on the street about it?"

"Not really," he said. "People just saying that nigger done it."

"Tell me," I said. "You ever see a break-in where there weren't signs of a forced entry?"

"Hell yeah, man. That ain't nothin."

"How would that work?"

"It could happen all kinds of ways, I guess," he said. "Pickin a lock ain't no thing once you get good at it. And some people just leave their shit unlocked. People are stupid motherfuckers, man. Or they leave a key under the matt. Like we ain't never seen that before."

"Hell," he said. "I even had a guy once who left his keys in the fuckin door. Car keys and house keys and every damn thing. I figure he just went to sleep and forgot about em."

"And you robbed him?"

"I come in sometime after midnight," Kenny said. "And he's got his wallet and gold watch laying there on the table, so I put that shit in my pocket. Went on out into his garage and drove off in his Cadillac. That was one sweet ride, man. He had a badass gun in there too, man. It was one of them silver 1911's with the tricked out grips."

"You're lucky he didn't shoot your ass," I said.

"He never even waked up, man."

"Did they get you for that one?"

"Yeah they got me," he said. "Got me over in Chapel Hill. I was over there stoned. I guess he reported the car stolen by then. They gave me a bunch of warrants but I didn't end up pleadin to nothing more than some stolen goods or somethin."

I reached in my pocket and took out my wallet. "Here's twenty bucks," I said. "Try not to spend it all in one place."

I got up.

"Come by any time, Egan," he said. "It's always good to see old friends."

CHAPTER SIX

I T WAS STILL EARLY and I was up for some adventure so I drove over to the open air drug markets on Alston Street. According to Kenny, this was Bernard Little's turf now, and that meant that so was most of the rest of Durham. Nobody that mattered cared, as long as the hard drugs, the robberies, and the murders stayed out of the suburbs.

The neighborhood hadn't changed one bit since the last time I was there. The houses still had decaying walls with holes in them, the paint had peeled away from them a little more, and pieces of plywood still covered the windows. Gang graffiti decorated several of the houses, the stop sign at the end of the street, and a broken fence separating two houses that couldn't have been more than ten feet apart.

There were bags of trash on the curb and random pieces of trash littering the yards. Black men in tank tops sat on overturned box crates, their faces glistening with sweat. When I pulled up to the curb in my truck, I saw the signalman throw up one hand and make a circling gesture with his fingers and the dealers scattered into the alleys.

I saw Marvin Martin walking away slowly toward the alley between two decaying houses. He was wearing a heavy winter coat. I knew him from way back. He was in court so much everybody there knew him and called him Marvin the Martian.

"Hey Marvin," I said.

He turned around.

"You learned your lesson yet?"

He gave me an angry look.

He said, "Yeah I learned it," and turned back around and kept walking.

Marvin was a career supermarket shoplifter. He liked to go into grocery stores wearing a winter coat, even if it was July, and load the coat up with whatever he could fit in there. He usually got arrested, but if he didn't, he'd come back to the projects and try to trade groceries for crack. He'd probably been arrested for shoplifting two hundred times before it occurred to him that Food Lion never sent a witness to court, which meant as a practical matter it was legal to steal from Food Lion.

Before Marvin figured that out, he probably spent six or seven years in jail, thirty days at a time.

I walked over and talked to the old men playing cards on the stoops. They were drinking malt liquor and they gave me that look of disgust a cop always gets in the ghetto.

"Why you got to come up in here scaring all them boys like that?" one of them said.

"I didn't do anything," I said. "I'm not here to arrest anybody. They can sell rocks like Now & Laters for all I care."

"Man, you know you busting up their game."

"The game ain't going nowhere," I said. "They'll be playing ball tonight. And tomorrow night. And the night after that."

I heard a whizzing sound from a car engine and I turned and saw a black Porsche Cayman turning the corner and driving down the street in my direction. I started to reach in my coat for the .38 caliber revolver I had there.

I watched the car coming toward me. It had blacked out windows and the window on the driver's side rolled down as it approached. It stopped in front of me. I walked over to the car and said, "Bernard, it's been a while."

"Been about two years."

"I hear you're big time now."

"I hear you small time now."

"You heard right."

"You did too."

I leaned against the car because I knew it would piss him off. He was wearing a black throwback Adidas track suit and several gold chains around his neck. He had a brand new Yankees cap sitting up sideways on his head like a saucepan. When he smiled, I saw that he had what looked like diamonds in his teeth. "Congratulations," I said. "You won the lottery."

"Oh, man, don't even play me like that, Egan," he said.

"This car had to cost what, sixty, seventy grand?"

He shook his head and started talking with his hands. "I'm a businessman, Egan," he said. "You see one of them Warren Buffett niggas riding in a Cayman, you don't say shit. But you profile my black ass, don't you? Some people would say that's racist. But I ain't about all that."

"I'm not a moron," I said.

"It's just basic market economics, Egan," he said. "You ever read The Wealth of Nations by that Adam Smith motherfucker?"

"Nope."

"You ought to read that shit, man. See, what that Scottish nigga would tell you is that when demand outruns supply, that creates what they call a seller's market. Drives the price of shit up."

"That's great for you," I said. "Sucks for the buyer though."

"Fuck the buyer," he said. "When it's the other way around, you think the buyer gives a fuck about the seller? Naw, man. He's just happy he can get shit for cheap."

"Besides," he said, "I've got other problems."

"Like what?"

"Investments and shit, man. It's hard to know where to park your money these days. All this uncertainty in the world."

"That's a nice problem to have," I said.

"I was thinking on getting me a tiger for the crib. You know? Like Mike Tyson had back when he was fucking Robin Givens. I almost got me one too. Can you believe it's legal in the state of North Carolina to buy a fucking tiger and put it in your house?"

"No," I said. "I didn't know that." I can't say I was surprised to learn it, though.

"I decided I didn't need one. I did what they call a cost and benefit analysis and decided that the cost of having the tiger outweighed the benefits."

"What are the benefits?"

"It's fucking gangsta, man. Nothing says you a real nigga like having a tiger in your house."

"I can see that."

"I been reading a lot of books lately, man. Broadening my horizons, you know? You ought to check that shit out sometime. See, most motherfuckers spend their whole lives working for their money." He put his finger to his temple. "A smart motherfucker figures out how to make that money work for him."

"It takes money to do that," I said.

"You ain't got none?"

"Not enough to play around with," I said.

"Shit, man. This America," he said. "All you need is ten dollars and a good idea."

He picked at the diamonds in his teeth and said, "Man, I watch TV sometimes and I see them motherfuckers on there talking about the rich and the poor and how the rich getting too rich and shit. That shit pisses me the fuck off. Those motherfuckers don't know shit. I say, fuck them socialist niggas."

"You sound like a Republican."

"Man I ain't even political. But those motherfuckers don't know how shit really is, man. You know Wormy?"

"I don't know. Maybe."

"Little motherfucker. He stay with his mama over in the towers."

"Looks like a like a worm? Moves real slow? Wears a Gilligan hat?"

"Yeah. He look like a worm. That's why they call him that."

"I think I busted him doing hand to hands once," I said.

"He do what he got to do but he ain't no hustler."

"What about him?"

"If you know Wormy, you know he don't want shit out of life," he said. "He just wants to sit on the corner with a bottle of wine in his hand. That shit's enough for him and he's perfectly happy doing it. Me? I got more expensive tastes."

"I doubt you're paying out much in taxes," I said.

"Bullshit, man. I've been diversifying my portfolio. Spreading shit around. I got stocks, bonds, angel investing, real estate, a couple of clubs. Most of my shit gets taxed at that capital gains rate and I'm paying those motherfucking taxes. Those bitches ain't going to Al Capone my ass."

"Aren't you worried about the cops?" I said.

He gave a dismissive wave with his hand and said, "Every champion got his time, Egan. Used to be Magic and Bird ran things. Then Jordan was the boss. Then there was kind of a power struggle and you had Akeem and Shaq and Duncan and all them niggas. Then you had Kobe and now you got LeBron. Nothing good lasts forever, man. But I'm planning on retiring a champion."

"You staying around here or moving someplace else?"

"I'm considering my options but I probably go somewhere exotic. Too much bullshit around here, man. They don't call it the Bull City for nothing. I hear there's nice places down in Honduras even though motherfuckers be killing each other like Scarface down there. Costa Rica is cheap and you can live like a king right on that beach and you know I always liked them fine ass South American tica bitches. But I'm also thinking on going back to the motherland."

"The motherland?"

"Kenya, probably," he said. "Did you know it's always seventy degrees with a nice breeze there? Even in the wintertime. And those fine Nubian bitches love them some American brothas with money. You know Mike? African dude works over at the BP station?'

"Yeah," I said.

"He came over here from Kenya five years ago and all he wants to do is save enough money to go back. Makes you wonder why he ever left in the first place."

"Maybe it sucked there."

"Man, any place sucks if you broke."

I tapped my fingers against the top of Bernard's Cayman. He said, "Hey man, don't be scratching my paint and shit."

"You know about Ray Marks?" I said.

"Hell yeah. That nigga can fight now."

"You seen him?"

"I had two tables ringside at his last fight in AC, man. That nigga the pride of Durham. And that's some bullshit they got him locked up on too."

"Why do you say that?"

"Man, why he want to kill a bitch? He can have all the pussy he want. Every sista in Durham want to suck that nigga's dick. But that's what he gets for fucking around with some white girl from the TV."

Bernard put his car back into gear. "Police always trying to take us down, man. They can't stand to see no brotha have some success. They did that shit with O.J. Tried to frame Kobe for raping that white bitch in Colorado when you know that bitch was just trying to get paid. Man, nothing surprises me no more when it comes to cops locking up brothas."

"Thanks for the economics lesson," I said.

"The Wealth of Nations, man. Check that shit out. I'm telling you. It'll change your whole mindset."

"You keep it real, Bernard," I said.

"Yeah, you too," he said.

CHAPTER SEVEN

I HAD NEVER been inside a television studio before and I was surprised to see how small it was. The production set with the desk and the backdrop of the city and the cameras and the lights could have easily fit into a two-car garage.

I had talked to both of the weekday anchors, all the weekend and substitute anchors, the other reporters, the producers, and the station chief, and none of them seemed to know anything about Sheryl Rose's personal life. They all said she was a professional, that she was always on time, and that she could sometimes be aggressive in the pitch meetings and had a tendency to pout when her story ideas got shot down. None of them had ever even had so much as had a drink with her.

Then I interviewed her cameraman. When I asked him what he thought of her, he said she was tough to work with.

"Why?" I said.

"She could be a bitch," he said.

"How so?"

"She was just one of those people. Don't get me wrong. She was good at her job. But she made it harder than it had to be."

"What do you mean?"

"Either she was all in or she acted like she was doing a hostage tape. That shit gets old when you're trying to just get the damn story done."

"She always seemed like a nice girl on TV," I said.

"She was a drama queen," he said. "I mean, rest in peace and all, but she was."

"She ever mention anything about fans stalking her or creeping her out?"

"Not really, but we've had that here before," he said.

"When was that?"

"Maybe five or six years ago."

"What happened?"

"Some nutcase thought he and the weather girl were meant to be together," he said. "He kept showing up at the station. I think they finally committed him to the nut house."

"Nothing since then?" I said.

"Nothing worth mentioning. Sheryl did say something once about being weirded out by this car that was parked across from her house, but that's all I remember."

"A car?"

"Yeah," he said. "A black car."

"When was this?"

"I don't know. Maybe a month before she died."

"Where was this car?"

"It was across the street. She saw it when she went out jogging and it was sitting there when she came back."

"Was anybody inside it?"

"She didn't know. She just said she had a weird feeling about it. She said the windows were all black but she felt like somebody was in there watching her. But like I said, she was dramatic."

"Did you tell the cops about this?"

"Yeah," he said. "I told Detective Fields."

"She didn't get the license plate number or anything?"

"No," he said. "All she said was that it creeped her out. She said she went into her house and locked the door and when she looked back out, it was gone."

"Did she ever see it again?"

"If she did, she didn't say anything about it to me," he said.

"What kind of stories were you guys working on then?"

"Just beat stories and features, mostly. If there was a fire, we covered it. If there was a murder, we covered it."

"How about features?"

"Mostly softball shit," he said. "Profiles of local people. Athletes, singers, teachers who won some award. That kind of shit."

"Anything else?"

"She was pushing to do this series about the influx of illegals because there was so much in the national news about amnesty and building a fence at the border and all that shit."

"What did the producers say?"

"They told her no unless she could find a local news hook to frame it," he said. "She talked to some of the locals and we shot a couple interviews with the activists. But all she really got was that they couldn't get a driver's license and they worked off the books. But everybody knows that already."

"Was she mad when they killed it?"

"She was pretty hot about it," he said. "She had a name for it and everything. Living in the Shadows."

"What did you think about it?" I said.

"I didn't really care one way or the other," he said. "But then again, she and I didn't even agree on what our job was."

"What do you mean?" I said.

"Maybe I'm simple minded, but I don't see what's so hard about just reporting the damn news," he said. "These kids today don't want to do that. They want to crusade against racism or global warming or whatever. I always thought you should go into politics if you want to do that."

I nodded and said, "I noticed she didn't have a journalism degree. Is that unusual?"

"Not really," he said. "Her major was social justice. I don't even know what the hell that's supposed to mean. I didn't have to go to college to learn what justice was. I got that from watching Andy Griffith and the Lone Ranger."

I liked the cameraman. He seemed like he'd be fun to have a beer with.

"You must be a big fan of Reverend Worthdale," I said.

Reverend Worthdale was Durham's answer to Al Sharpton.

He gave me a disgusted look. "Let me tell you something," he said. "You show me somebody that makes their living crusading for the poor and I'll show you somebody that doesn't tip, doesn't give to charity, and doesn't pay their taxes."

CHAPTER EIGHT

W HEN I GOT back to the office, I read through the witness
statements again. There was nothing in the cameraman's
statement about the black car. The statement was just a short sum-
mary describing Rose as passionate and temperamental.

I sat back and thought about the people I'd interviewed at the station. You could see a clear line dividing them. The production staff
acted like they were working a construction site and the editorial
staff acted like they were actors shooting a movie. I figured the production staff probably hated the editorial staff and the editorial staff
probably looked at the production staff as something like servants.

Social institutions had always fascinated me. As a student of
human nature, I knew that most people were prisoners of institutional bureaucracy in one way or another and didn't even realize it. This wasn't just true of people who worked in institutions
like government or academia or the legal system. It was true of all
people everywhere.

Even criminals have social institutions with their own bureau-
cratic structures. And those structures function like they do in all

the other institutions in the world. Working in the crime business teaches you a lot about people because you get to watch the same social experiments over and over again and see them generate the same results.

There are cultural differences, but the human animal is pretty much the same everywhere. Human nature isn't like biology or scientific understanding. It doesn't change or evolve, ever.

The criminal class includes people from all races and nationalities, but there are some differences among the tribes as to the crimes they tend to commit. You see it on the court calendars every day. Blacks sell crack and rob gas stations. Mexicans drive drunk and bet on cockfights. Whites molest little kids and forge checks. I don't know what the Asians do. I guess probably just math and karate.

The criminal class itself is fairly small. You realize that when you walk a beat and arrest the same people for the same things again and again. When you get to know them, you began to understand that they aren't that much different from the rest of us. There is usually some good even in bad people, just as there is some bad in all of us.

Your average criminal doesn't wake up in the morning and plot evil. He has the same wants and needs and dreams as everybody else. Mostly, he just wants to have fun and be happy. The only thing that makes him a criminal is that he doesn't mind taking shortcuts to get there. That's why most criminals I've known are people you wouldn't mind sitting next to at a ball game.

That's not to say they aren't annoying or antisocial, because a lot of them are. They break into houses and steal money or they sell drugs or fence stolen goods at pawn shops. They waste your time, but they aren't really dangerous. When you encounter them every day, you start to understand them and you even like some of them. The only ones I ever really hated were the ones who had cruelty in them.

When I was a cop, I tried to look the other way on all the victimless crimes. If I saw somebody smoking a joint on his porch, I just nodded and kept walking. If some stripper in one of the clubs was trading blow jobs for cash in the champagne room, I didn't give a shit. This occasionally caused friction with my bosses when I was in Vice, but you had to look the other way on the small stuff if you wanted to get anybody to ever talk to you about the bigger stuff.

I remembered a small time crack dealer named Levi who sold five and ten dollar rocks in the open air markets on Alston Street. I could have sent a CI with a camera and wire to do as many controlled buys from him as I wanted. And since he had three felonies on his record, I could have habitualized him on every transaction and put him in Central Prison for life. But I didn't.

Instead, I did the controlled buys and showed Levi the videos and told him he could do life in prison or become a snitch. He chose to become a snitch and I ended up using him to bust a big time trafficker who went by the street name Murder. When we went raided Murder's house, we found nine kilos of cocaine and almost two kilos of uncut heroin. Murder was now doing pushups in the federal lockup in Lewisburg, Pennsylvania, and he would be doing them until the second coming of Jesus Christ. We even cleared several cold case murders from the guns we found in his closet.

The Sheryl Rose murder didn't have the markings of a street crime, but I knew that whoever killed her had the same thoughts and behaviors and instincts that anyone has. And if I was careful to look at the evidence in that light, I might be able to understand that person and find him.

The piece of evidence that bothered me the most was the mystery phone number because it meant that she had a secret with somebody. I knew that if two people had a secret, it was probably a secret for a reason. I wasn't going to believe Ray killed her until I knew what that secret was and who she shared it with.

CHAPTER NINE

$\mathbf{M}$AX BOLUS' GYM was old school as hell. There was none of the fancy new age equipment in there. Just two rings, a series of heavy bags, four or five speed bags hanging from the wall, mats with jump ropes, a crazy ball suspended by bungee cords, and a wooden bench next to piles of gloves and headgear of all different sizes. Even though he knew better, Max still made himself believe that headgear was for pussies.

The walls of the gym were filled with posters from old fight cards. There was Ali-Frazier. Louis-Braddock. Marciano-Walcott. Hagler-Hearns. Behind the counter was a framed Pabst Blue Ribbon poster from one of the Ray Robinson-Gene Fullmer fights that Fullmer had autographed but I guessed that it wasn't from the one where Robinson flattened Fullmer with a single perfect left hook.

Max had the physique of a man half his age. He was in his sixties and was still fit and trim. He had that ramrod straight posture that only Parris Island could give you. He looked like he could still make the welterweight limit if the weigh-in was tomorrow. His shoulders were set close together, but his arms were veiny and muscular and the skin around his face was tight and covered in scars. His gray hair was buzzed in the style of an eternal jarhead.

He was standing behind the counter when I came in. Behind him a handful of boxers were working the bags. Two of them were sparring in one of the rings.

"So when are you and your shyster friend going get Little Ray out of there so we can get back to work?" he said.

"It's a little more complicated than that," I said.

"Fucking lawyers. I always hated them. People say boxing is dying and they're right. You know why? The best fights don't get made no more. You know why? Because of the fucking lawyers."

"What do you know about steroids?" I said.

Max gave me an angry and disgusted look. "I run a clean gym," he said. "I tell my fighters to stay away from that shit."

"You've seen the news."

"I seen it."

"So what do you make of it?"

"I think Little Ray listened to the wrong fucking people."

"Who are the wrong people?"

"The managers, the promoters. The scumbags ruining this sport."

"Can you give me some names?'

"What do I look like, a fucking stool pigeon?"

"You want to help Little Ray or not?"

"Sure," he said. "But I don't know if you know who runs the boxing management and promotions business, Egan. I can assure you it's not the fucking Indian Guides."

"The mob?"

"They organize violence for a living. Who else could do it?"

"You know something, Max? Merle Haggard music should automatically start playing when you walk into a room," I said.

He shook his head. "People don't know shit about boxing anymore," he said. "You ask them to name the best Hispanic fighter ever and they'll tell you Oscar De La Hoya. Roberto Duran ain't even dead yet and people already forgot about him. Ask them who's the best fighter ever and they'll say Tyson. That son of a bitch wasn't even one of the ten best heavyweights ever."

"It's a dying art," I said.

"It's not an art, you stupid ass mick. It's a science. That's why they call it the sweet science. And this ain't a fucking art studio. It's a laboratory. Being a fighter ain't just something you're inspired to do one day. It takes years of hard work and dedication to learn the craft. Big Ray understood that. Why do you think he went 21-2 as an amateur?"

"Because he's black?" I said.

"No, dumbass. Because he learned the science, which is something you never did. Ray taught his boy that too. He didn't want Little Ray to be like one of these Macho Comacho spics who takes two shots to land one. He wanted him to learn defense, and that shit takes time. And the kid did it. That kid's the best defensive boxer I ever trained. He's got it all. The lateral movement, the shoulder roll. He knows how to open and close the distance, how to change up the angles, how to fight on the inside with one arm."

"You taught me the shoulder roll," I said.

"You don't know shit about boxing," he said. "You wouldn't know a left hook from your dick."

"You are like dandelion wine, Max," I said. "You just get sweeter with age."

He sat down on his stool and said: "Listen, I'm sorry that pretty little reporter girl got killed. I liked her. She seemed like a nice girl when she came in here to interview him. But that kid didn't kill her. He didn't have that in him. Hell, I had remind him all the time that he was in the dishing out pain business. He's got all the tools but he ain't got the viciousness. What you and me see as a contest of blood, he still sees as just a sport like football or basketball. If he ever does learn to be mean, there's not a middleweight on this planet that can stand in the ring with him. That roid rage crap is a bunch of goddamn bullshit. I'm going to kick his fucking ass next time I see him for using that shit, but it didn't make him crazy. Trust me, I'd have seen it in here and been happy to see it. But I never saw it. Not once. If anything, the kid is too fucking nice for this business."

"The Durham Wrecking Ball," I said. "You gave him that nickname."

"So fucking what?" Max said. "He needed a nickname. This business is more ridiculous than professional wrestling now. You got guys calling themselves shit like The Hispanic Causing Panic. But that don't mean shit. Look at James Toney. His nickname is Lights Out. When's the last time he ever knocked anything out besides a goddamn all you can eat buffet?"

"The cops have Little Ray dating the girl," I said. "They've got a violent death. I've seen the pictures and they're not pretty. They've got no sign of a struggle or forced entry. They've got sex right before she died. Max, they think they have their guy and they are going to put him on trial and he is probably going to be found guilty."

"Then what the fuck are you doing here?" he said. "You in the grief counseling business now?"

"You mentioned the mob," I said. "Any reason they'd have to frame him?"

Max shook his head. "Nothing in it for them. They were invested in him winning."

Max looked down. His eyes were sagging. He thought a long time before he spoke, which was uncharacteristic of him. He said, "You ever tell yourself you won't believe something? Even if you do? Just because you can't?"

"Sometimes," I said. "I think we all do that."

"That kid," he said. "I trained him since he was six years old. His daddy was still fighting then. He'd come in here and play on the equipment and fuck around on the heavy bag and I'd get up to my cranky old ways and wouldn't be able to stand watching the little bastard do it wrong. So I made him learn how to throw a jab and made him throw it over and over. Then I taught him the straight right hand. Then the left hook and the uppercut. That kid worked harder than any fighter I ever had. We literally built him one piece at a time. And what we built is a goddamn good fighter."

"I thought he had a real shot," I said.

"He had a goddamn good shot. A clear shot. After he demolished Porter, I had him lined up to fight at a casino down in Biloxi against Hernandez. He wins that one and he gets a shot at the title eliminator as the main undercard on an HBO fight. He wins that one and he fights for the middleweight championship of the world. The lineal middleweight championship. Not the goddamn fucking junior middleweight or the super middleweight or one of those bullshit weight classes they made up just so they can give belts to everybody. But the goddamn middleweight title. The guy who beat the guy who beat Bernard Hopkins. Who beat Monzon. Who beat Hagler. Who beat Ray Robinson. Now that might not mean shit to most people, but it's a big goddamn deal."

"I know it is," I said.

"You think he'd throw that away for some TV broad?"

"I'd like to think he wouldn't."

Max put his hand on my shoulder and pointed at me, looking me in the eye. He said: "Egan, I'm a hardheaded man and this sport is the only thing I know about in this world. But I'm not so hardheaded that I can't see what's right in front of me. So do me a favor, okay? Either prove he didn't kill that girl or prove he did."

CHAPTER TEN

I WAS WAITING in the small glass interview room in D Pod of the Durham County Jail. I was sitting in one of the plastic chairs and leaning forward with my elbows on the table. I hadn't been there ten minutes and I was already bored to death.

I looked through the glass and saw the pod. It was full of inmates shuffling back and forth. Some of them were standing under the TV watching reruns of Walker, Texas Ranger. Some were sitting at the steel picnic tables eating baloney sandwiches and drinking little square boxes of milk. And some of were just wandering around muttering nonsense to themselves.

I decided that the next time somebody complained to me that jails were too much like country clubs, I was going to punch them in the face. The worst part about jail wasn't the filth or the violence or the other things people usually imagined. It was having to live in a small confined space with a bunch of crazy morons.

Everybody in jail was there because they had been denied bond or didn't have anybody to post for them or had missed so many court appearances that the judge had just decided they couldn't be trusted to find their way to court without the sheriff's help.

At least half of them were mental cases. When we stopped putting people in loony bins, jails and prisons became dumping grounds for the insane. I thought about what it would be like to live in that environment and decided I'd rather just kill myself.

Eventually I saw one of the jailers bringing Ray toward the portal with the pneumonic steel door. The door made a hissing sound and slid open and Ray came through it and opened the door to the visitor's room and reached out to shake my hand.

"Just let me know when you're done," said the jailer.

"Will do," I said.

I told Ray to have a seat in the plastic chair on the other side of the table and he did. I sat down in the chair across from him.

"Good to see you, kid," I said. "I wish it wasn't under these circumstances."

"Thanks for coming, Mr. Egan," he said.

"Mr. Roth sends his regards."

"Please tell him I said thanks for all the work he's doing for me."

"I'll tell him," I said.

Ray looked like a child sitting there across from me. His shoulders were narrow and the only thing about him that looked like a fighter was the size of his hands.

"I watched the interrogations," I said. "There's nothing on there that can hurt you."

"What are they looking for?"

"Whatever you give them. Most guilty people end up telling them some story about what happened. It might be the truth or it might be some half-truth that slants things so that it's not their fault."

He nodded.

"We got discovery from the state," I said. "So I've seen your interviews with Detective Fields. Nothing surprising there. All you said was that you were innocent."

"I am innocent," he said.

"Whether you're innocent or not doesn't matter right now," I said. "I could tell you I believe you but that doesn't help you any. What matters is what the evidence is going to look like to a jury."

"I wouldn't never hurt Sheryl," he said. "I told them that."

"You told them that a bunch of times," I said.

"They didn't believe me."

"If you're in that interview room, they don't believe you, kid. Nobody has ever talked their way out of that room."

"Why do they think I did it?"

"There's no sign of a break-in and it's unlikely she would let somebody in that she didn't know," I said. "You were the last person to see her alive, as far as they know. What time did you leave her apartment?"

"Probably seven thirty, eight," he said.

"How do you know?"

"I'm in bed by nine. I get up to go running at five in the morning."

"Did you have sex with her?"

"Yeah, we had sex."

"Did you have rough sex? Be honest with me, now."

"No, sir. It was just normal sex."

"She ever say anything about being into rough sex?"

"No, sir. Not to me."

"You sure?"

"Yeah."

"What kind of sex did you guys have?" I said.

"What do you mean?"

"Did you have oral sex?"

"Yeah, we did that."

"Anal?"

"Naw," he said. "She don't get down like that. Me either."

"So just oral and vaginal?"

"Yeah. Why?"

"Just asking."

Ray put his hands up over his face and looked like he was about to cry. "Why would somebody do her like that?" he said.

"I'm more concerned with question of who did her like that," I said. "Did she ever mention any other men?"

"No."

"Any ex-boyfriends you know about?"

"No, sir. She said she dated a guy in Miami but they broke up a few years ago. That was her last boyfriend as far as I know."

"And you two got together after she did that piece on you for the news?"

"Yeah. She came back to the gym about a week later. Asked me did I want to go to lunch. I said yeah. I liked her. She was real sweet."

"How many times did you see her?"

"Nine, ten times, I think."

"Where did you go?"

"We went to a baseball game once," he said. "We went to the movies a couple times. Went out to dinner."

"When did you first have sex?"

"I think it was the second time we went out," he said.

"Did you know who she was before she came to interview you?"

"Yeah," he said. "I seen her on the news."

"Did she ever mention seeing a black car outside her house?"

"A black car?" he said.

"Yeah."

"No. I don't think so."

"How you getting along in here?" I said.

"I'm about to go crazy, man."

"Your mom and dad are worried sick about you. But you know that."

"Yeah."

"There's nothing we can do to get you out before the trial," I said. "Roth asked them to lower the bond to a hundred grand but the judge denied you bond on account of the DA threatening to make this a death penalty case. You can imagine the play this is getting on TV."

Ray shook his head and said, "I can't even imagine, man. It's like a nightmare I can't wake up from. I go to sleep and sometimes I wake up thinking I'm in my own bed. Then I look around and see I'm still here."

"Make the best of it," I said. "Don't start any shit with anybody but don't take shit off anybody either. Nobody's tried to fuck with you, have they?"

"No," he said. "Some of them asked me to teach them how to fight."

"Did you?"

"I showed them some moves."

"No harm in that," I said. "Remember to be polite and respectful to the CO's."

"They won't have no trouble from me," he said.

"Good."

"The cops said there was a surveillance camera on her door," he said. "So she couldn't have died when they said she did."

"That was bullshit," I said. "They were just trying to get a confession out of you."

"They can just lie like that?"

"The cops can lie about anything. It's in the constitution."

"So what happens now?" he said.

I leaned back and crossed my arms. "Now we try to build you a defense," I said.

"How long does that take?"

"How long did it take you to learn defense."

"Years."

"Hopefully it won't take that long."

"Man, I hope not. I'm ready to get up out of here."

"Ray, somebody killed Sheryl. If it wasn't you, it was somebody else. They're not looking at anybody else. So if there's somebody else, I've got to find them and deliver them to the cops on a silver platter. Anything you can think of that you haven't told me, no matter how insignificant it might seem to you, might be helpful."

"I've been thinking about it over and over," he said. "I didn't know her well enough to know anything. All I knew was from the times we went out."

"She never talked about boys or engagements or anything like that?" I said.

"No sir," he said. "I mean, we talked about who we been with, you know? Like, you ever been in love? That kind of stuff."

"What'd she say?"

"She just said she had a boyfriend through most of college but that she didn't date much since then cause she worked all the time."

"Did she say she'd been on any dates since she moved to Durham?"

"No. She didn't say anything about it. She just said her schedule was crazy, you know? Like she had to be up early for the news and then she had to be back at work at night for the news. That's why mostly we went out on the weekends. She said she did most of her sleeping in the afternoon."

"She say anything about getting any calls or letters or anything from fans?" I said.

"She said people recognized her sometimes like in the grocery store or something and said hi but she didn't say nothing that made me remember nothing like that."

"She was a very pretty young woman," I said. "Everybody in the city knew her name and her face. She had to have lots of admirers."

"She didn't really talk about it. She mostly talked about her work."

"What'd she say about it?"

"Just that she liked it. She said she missed Florida but she liked the weather here better than Ohio."

"Did she tell you about her career goals?"

"She said she wanted to get on with one of the national networks eventually and be behind the desk."

"And she approached you about going to lunch?"

"Yes sir."

"What did she want to know about you?" I said.

"She just asked me about being a fighter and stuff. She was interested in what my training's like. She wanted to know about the promotions side too. She asked me if I knew anybody in the mob."

"What did you say?"

"I said not that I know of," he said. "I mean, there's some guys you think might be, but I never saw them do none of that kind of stuff and it wasn't my business to be asking them no questions like that."

"What else do you remember talking about with her?" I said.

He shrugged. "I told her about my training schedule," he said. "She liked to run too. She asked me about some of my fights she'd watched on Youtube."

"What did you say?"

"I told her about how my dad always told me to focus on defense first. That way, I wouldn't end up brain dead and broke. I told her it was frustrating sometimes because people boo you if you're not a banger. But if you look at the guys that last, they always protect theyselves."

"Anything else?" I said.

"She wanted to know what it felt like to knock somebody out."

"She did?"

"Yeah. She'd seen me knock out Porter in AC and wanted to know what it felt like to hit somebody that hard. I told her it's the mechanics that makes the punch and there won't no meanness behind it like people think."

"Did that make any sense to her?" I said.

"I don't know. I told her it wasn't nothing personal. I felt bad for Porter when they had to take him out of there in that ambulance. I was afraid I'd killed him."

"Did she seem fascinated with the violence?"

"I guess so," he said. "She said she'd done some kickboxing classes."

"What did you tell her about your history with women?"

"Just said I had a girlfriend all through high school and about playing football and stuff."

"The girl I remember?" I said.

"Chantel."

"Yeah."

"She in school in Atlanta now," he said. "I still talk to her on Facebook sometimes but she's dating another dude now. We still friends though."

"She wasn't the jealous type, was she?"

"No," he said. "She was real cool."

"Did any of your friends think anything about you seeing a white girl?"

"Nobody said nothing bad about it. A couple of them teased me if they saw her come on TV and I was watching it with them."

"Anything else?"

"She asked me how I got my nickname," he said. "I told her Max came up with Wrecking Ball cause the first part rhymed with Ray. She asked me why not Sugar Ray and I said Ray Robinson and Ray Leonard had already worn that one out and I didn't want to compare myself to them anyhow."

"Did she ever come to watch you train?"

"Just when she interviewed me and when she came back the second time to ask me out," he said.

"I know this is a personal question, but what kind of sex was she into?" I said.

"She liked to feel on my muscles and she liked to give head."

"How'd you do it?" I said. "Missionary? Doggy style? Reverse cowgirl? What?"

Ray blushed and laughed and looked away. "She kind of wanted it a lot, to be honest with you. She liked it a lot."

Ray stopped. "I feel bad even talking about this since she's deceased," he said.

"There's nothing we can do about that now," I said. "The only life we can still save is yours."

CHAPTER ELEVEN

I LEFT MY APARTMENT on University Drive and drove downtown to Roth's office on Main Street. As I drove through the city, I thought about its new split personality. The old Durham was still there. You could see it in the faded tobacco warehouses and rail yards, in the decaying houses with the paint peeling away and the weeds growing high in the yards. In the open air drug markets with the pushers and the junkies wandering around like zombies and the corners where you knew not to stop unless you wanted a gun in your face and a hand in your pocket.

Then there were the gleaming new buildings of the American Tobacco Campus. The performing arts center, the yuppie bars and restaurants, the new Durham Athletic Park, the pristine walkways and gothic buildings on the Duke University campus, where future senators and congressmen and CEO's studied late into the night and plotted to take over the world.

Durham had reinvented itself with the influx of northern transplants fleeing the cold and gloom of the Rust Belt for the Triangle's warm weather and thriving economy, turning it into a booming economic engine with more Ph.D's per capita than any-place not named Silicon Valley.

It called itself the City of Medicine and it was. But that was a slogan with two meanings. It encompassed the medical research breakthroughs being made by Nobel Prize-winning scientists at Duke Hospitals, but it also encompassed the street drugs being sold every minute in the south and east side ghettos. The heroin, the cocaine, the pills, the methamphetamines.

While young millionaires sipped champagne and discussed the latest economic and political theories in their Forest Hills mansions, addicts lay dying next to dumpsters on Alston Street with needles in their arms.

I parked in the parking garage on West Main Street and walked down to Roth's office. I sat across from Roth and told him about the interesting shit I'd found. He was especially interested in the mystery phone number. He was also interested in the lack of DNA under Sheryl Rose's fingernails and the lack of scratch marks around her neck. He said, "All that plays into my kinky sex theory."

"It does," I said. "But that still means he's guilty."

"Yeah, but if he takes the stand and says she was into being choked and it was an accident, we'll get a jury instruction on involuntary manslaughter," he said. "That's only a Class F felony. The max on that is three years."

"What if he won't say that?"

"Then he's a fucking idiot," Roth said. "If it's not an accident, it's an intentional killing. You know how much time you get for that?"

"More, I would imagine."

"You bet your ass."

I took a seat on Roth's couch and made myself conformable. I said, "He didn't confess to Fields."

"So fucking what?"

"I never saw an accidental killer who didn't confess."

"First time for everything," Roth said.

"I want to know more about that number."

"What do you have so far?"

"It's a cell phone with pre-paid minutes," I said. "It was purchased in a mobile phone store in Northgate Mall. They have surveillance cameras in there but the tape records over itself every three days. I thought I'd need to get you to do a subpoena to get the records of the transaction but I sweet talked the girl into giving me what they have."

"And?"

"It was a cash transaction," I said. "I asked who was working that day and she said she didn't know. They don't have any employee logs, either, so it's impossible to know who sold the phone. She said it was probably her because she was working days back then from eight till five."

"I don't guess she remembered anything."

"No. She said they sell those things all the time. I asked her if she ever sold one to a guy who looked like he might choke a woman to death and she said no."

Roth put his jacket on and then stopped just as he was about to push his left arm through the sleeve. He said, "What about additional minutes?"

"You can buy airtime cards to add minutes. We might need to get a subpoena to get those records because the phone company has those cards keyed to that phone. But I'm guessing those were probably all cash purchases too."

Roth straightened his jacket and shot his cuffs. He said, "So this guy starts calling about six months before she dies using a prepaid phone that was purchased with cash?"

"Assuming it's a guy, yes."

"That is interesting."

"That's why it made my list of interesting shit," I said.

"How many calls were made from that number?"

"I haven't counted them," I said. "It was a lot."

I took out the logs and started shuffling through them. "It's the pattern that's interesting," I said. "One call on November the 13th in the morning. Two more the following day. After that, you're looking at three or four calls a day. And that's not counting the times she called that number."

Roth gave me a troubled look.

"Why do you buy a prepaid phone?" he said.

"I saw them a bunch when I was in Vice," I said. "Makes sense for a dealer to change up his number from time to time so we can't put a trap and trace on it. But there's other reasons. Let's say you're married and having an affair and you're scared your wife is going to go through your phone."

"That's how my ex-wife caught me fucking around," Roth said. "Well, one of the ways. She also put a PI on me. Damn, that was some expensive pussy."

"Whatever the reason, this is a conscious effort to avoid detection," I said.

Roth settled back in his chair and smiled, which was rare for him. "And there's nothing about this in any of the police reports?" he said.

"No," I said.

"Why would they leave that out?"

"I guess they didn't think it was that important," I said. "But I'd sure as hell like to know whose number this is. Wouldn't you?"

"Damn right I would," he said.

I WENT ONTO Amazon.com and purchased DNA for Dummies and read it and was still confused. It was still too complicated for me, so I did a Wikipedia search for DNA and read about it. Jill had told me to look beyond the SBI lab report and to focus on the slides themselves. I passed that information on to Roth and he said he'd file the discovery motion as well as a subpoena to get the phone records for the mystery caller.

I had a lot of questions. The first one was, "What the fuck is DNA and why is it so convincing?" When I was in Major Crimes, I dealt with it in passing but I had never really tried to understand it before. I left the science stuff it up to the CSI nerds.

I read in the book that DNA was a genetic code that was particular to each person and that while people who were related might have similar DNA, complete strangers would have totally different DNA. Except that they didn't always. I read on the Internet about a study they had done on DNA samples taken from felons that they ran through a cold case database and got hits matching felons who were not yet born when the crime was committed. So that was something. It meant that DNA matches didn't always tell the truth. Like anything else, DNA evidence wasn't perfect. But as I found out, it was pretty damn good.

I did more Internet research and found a report by the American Academy of Science, which sounded pretty official. It had been commissioned by Congress to examine the use of forensic evidence in criminal court proceedings. When I read it, I was startled to learn that much of what I thought I knew about forensic police work was complete bullshit.

Fingerprints are bullshit. I'd always been told that they were like snowflakes and that no two sets were ever alike. But where did that come from? It turns out it was just something the FBI made up years ago and got repeated so often that everyone now just accepts it as fact. Fingerprint science, it turns out, is a highly subjective thing.

In fact, they even did a study where they gave examiners sets of fingerprints and asked them to match or exclude them from crime scene samples they provided. But the testers introduced contextual bias by telling the examiners things like, "This guy has already confessed and we just want to corroborate his confession."

Or, "We're pretty sure it wasn't this guy because we think he was dead when the crime was committed."

What the examiners didn't know was that the prints they were evaluating were prints they themselves had evaluated earlier in their careers. In about half of the cases, the examiners reached the opposite conclusions they had reached when they studied them the first time.

I learned that ballistics is bullshit, hair and fiber evidence is bullshit, tool mark evidence is bullshit, and arson accelerant evidence is bullshit. Pretty much everything is bullshit. It seemed that the only things that are not bullshit are drug testing from blood samples and nuclear DNA, and even those things are subject to human error.

But despite all I learned, none of it helped Ray. I had a blood test showing he had performance enhancing drugs in his system and a semen sample that matched his DNA. The report mentioned fibers and hairs that were unaccounted for, but I'd already learned to distrust fiber evidence and learned that the hair could have come from contact transfer, which would be common for a reporter who came into contact with numerous people every day. There were still the fingerprints they hadn't accounted for, but I didn't have anybody to match them to.

Roth had filed a motion seeking the underlying data for the lab reports, and Jill said she'd call her old college roommate Ellen Page, who now answered to Dr. Ellen Page, to ask if she'd review the data and give me a second opinion. Ellen was the director of a lab that did research on the human genome for pharmaceutical companies. The lab had previously done contract lab work for the SBI before the state started doing all of its lab work in-house, so she was experienced in criminal forensics.

I was in Jill's living room and we were watching The Third Man. I had seen it a million times but it never got old. Jill rented it from Netflix because she had this thing now for Joseph Cotton after seeing him play the serial killer in the Hitchcock movie. I told her he was probably old and wrinkly and dead now and she said she didn't care.

"You have any bourbon in here?" I asked her.

"I bought some just for you," she said.

She was sitting next to me on the couch wearing gym shorts and a throwback UNC t-shirt with the strutting ram mascot. Louie was in her lap and he jumped off and turned around and hissed at me when she got up.

"Sorry, bud," I said to him. He scampered off in anger and curled up in a chair across the room.

She returned with a glass that had two ice cubes in it and a bottle of Gentleman Jack. I said, "That's my girl," and poured myself half a glass of bourbon. On TV, Orson Welles and Joseph Cotton were up on the Ferris wheel and Welles was asking Cotton how many people he would allow to die if he got a thousand bucks apiece for them. "Free of tax, old man. Free of tax," he said.

"You know anything about DNA?" I said.

"I know a little," she said.

"It had to be easier to be a murderer back in the old days," I said.

"I'm sure it was."

"Jack the Ripper didn't have to worry about DNA."

"No he didn't."

"What are the chances Ellen actually finds anything helpful to us?" I said.

Jill put her arm around me and said, "About the same as the chance I'll sleep with you if you keep interrupting this movie."

"I'll shut up then," I said.

"Smart boy."

We watched until the end and then started kissing until we ended up in her bedroom, but the whole thing was ruined when

I couldn't get the zephyr music from the movie out of my head. It just played in a loop over and over and the sex was no good.

"What's the matter?" she said.

"All I can hear is that music," I said.

"Oh. I know. It's stuck in my head too. You want another drink?"

"Sure."

She got up out of bed and put on her t-shirt and came back with the Gentleman Jack bottle and two glasses. She poured them and we lay in bed sipping the whiskey.

She said, "You think this is what it's like when you get married?"

"Probably," I said. "Except the people are probably in different rooms."

After awhile Louie came in and jumped up in the bed and began rubbing and purring on me. I petted him and said, "Does it ever seem strange to you that you have this wild animal that goes out into nature and just tears birds and chipmunks to pieces with its bare teeth and then comes into your house and snuggles with you in the bed?"

"No," she said, reaching over to pet him. "He's a sweet boy."

"Sweet, my ass," I said. "I pulled into your driveway once and saw that son of a bitch with a full adult gray squirrel in his mouth. Had it by the neck. The squirrel was deader than shit."

"That's nature," she said. "Every prey has a predator and every predator a prey."

"Except for man," I said.

"Man has a predator too," she said.

"Oh yeah? What's that?"

"Man," she said.

CHAPTER TWELVE

THE NEWS TRUCKS crowded the front of the Durham County Courthouse. They were waiting for Stuart Roth as soon as we came out of the garage. They stuck their microphones in his face and aimed their large camera lenses at him. Roth was dressed impeccably in a black suit with purple pinstripes and a matching purple tie. He wore Armani sunglasses and carried his briefcase. I followed behind him in jeans and a gray blazer.

"Mr. Roth, Chief Jaggers has described this as one of the most savage murders in his thirty years on the force. Do you care to comment?"

Roth stopped walking. He stood there holding the briefcase at his side.

"The chief can make all the irresponsible comments he wants to," he said. "In fact, I believe that his comments have already irreparably compromised my client's right to have a fair trial in this county. And I will be taking this matter up with the court and seeking a change of venue."

"The police say they have DNA linking Ray Marks to the killing."

"As I have said before and will say again," Roth said. "Unlike our police chief, I intend to try this case in a court of law and not in the press. A jury of my client's peers will look at the facts, all the facts, evaluate them without passion or prejudice, and then render a just verdict that speaks the truth. We are very confident they will find Mr. Marks not guilty of this terrible crime."

Roth walked through the cameras toward the courthouse doors and I followed him.

"What do you have to say for the roid rage allegations," one of the reporters shouted.

Roth ignored the question and walked inside. We took the elevator to the fourth floor and walked into courtroom 403, where they were getting ready to do calendar call for the afternoon Superior Court administrative session. Roth crossed the swinging gate separating the gallery from the bar and took a seat in one of the jury chairs. I took a seat in the front row of the gallery where I could hear the conversation between Roth and the prosecutor.

Peter Stricker saw Roth there and pointed toward him and began whispering something to his assistant, Shawn Taylor. Stricker stood up and walked over to Roth, who taken taken off his sunglasses and was cleaning them with his tie.

"You really need to put a muzzle on that idiot police chief of yours," Roth said.

"You mind your shop and I'll mind mine," the prosecutor said.

"You want to drive to Forsyth County to try this thing?" Roth said.

"This case isn't going anywhere and you goddamn know it."

"Whether it does or doesn't, I already have an issue for appeal."

Roth opened his briefcase and handed Stricker a copy of his motion to suppress Ray's statements to the police and the physical evidence gathered as a result of the police examination of him.

"We haven't even set a deadline for motions yet," Stricker said.

"It doesn't matter," Roth said. "Have you watched that police interview? Looked pretty custodial to me. My client was even hand-cuffed during part of it."

"Assuming this is not a bullshit motion, which it is, the physical evidence still comes in. I have U.S. Supreme Court case law on that."

"I can distinguish it from this case," Roth said. "In this state, we have statutory procedures for getting nontestimonial physical evidence. And your cops, in their zeal to railroad my client, drove over those procedures like a drunk knocking down traffic cones."

"Look," Stricker said. "You know what's going to happen. Your client gets one chance and one chance only. He pleads guilty and I'll take the death penalty off the table today. He doesn't and I'll file my motion of intent to seek the death penalty this afternoon."

"Are you joking?" Roth said.

"There are aggravating factors here."

"Name them."

"Your client took advantage of a position of trust," Stricker said. "That's one. And this crime was particularly heinous, atrocious, and cruel."

Roth laughed and said, "Peter, try the tough guy shit on the kids who haven't sat at the big boy table before. You and I can posture all we want, but let's just cut through the shit and be honest about this. Do you have a case? I'll concede that you do. Will you likewise concede that you'll be lucky to get murder two and would be offering me voluntary manslaughter if your victim wasn't a TV celebrity?"

"No."

"Well then I think you're either lying or you're delusional. I like to think the best of people, so I'll assume you're delusional."

"Listen to me," Stricker said. "I don't want to do it, but I swear to God I'll kill that boy if I have to."

"That's why we have juries, Peter. To say which one of us is right and which one of us is wrong."

Judge Watson came out of the side door and the bailiff stood and said, "All rise. Oyez, oyez, oyez, this Superior Court for the county of Durham is now open and sitting for the dispatch of business. The Honorable Benjamin J. Watson presiding. God save this state and this honorable court. Be seated."

The judge began calling the calendar. When he got to our case, Roth and Stricker both stood up. Stricker said, "Judge, we have provided discovery in this case and have had preliminary discussions regarding a plea. So far, it looks like we're pretty far apart. The state would ask that this case be put on the trial calendar sooner rather than later."

"We're still waiting on some discovery, your honor," Roth said.

Stricker shot a confused look at Roth and said, "I'm not sure what discovery counsel is referring to, judge."

Roth thumbed through the file and took out his motion. He said, "Judge, we have the police report, the SBI report, the medical examiner's report, witness statements, all the usual stuff. But what we don't have, and what we have specifically requested, as Mr. Stricker will see if he bothers to read my motion, is the data supporting the SBI lab report. We have also issued a subpoena, which we have filed with the clerk, seeking certain telephone records. I anticipate getting those in the next month or so, but I don't feel that we can proceed until Mr. Stricker gives me the SBI records and we have a chance to have it independently evaluated."

Stricker looked down at the motion. "Judge," he said. "They have the lab report. I don't see how all the rest is necessary."

"It's necessary because if you'll remember a few years back, judge, another man in Mr. Stricker's position handed the defense a lab report that didn't match the data underlying it and it took the defense lawyers and their experts to catch it. Now I'm not suggesting Mr. Stricker is doing anything like that, but we'd like to see the raw data so that we may have it independently verified."

The judge looked at Stricker. "Any reason you can't accommodate Mr. Roth's request in a timely manner, counselor?" he said.

"The SBI has all kinds of backlogs these days, judge. I can request it, but I'm sure Your Honor is very aware of how underfunded and overworked that agency is at the moment."

"Mr. Stricker just notified me that he intends to make this a death penalty case, judge," Roth said. "If a man's life is going to be put at stake, I don't see how we can be denied those records."

The judge nodded. "I'll give you a month to turn over the records, Mr. Stricker," he said.

"Thank you, your honor," Roth said. "We do have one more discovery request, judge."

The judge rifled through the motions in the file. "Give me one moment, Mr. Roth."

"Take your time, judge."

"Okay. Go ahead."

"The state has complied with our discovery request for e-mails and other information obtained from the victim's computer. Your honor has placed those matters under seal in order to protect the privacy and reputation of the victim. However, the state contends that in retrieving that information from the victim's computer, the computer's hard drive was irrevocably damaged. We would like to get an independent analysis of that hard drive."

"What makes you think you can fix it if they can't?" Judge Watson said.

"We believe it's worth a try, judge."

"Who is your expert you intend to use?"

"Eliot Goodson, your honor," Roth said. "I'm sure you're familiar with him. He worked in computer forensics for the Durham Police Department before he was lured away by the big money over in the Research Triangle Park."

"Any objection, Mr. Stricker?"

"This is another fishing expedition, but if they want to look, we don't object," Stricker said. "However, we would like for anything they find to be turned over to us in reciprocal discovery and of course be placed under seal."

"Very well, gentlemen," said the judge. "Peace among God's children. The state will provide the defendant with the SBI data supporting the lab tests and will make available to the defense expert the hard drive from the victim's computer. I'll further order that anything found on that hard drive be placed under seal. Any further business?"

"No sir," said Roth.

"None from the state," said Stricker.

"All right, then. Looks like the earliest we can put this on the calendar is about six months from now. Does that work for both parties?"

Roth closed his briefcase. He said, "Assuming there are no additional discovery matters that come up between now and then, that works for us, judge."

"Works for us too, judge," Stricker said.

CHAPTER THIRTEEN

S INCE THE MEDIA CIRCUS was in full swing, I figured it was about time the race hustlers got in on the action and they didn't disappoint. When I came out of the courthouse, I saw them standing on the steps holding signs and chanting slogans. I crossed the street and stood under a tree and watched them. The sun was declining in the sky, turning the blue into a light pink, and the street was busy with people leaving their government offices and heading to their cars.

It was a pretty small crowd but they made a lot of noise. There was a lot of yelling about lynching and institutional racism which, to be honest, were pretty legitimate concerns given that this was Durham. Some cities dabble in race scandals from time to time, but we do them for a living. Race scandals are to us what Coca-Cola is to Atlanta. They are our biggest and most-reliable industry.

The Reverend Marcus Worthdale was leading the mob and playing it up for the cameras. He reminded me of Al Sharpton back when Sharpton was fat. He had that wavy Southern Baptist preacher hair and was always dressed in an expensive suit. Any time a camera was around, you would find him fulminating about rushes to judgment and racial profiling, giving his full throated oratories with a righteous defiance befitting the leader of an angry mob.

But the fact that he was an opportunistic phony didn't mean he was wrong. The cops pretty much set up shop in what some of them still called Nigger Town and arrested the blacks for everything they could think of while ignoring the white kids committing crimes in the suburbs. You didn't even know crime was happening in the suburbs until some meth lab house blew up and killed some people.

Unlike most of the local agitators, including much of the Duke University faculty, Reverend Worthdale had come through the lacrosse scandal without a scratch on him. Three innocent kids got arrested and indicted for raping a black stripper, even when nobody in their right mind believed the charges.

Reverend Worthdale led the rush to judgment in that case and cheered as his supporters shouted death threats at the three kids when they arrived at the courthouse to turn themselves in. And he never apologized for it or suffered any noticeable hit to his reputation even after the attorney general declared them innocent on national TV.

He at least had the good sense to keep his mouth shut when the stripper stabbed her boyfriend to death a few years later. But the Reverend was back now and full of righteous fury. Of course, the media had come out with their cameras ready.

"We will not be silenced by a culture of intimidation and oppression," he shouted to his supporters. "We will not stand by quietly as this police department and this city demonstrate, once again, that there is a double standard for justice here in the city of Durham, North Carolina. The evil specter of segregation is still alive and well in this city. White folks get rich and black folks get lynched."

The crowd cheered. I stood watching from across the street. He continued: "We all mourn the tragic murder of Sheryl Rose, as we mourn the passing of any innocent human life from this earth and we pray that our merciful father in heaven will welcome her home and comfort her family and heal their wounds in their hour of grief. But we will not stand by and silently watch another rush to judgment or allow another young black man to be convicted by the police and the media before he has even had his day in court. Ray Marks is presumed innocent under the law, but he has already been judged and condemned by all."

You had to admire the guy. He could put the words together and he had a great racket going. Next came the part I was waiting for. "Today I am calling not just on my brothers and sisters in the African American community, but on all members of this community who seek justice and equality, to give and give generously to the Bull City Coalition for Social Justice's campaign so that we may fight for true justice for both Sheryl Rose and Ray Marks. They may be waving the noose, but we going to fight em with the truth."

You had to love it. And, goddamn him, he was right. Slavery in America had actually died its final death in this very city when General Johnston met General Sherman over at Bennett Station to surrender to him the Confederacy's last army. But since that day, Durham had recorded an appalling history of race relations and was still rife with segregation, racism, poverty, crime, and corruption.

In the days that the media had been obsessed over Sheryl Rose's murder, there had been other murders in the projects. I only knew this because I read the crime blotter in the Herald. If you only got your news from Channel 5, you'd think Sheryl Rose had been the only person murdered in Durham this year.

The key word in Reverend Worthdale's speech was "fund." Behind every injustice was a collection plate. I watched as Reverend Worthdale opened his briefcase and took out some papers. He held them up high for the cameras. He said, "Here in my hand I have a petition demanding a full and impartial investigation into the railroading of yet another young black man. I am personally going to take this petition into this courthouse and place it on the District Attorney's desk."

He walked over and reached for the door. I looked at my watch. It was five minutes past five. He pulled on the door and it didn't move. He pulled on it again and it still didn't move. He turned back and looked at his assembled supporters.

"They playing games with us," he said. "They playing games. But they can't stop our voices from being heard. We are going to take our petition and we are going to put it on the door of the halls of justice just like Martin Luther took his letter and nailed it to the door of the Sistine Chapel."

The crowd exploded in cheers. Reverend Worthdale placed the petition on top of the door handle and it fell off and landed on the ground. He bent down and picked it up and carefully put it back.

I stood across the street waiting for him to finish and watched the crowd thin out and then I decided to go over and ask him some questions. He was surrounded by a group of young Nation of Islam looking guys in suits and bowties and I had to say, "Excuse me," to get through them so that I could speak with the Reverend.

I put out my hand and he shook it. I said, "Howdy Reverend. I'm working for Ray's lawyer. I think it's great you're creating a fund for him."

"Justice delayed is justice denied, Mr. Egan," he said.

"The cameras are gone," I said.

"This isn't about the cameras," he said. "This is about our long and continuing struggle against racism and inequality."

"I said the cameras are gone."

"Clearly you misunderstand my motives, sir."

"Okay, when can I pick up the money?" I said.

He stood there and gave me a scornful look.

"You got a fund going," I said. "I think that's jim dandy. What's it for again? The Coalition for Justice and the American Way or something like that?"

"You are mocking me, sir. And I don't appreciate that. This isn't a joke to my community or my organization."

"No, really," I said. "I'm excited about it. I just want to know when I can come pick up the check?"

He gave me a confused look. I said, "You know, on account of how his lawyer and I are actually doing all the work to fight this rush to judgment."

"When we raise the money, we will distribute it appropriately," he said.

"That's interesting," I said. "Where else would it go but to Ray's defense?"

"Listen, Mr. Egan. We have bills and expenses to continue to make sure our movement sustains itself so that it may prosper and grow. But as a police officer, I don't expect you to know how any of that works."

"Reverend, we're both grown men here so let's cut the shit. First, I'm not a police officer any more. I'm on my own now. Second, I admire you. You've got a great thing going here. But it'd be a shame if the media and Ray's family found out you had raised a bunch of money for Ray's defense and none of it actually went to him."

He stared at me.

"What you driving these days?" I said. "You still rocking that red S Class or did you get something new?"

"I'll have my treasurer give you a call," he said.

"That's super awesome," I said. I started to walk away and then turned back.

"Keep up the good fight," I said. "Maybe one day we'll overcome all these problems and achieve true equality and racial harmony. That'd be great. But it makes me wonder. What will you do, then?"

"I don't like your insinuation, Mr. Egan. But the thing about white privilege is that those who have it don't even know they have it. So I'll turn the other cheek and just pray that someday you'll see the truth."

"No offense intended, Reverend," I said. "I'm just a curious person and it's something I wonder about. I hope I live to see that day. I really do."

I reached into my wallet and took out a card.

"Here's my number," I said. "I'll be waiting on your treasurer's call."

CHAPTER FOURTEEN

J ILL AND I were sitting in the bleachers along the right baseline
of the Durham Athletic Park. We were watching the Durham
Bulls play the Lehigh Valley IronPigs. It was a beautiful summer
day with temperatures in the low 80's and the blue sky was full of
big white clouds. Over the left field fence, the sun was glistening
off the blue glass of University Tower and the old Central Carolina
Bank building was rising up above the rest of the downtown sky-
line behind the giant bull in the outfield, which stood there snarl-
ing and taunting batters with its prize: "Hit Bull Win Steak."

I was wearing a Boston Red Sox cap and Jill was wearing a UNC
baseball cap and dark sunglasses and had her hair pulled back in
a ponytail. We were both drinking large cold beers in plastic cups
and I had a bag of popcorn in my lap.

"I hate that fucking movie," I said.

"Why's that?"

"We would still be playing ball in the old stadium if it wasn't
for that."

Jill reached over and grabbed a handful of popcorn. "You're an idiot," she said. "This place is great. That old stadium was a dump."

"It might have been a dump, but it had character," I said.

"It smelled like the New York City subway," she said.

"I still miss it."

"Besides, look at all the other developments that sprang up here," she said. "We got the American Tobacco Campus. We got good restaurants, bars, a performing arts center. You can't blame that movie for ruining this city."

"Yes I can," I said. "I still hate Kevin Costner and Susan Sarandon for that. I grew up trying to catch foul balls in that old ballpark. And they came along and just burned down all my childhood memories."

"Did you ever catch a ball?"

"Yes," I said. "Well, I didn't catch it, but I chased it down and found it under the bleachers and took it home with me. I still have it."

Jill leaned back in her seat and crossed her legs. She said, "What about Tim Robbins? You hate him too?"

"I used to," I said. "But how can you hate a guy who crawled through a river of shit and came out clean on the other side and then ran off with all of Warden Norton's money?"

The last Bulls hitter of the inning struck out and the IronPigs jogged back to the dugout. The organ music started playing and the Bulls mascot came out onto the field and started dancing for the kids.

"I hate triple A baseball," I said.

"Why?"

"If I wanted to go to a real baseball game, I'd just go to Atlanta or Washington. Well, bad examples. New York, maybe."

"You've been to New York?"

"Yeah. Is that surprising to you?"

"You just don't seem like the type," she said.

"My dad used to take me when I was a kid. We'd eat at this little Italian speakeasy type place on 61st Street and we'd ride the subway up to the Bronx and watch the Yankees play. You ever been to a major league game?"

"My dad took me to Yankee Stadium too," she said. "And Camden Yards."

"I've been to a bunch of them," I said. "I have to say that Fenway is the best."

"I don't care about the game," she said. "I just like being outside on a beautiful day. Usually it's more fun if I don't have Oscar the fucking Grouch sitting next to me."

"I still like all that too," I said. "But for a real minor league experience, you've got to drive down to Wilson to see the Tobacco Worms. You ever been there?"

"No," she said.

"I should take you sometime. It's great. The stadium is a real dump. The local high school kids sell hot dogs for fifty cents apiece and they even have a whole section along the right fence line with tables that are just giant wooden spools. They have a bar set up right there behind them."

"How far away is it?" she said.

"About an hour and a half."

"No thanks."

"You'd love it," I said. "It's like going back in time."

"I don't go east of Raleigh unless I'm going to the beach," she said.

I finished my beer and started looking around to see if the beer man was anywhere in sight. I put my hand on Jill's leg.

"You talk to Ellen?" I said.

"I talked to her."

"What'd she say?"

"She said she'd look at the data if you gave it to her. It'll cost you though."

"What'll it cost me?"

"She wants two tickets to Cosi Fan Tutte at the DPAC."

"She should wait for The Marriage of Figaro. It's better."

"That's not on the schedule this season," she said. "Besides, Mozart is Mozart."

"Tell her it's a deal," I said.

"I'll tell her. She said to tell you she wants seats at the bottom of the upper level with a view to the middle part of the stage."

"What if they don't have any of those left?"

"Then your kid fries in the electric chair," she said.

"Do you know when the tickets go on sale?"

"I don't have a clue. Look it up yourself."

"I'll get right on it," I said.

CHAPTER FIFTEEN

ROTH CALLED ME and told me that Stricker's office had given him the data from the lab report. I drove over to his office and picked it up and took it to Ellen at her spacious lab in the Research Triangle Park. She called me the next day and told me to come back to the lab. I got in my truck and drove down 85 until it merged into 40 and I took the Harrison Avenue exit and parked in front of the giant brick and glass building that housed the lab. The lady behind the desk waved me back. Ellen had the slides out on a table and was looking at them.

"These slides are interesting," she said. She pointed to pictures of scientific markups that might as well have been tablets written in Urdu as far as I was concerned.

"Roth said most defense lawyers don't request the data," I said. "They just rely on the report."

"That's a shame," she said.

"I thought DNA was pretty straightforward."

"Not as much as you might think."

"I read this report that said DNA is one of the few real objective forensic methods," I said. "I thought it was supposed to be rock solid."

"It's an objective method," she said. "But interpreting the data requires more subjectivity than people realize."

"You see right here," she said, pointing to a table of numbers with a corresponding chart next to it that looked like an EKG reading.

I looked at it. "What am I looking at?" I said.

"Different analysts might tell you different things," she said.

"What do you mean?"

"Well, you see these markers here?" she said.

"Yes."

"These are from your suspect."

She took out a page showing a vertical lineup of black, gray, and white lines on what looked like a ladder.

"Okay."

"Here you have the sample. You see that?"

I nodded.

"But then you have this," she said, and pointed to the page with the table and the charts.

"These could be indicators of alleles present that aren't strong enough to be counted as true additional alleles, at least according to the SBI lab's criteria for matches."

"What the hell is an allele?" I said.

"It indicates the presence of a particular person in a source sample," she said. "When you have multiple alleles, that tells you that you might have more than one contributor to the sample. See, some analysts in some labs would say this sample is a mixture with multiple contributors. The SBI analyst who made the report evaluated it using the state crime lab's criteria and interpreted it differently. He or she saw only a single contributor. Obviously, if it's a mixture, that means your victim was having sex with more than one person."

"Why wouldn't they include that in the report?" I said.

"They probably interpreted the other indicators as something like background noise in the test," she said. "It gets very tricky when you have a mixture where one contributor's DNA is more pronounced than another's. You could get ten analysts to look at these slides and you might get ten different opinions. I reviewed the SBI standards and under their protocols, the analyst made the right call. That's why there's no mention of a possible second contributor in the report."

"So DNA is bullshit too?" I said.

"No," she said. "But it's open to different interpretations."

"The person who evaluated this knew the cops already had a suspect in custody," I said. "They had a rush order on it."

"Contextual bias can factor into it," she said. "Consciously or subconsciously, the analyst might have been looking to confirm what the cops already knew or thought they knew."

"But you have these other indicators," she said. "These things right here and here." She pointed to the spikes in the EKG reading on the chart.

"Okay," I said.

"I think those readings show a second contributor in the source sample," she said. "I think they got it wrong."

"Can you get a DNA profile from that?"

"Probably," she said. "But it would be worthless unless you had someone to match it up against."

"There's the database of convicted felons," I said.

"That'd be a good place to start."

"But you can build a DNA profile with what you've got here?"

"I think so," she said. "If the markers are weak, it tells you that you have a somewhat degraded sample. That might mean that it's older or weaker for whatever reason. But even though the markers are weaker, they are still consistent. If you had a second suspect who had sex with her, his markers would match these markers."

"Okay."

"There's a lot more technical shit to it," she said, "but I know you're not a scientist, so I'm trying to give you the simplest version I can."

"I read DNA for Dummies," I said.

"That's a good start," she said.

"But bottom line," I said. "Ray wasn't the only contributor to the semen sample taken from the crime scene?"

She nodded and said, "That's my professional opinion."

CHAPTER SIXTEEN

E LLEN WAS SITTING on the first row in the courtroom when Judge Watson called the case. Roth had put it on the docket for a hearing on his motion to continue the case to a later date. Roth stood up and asked to be heard at the appropriate time.

The judge looked over the motions and you could tell from his face that he was thoroughly confused.

"Mr. Roth, I. . . . Sir, I thought we had a trial date set," said the judge. "I thought both parties had agreed on it."

"Judge, Mr. Stricker just provided me with the data from the SBI forensic report, and in that data, we happened to find something very interesting. It turns out the SBI report isn't worth the paper it's written on."

"Object to that characterization, your honor. I find offensive Mr. Roth's insinuation that I've tried to somehow misled him or hide any exculpatory evidence," said Stricker, rising in anger. "I have an ongoing duty of disclosure and I fulfilled that duty."

"Judge, I've been requesting these DNA slides since this case began. I made informal requests and got nowhere. I filed a motion asking the court to order the state to give them to us and Mr. Stricker objected. He only gave us the data after this court ordered him to. And what we found in that data is simply amazing. We found that the data are not only inconsistent with the conclusions in the report, but that they actually exculpate Mr. Marks and implicate another individual whose identity is unknown to us at this time. In light of this, I think justice demands that we postpone this trial until after we have had the chance to fully investigate this matter."

"Judge, this is a delaying tactic," Stricker said. "We've previously stipulated to the analyst's report. The reports are comprehensive and say nothing that would exculpate the defendant."

"He's right, your honor, they don't," Roth said. "And that is an outrage. Because we contend that the DNA slides used to generate those reports show the existence of at least two contributors to the semen sample taken from the vagina of the victim after her death. This fact was left wholly out of the analyst's report and never disclosed to us."

"What is Mr. Roth even talking about, your honor?" Stricker said. "You have the report. It's clear as day. All that was missing were the slides corroborating that report."

"The slides do nothing of the sort, judge," Roth said. "They contradict the report. They annihilate the report. They blow the report out of three dimensional space."

Stricker had an incredulous look on his face. He said, "Are we to believe that Mr. Roth is now an expert in the field of nuclear and mitochondrial DNA, your honor? This is absurd."

"I don't want to get lost in the weeds here, Mr. Roth," said the judge. "I'm not a scientist. Mr. Stricker's not a scientist. You're not a scientist. If you're asking me to delay this trial, I'm going to need more than just allegations of inconsistencies."

"Well, judge," Roth said. "It just so happens that I found a certified DNA scientist hanging out around the snack machines and she can explain all of this to you in detail. I'd like to call her in support of my motion. Dr. Ellen Page, would you please stand."

Ellen stood. Stricker turned back and looked at her in the gallery.

"This is outrageous, judge," Stricker said. "Even by Mr. Roth's standards. I've had no notice of this witness, no opportunity to prepare to cross examine her, no copy of her curriculum vitae. . ."

"Here you go, buddy boy," said Roth. He handed Stricker a copy of Ellen's CV, complete with details about her education, experience, and citations to articles in scientific journals that she authored, co-authored, or peer reviewed. After asking to approach, Roth handed a copy of her CV to the judge.

"I. . . judge, I object," said Stricker. "This is trial by ambush."

"It's more like an ambush of an ambush, judge," Roth said. "You see, Mr. Stricker was in possession of this material earlier than I was. He had a duty to disclose it to me and to do so in a timely manner. I have the ethics opinion on that handy, if you'd like to see it. He tried to ambush me by not turning it over until it was too late for me to have it thoroughly examined. I can only presume, given its nature, that he was either incompetently unaware of the data's significance or simply hoped I would miss it. But we didn't miss it. And oh man do you want to hear the results."

"Judge, I. . . this. . . ."

"He can't complain that his ambush failed because I got there ahead of him and killed him first," Roth said.

The judge looked at the CV and then gravely studied the motion. "I'll hear from the witness," he said.

Ellen took the stand and swore the oath and Roth asked her the series of questions necessary to qualify her as an expert in the field of DNA. Then Roth got to the good part.

"Have you had the opportunity to evaluate these slides, Dr. Page?" he said.

"I have."

"And what did you find?"

"I found what I believe to be two sets of DNA," she said.

"Two sets, you say?"

"Yes. Two sets."

"How would that happen?" Roth said.

"The SBI analyst singled out the dominant contributor and concluded that it was the only contributor to the sample. A closer examination led me to conclude that the sample was actually a mixture. Although it is not as pronounced as the dominant sample, I was able to identify a second contributor to the sample and develop a second DNA profile from that."

"Did either of the sets match the sample provided by Mr. Marks," Roth said.

"Yes, sir," she said. "The dominant sample matched Mr. Marks' DNA."

"How could you tell?"

She held up the slide.

"Right here you can see the markers," she said. "This is a sample of DNA taken from the semen sample and next to it is a slide showing Mr. Marks' DNA profile. At least, according to the data furnished by the SBI. You can see that the markers line up in twelve places. So that's a match."

"Okay, how about the second one?" Roth said.

She turned the page and held up the second slide.

"Upon evaluating the sample, I found a second allele, which indicates the presence of a second contributor," she said. "I was able to develop a profile from that. As I said, it's less pronounced, but it's there."

"What does that tell you?" Roth said.

"It tells me that the semen taken from Ms. Rose's vagina after her murder was a mixture that came from two separate individuals."

"Wait a minute," Roth said. "Are you telling me that Sheryl Rose had sex with two men on the night she was killed?"

"It appears so," she said. "Yes, sir."

"Why would one sample be more pronounced than the other?"

"It could be any number of things. The unknown contributor might have worn a condom or he might not have ejaculated during intercourse."

"No further questions," Roth said.

Judge Watson looked at the DA. "Mister Stricker?" he said.

"Judge, I'd like some more time," Stricker said.

"How's ten seconds sound?"

"I can't possibly be expected to rebut this. . ."

"Motion to continue is allowed," said the judge. "I find all this highly troubling and I'm not going to put a man on trial for his life until Mr. Roth has had the chance to get to the bottom of this."

"Thank you, your honor," said Roth. "I'll draft the order."

CHAPTER SEVENTEEN

THE STATE TURNED OVER Sheryl Rose's hard drive and I took it to Eliot Goodson. It took him about ten minutes to recover the information the state said was unrecoverable. He gave a disgusted laugh. "Fucking amateurs," he said.

"If something's been erased, can you get it back?" I said.

"Nothing is ever really erased on a computer," he said.

"How long will it take you to go over her Internet searches and all that?"

"Give me a day or two," Eliot said.

I drove to a local strip mall and found a bar and settled in to drink a couple of beers but I had only finished one when Eliot called me and told me to come back to his office.

"I think I've got something you'll be interested in," he said.

I drove back to his office at Global TecTonic and parked in front. It was after six and the place was empty. The front door was locked so I called him on his cell phone. He came out to meet me at the door and let me in and I followed him back to his office. He took a seat in front of his computer. He said, "This is what I wanted to show you."

On the screen was a website called SMhookups.com. On his computer screen was a profile for a woman calling herself lilsubmissive83.

"What's that?" I said.

"That," he said, "is an account that was created on this computer."

I looked at the profile. There was a black and white silhouette of a woman kneeling before a man that looked like it had been uploaded from the Internet. The profile said, "Young, fit professional seeks sadistic but sane older man. I'm new to the area but not the lifestyle. No drunks, no druggies, and no fatties."

There was an area where you could list your likes and dislikes. She liked breath control, spanking, daddy/daughter play, and shibari rope bondage. She disliked having people piss on her, corner time, and cages.

"Jesus suffocating Christ," I said.

"Pretty extreme stuff," Eliot said. "But I've seen a lot worse."

"It's a hookup site, right?"

"Yes."

"Can you tell if she communicated with anybody else on the site?"

"Her inbox was full of messages but she only responded to one other profile," Eliot said. "They exchanged several e-mails and talked about meeting up."

"What's the other profile look like?"

Eliot clicked some buttons on his keyboard. "It's right here," he said. Another profile came up. "The guy calls himself PaleKing97."

"He says he lives in Durham," I said.

"According to her profile, they only lived seven miles apart," Eliot said.

I studied the profile. "Experienced, hardcore sadist looking for petite submissive slavegirl. This isn't just about sex for me, but a way of life. You must be serious about meeting in person as I do not engage in endless email exchanges. Either you're real or you're not. I am 35, own my own company, and very experienced in dominating submissive little playthings. I am unattached and can host."

His likes included collar and lead, daddy/daughter play, shibari rope bondage, eye contact restrictions, breath control, and discipline.

Eliot got up and went over to his computer and said, "I printed out these profiles as well as the e-mails they sent each other. It was mostly fantasy shit. He sent her a picture but you can't see his face. It's in there. She never sent him a picture. You can probably guess why. He also sent her a phone number."

"So she could have called him?" I said.

"She could have. You'd have that in your call log."

"I haven't seen that number before, I don't think. I'd have to go back and check."

I sat there in disbelief. "The police never found this?" I said.

"They wouldn't have looked for it," he said. "In cases like this, they usually tear the suspect's computer apart, but they wouldn't have had any reason to go digging for dirt on the victim if they already had their perp."

"The only thing they found on Ray's computer was a bunch of boxing articles and naked pictures of some black porn star named India," I said.

"There's quite a bit of stuff on here relating to BDSM," Eliot said.

"The Internet is a dark fucking place," I said.

"It gets a lot worse than this," he said. "This is nothing."

Eliot began typing at his keyboard again. "I know what you're going to ask me next," he said, "and the answer is yes, she did Google searches on various things relating to sadomasochism, including sex with asphyxiation. That's what breath control is, apparently." We sat silently as he clicked through various screens.

"So she was into being strangled while she had sex?" I said.

He shrugged. "Just because you look nice on TV doesn't mean you don't have a dark side."

"I guess."

"That shouldn't be so surprising to you," he said. "Would you want the cops going through all your Google searches?"

"No," I said. "They'd probably think I was pretty strange."

"Me too," he said.

"What can you tell me about this Pale King guy?"

"He sounds like a charming individual."

"Can you get his address?"

"I can try to get his IP address," Eliot said. "Hold on a minute."

Eliot started clicking through screens and I sat there watching him. He shook his head and said, "He's using Tor or some kind of masking device. It's showing IP addresses from all over the world."

"Fuck," I said. "Can't you do something?"

"It'd take me some time," he said. "This guy knows what he's doing. He's created a cloud that's going to be pretty hard to see through."

I thought through it a second and had an idea. "You hacked into Rose's e-mail," I said. "Can you hack into his e-mail?"

Eliot looked at me like I was up to something.

"I got you a court order," I said.

"You got me an order to get into the victim's computer," he said. "Do you think this court order is broad enough for me to go hacking into other people's private information?"

"I'm taking the position that it is," I said.

He nodded. "Okay," he said. He gestured at the computer. On the screen was an e-mail page showing correspondence between PaleKing97 and several other women on the site. They had names like DefiledOne81 and Kajira11. He clicked on them one at a time and we read the messages. He stopped on one and we both read it and then looked at each other.

"They met each other," I said.

"It says they arranged to meet," he said. "Doesn't say it actually happened."

"She gave him an outside e-mail," I said.

"Kajira11@yahoo.com. Very creative," Eliot said.

"Can you tag that e-mail account?"

"What do you mean?"

"I don't speak Internet nerd language," I said. "Can you get a name and address from it?"

"Can I do it legally or can I do it?"

"Can you do it?"

"Egan, fuck you," he said.

"I'll be discreet," I said. "I promise."

"Discretion isn't in your vocabulary. Just promise me you won't hire a skywriter to broadcast that you got this from me."

"I won't," I said.

He reached over and grabbed a stack of yellow sticky notes and peeled one off and wrote down a name and address on it and handed it to me.

"You are the fucking man," I said. "You know that?"

"I'm pretty special," he said. "But I try to be modest about it."

CHAPTER EIGHTEEN

THE E-MAIL ADDRESS was registered to someone named Jennifer Coats and the house matching the IP address was recorded in county property tax records as having been purchased in 2010 by David Coats and Jennifer Coats. I looked her up online and found out that she was a 37 year old married stay at home mom.

I knew I had to talk to her but I wanted to know more about the domination and submission lifestyle before I did.

I called Nikki Davis and left her a message. She called me back an hour later and said she was at a motel in Garner. I told her I'd drive out there to meet her. It took me about an hour because I ran into traffic bottlenecking the interstate around Miami Boulevard near the I-40 split between Durham and Chapel Hill.

Garner is a little suburb on the south side of Raleigh. There is nothing there worth seeing except for a pretty decent biker bar called the Locked & Loaded that has surprisingly good food and cold draft beer. I stopped in and had a couple of beers and some Buffalo wings and then went to Nikki's room at the Days Inn.

The room was on the third floor and it was a basic cheap motel room with a queen sized bed, a TV, and a small desk and chair. It smelled of marijuana and cigarette smoke.

Nikki moved around a lot, posting prostitution ads on Backpage. com and turning tricks in motel rooms. When I got there, she was smoking a joint and there was a bottle of Absolut Mandarin on the table. She was wearing only a black bra and matching thong panties. She opened the door and hugged me and told me to come in.

"Make yourself a drink, baby," she said.

"They got any glasses in here?"

"Over by the sink."

I went over to the sink and found a plastic cup. "You got anything to mix this with?" I said.

"Nope."

I poured half a cup of vodka and took a seat on the bed next to her.

"You want to hit this?" she said.

"No thanks. I'm good," I said.

She put the joint out in the ashtray and stood up and put on a pair of black pants. She was almost thirty now, and she was damn good looking.

In her younger days, she reminded me of Beyonce when Beyonce was fronting Destiny's Child. She was probably the most naturally beautiful stripper I'd ever seen. She had a small gold stud in her left nostril and a tattoo behind her left shoulder. For whatever reason, girls with piercings and tattoos got more and more attractive to me the older I got.

"You still posting?" I said.

"Unfortunately," she said. "I had a job in an office for awhile but I got laid off."

"You here permanently now?"

"No. I'm back and forth between here and Durham. My mama stay up here now."

"You know not to go to any hotels in Cary, right?"

"Yeah. I remember you telling me that."

"It's not exactly safe here, either," I said. "But I'm pretty sure the Cary PD doesn't do anything but set up stings for Backpage girls."

"I try to be careful. I got me a couple regulars. But this motherfucker took me for a hundred dollars the other night. Said he was going to the ATM and just drove off."

"You can't trust people," I said.

"No you can't."

"Tell me," I said. "You know anything about the domination and submission lifestyle? You ever get any of those types?"

"Not really. Those people scare me."

"I'm just wondering how common it is."

"I knew this girl that was into it. She still posts. She said she makes two hundred dollars an hour beating the shit out of men. She tried to tell me I needed to get into that but I don't like that kind of stuff."

"You have her number?"

She laughed and said, "I always knew you had a dark side, baby."

I smiled. "It's something I'm working on," I said.

"I don't have her number but she goes by Mistress Jasmine."

"And she posts on Backpage?"

"Uh huh."

"Under the Raleigh/Durham section?"

"Uh huh. The fetish section."

I always liked Nikki. I got to know her when I was in Vice and she was working as a stripper and a prostitute on the south side of Durham. She knew everybody and fed me information on everything and was the best snitch I ever had and probably the only one I actually had any respect for.

Through her, I learned that people treated hookers like confession booths. They didn't just pay them for sex. They paid them to listen to all the shit they couldn't say to the regular people in their lives. Her tips helped me bust drug dealers, pimps, murderers, you name it. She was a good hearted girl who did what she did because she came from a rough place and had limited options. She did what she had to do to survive. She had a tough side to her that I admired. She wasn't going to let anybody push her around.

I had to help her out of a jam once when she lost her temper at the Burger King on Fayetteville Road. It was her birthday and she and a friend had been partying at a club and some other girls started talking shit to her and wanted to fight. She did the smart thing and left the club but the girls got in their car and followed her to the Burger King. There were four of them and they went through the drive-thru, ordered their food and then waited for Nikki in the parking lot.

When she came out, they started screaming at her, calling her a bitch and a whore and saying they were going to kick her ass. She got in her car to leave, but they started pelting the back of her car with Whoppers and milkshakes and whatever else they could get their hands on. She didn't say a word. She just put the car in reverse and ran right into them, sending them flying skyward like bowling pins. Then she put the car in drive and smashed right through the Burger King menu board and drove away.

The arresting officer showed me the surveillance tape and I laughed my ass off watching it. I probably watched it a dozen times and it just got funnier and funnier every time.

They charged her with four counts of assault with a deadly weapon and hit and run causing property damage. She had a record, so she was looking at some active time, but I talked to the arresting officer and the DA and she ended up getting a year of supervised probation. I knew her probation officer, so I made sure she didn't get violated for anything.

"What you been up to, Egan?" she said. "I heard you wasn't a cop no more."

"That's right."

"How come?"

"It's a long story," I said.

"That's too bad," she said. "You were one of the good ones."

"What's it like out there these days?" I said.

"What you looking for?"

"I'm just trying to get a sense of where things stand."

"Everything is pretty much the same," she said. "Bernard has taken over the South Side."

"That's what I hear. What's he selling?"

"Cocaine and her-on."

"What about pills?"

"Everybody selling that shit. Weed too."

"Do the cops know about Bernard?"

"Don't see how they don't. It's not even like he trying to hide it."

"So he's the man, now?"

"Yeah. He think he is, anyway."

"I never liked him."

"Me neither."

"What are the cops up to?"

"Same shit. Corner busts. Stings. They taking down a bunch of Mexicans."

"If things keep going like they are, Mexico is going to be the one building that wall," I said.

"I'd go to Mexico if I spoke Spanish," she said. "I hear it's cheap as hell down there but them Mexican girls is crazy."

"Oh yeah?"

"Yeah. They'll kill you they catch you fucking their man."

"You don't deal with Mexicans much, I don't guess."

"Hell no. I don't get calls from nobody but white guys and black guys."

"You making any money?"

"Depends on the night. It's been slow lately. I got to post tonight just so I can pay for the room."

"How much is it?"

"Forty."

"Here," I said. I took out my wallet and put two twenty dollar bills on the bed.

"Thanks," she said.

"You mind if I make another drink?"

"Go right ahead."

I got up and poured another half glass of orange vodka and sat back down on the bed.

"You remember Crazy Ass?" she said.

"I had forgot all about that," I said.

"I'll never forget it. He be talking about how he gonna do this and he gonna do that and thinking he all bad."

"Yeah. And you texted me and said you thought he was going to rape you. I was drunk that night. I barely remember it."

"It didn't take you ten minutes to get there."

"I wasn't far away."

"I just remember you banging on the door and yelling 'Police' real loud and me opening the door and you coming in drunk as hell and punching him right in the face, knocking that stupid looking hat off his head, grabbing him by his braids and putting your gun in his face."

"God that felt good," I said. "I remember he was wearing one of those hats with the tag still on it."

"The look on that motherfucker's face was funny as hell. He thought he was getting arrested. He didn't know he was getting his ass kicked."

"I was going through a dark time then," I said. "It felt good to take it out on some no good asshole."

"It's good to see you again, baby," she said. "I think about you sometimes."

"Yeah. I think about you too."

"You didn't drive all this way just to catch up."

"I just needed to talk. I don't know who to trust in Durham these days. Things are a little bit crazy."

"I saw you on TV."

"Yeah?"

"You were walking into court with that lawyer who's defending that fighter."

"I try to stay off TV if I can."

"You looked good."

"Thanks," I said. "Say, if I need you to do me a favor, will you be around?"

"You know I'll help you if I can, baby."

"Thanks. I knew I could count on you."

She took out a cigarette and lit it and inhaled, then blew out the smoke slowly. "You think that fighter killed that girl?" she said.

"I don't know," I said. "It looks pretty bad. But it doesn't look like she fought back. The only thing I can think of is that maybe she liked being choked."

Nikki shook her head. "Like I said, that shit scares me," she said. "But you call Jasmine. Anybody know about that shit, it'd be her."

I got up. "I got to get back," I said.

"You got plans?"

"Dinner with the girlfriend."

"Who you dating now?"

"A girl who's too young for me. She's a scientist. She does clinical research over at RTP."

"What kind of research?"

"Microbiology stuff."

"I need to get back in school."

"I'd like to see you do that," I said. "You're too smart to be out here fucking around with these dummies."

"You call me anytime, you here? I'll text you if I change my number."

I stood up and walked to the door. "You be safe," I said.

"You too, baby," she said.

CHAPTER NINETEEN

I FOUND MISTRESS JASMINE'S postings under the fetish section on Backpage.com. I called her and set up an appointment. When she asked me what I was into, I said, "I like to be beaten and called whitey." She said she could do that no problem.

She had her "dungeon" in the living room of her apartment in a complex just across from Northgate Mall in north Durham. I figured I needed some alcohol before venturing into the world of sadomasochism, so I stopped at a nearby Tripp's and had a couple of glasses of Jack Daniels on the rocks.

Mistress Jasmine was a tall black woman in her early thirties. She advertised herself on the Internet as a BBW, which means a great big fat woman. She looked heavier in real life than she did in the pictures on her ad.

"You got the money?" she said.

"Right here," I said.

I took out an envelope with two hundred dollars in it.

"Put in on the counter and have a seat on the couch."

I did.

"So you into racial humiliation?" she said.

"Not exactly," I said. "Nikki told me to call you. I'm just looking for some information."

"She did?"

"Yeah. She spoke highly of you."

"You're lying."

"Okay, she just said you did domination and submission stuff."

"I do."

"On your ad it says you dominate men."

"That's what it says."

"Okay, here's the thing. I'm investigating a murder that I think may have been related to sadomasochistic sex."

"You a cop?"

"No."

"What are you then?"

"I'm a private investigator. I'm not trying to jam you up in any way. I promise not to reveal anything about you. No one will even know I talked to you. I gave you two hundred bucks and all I want is some background information on domination and submission."

"You'll keep my name out of this?"

"I will. I promise."

"And I ain't got to worry about no cops knocking on my door?"

"No."

"Okay. What you want to know?"

"What's this whole domination and submission thing about?" I said.

She took a seat in a chair opposite the couch. "It's about power exchange," she said. "Men come to me because they want to be dominated or humiliated or beaten."

"Why do they want that?"

"It's about giving up control. You'd be surprised at who some of them are. Most of them are in positions of power during the day and they want to let go and give up control to someone else for an hour or two. It's like therapy for them."

"What kind of things do they want?"

"Some of them like corporal punishment. Some like to worship my boots. Some are into being tied up or handcuffed. Some want me to make them do disgusting things that they fantasize about doing anyway."

"Like what?"

"Like dressing up in women's clothing."

"Really?"

"It could be anything. A guy wanted me to make him clean my toilet with his tongue yesterday. Some of them just want to be a house maid or a servant."

"A guy paid you two hundred bucks to lick your toilet?"

"Yes he did."

"Do you have sex with them?"

"Never. Domination is not prostitution."

"I didn't mean to offend you. I'm just trying to understand."

"Society still has this thing about it but it's just role playing. It's harmless. They have a fantasy and I fulfill it for them. It gives them a release. That's why they come back again and again."

"That's interesting," I said. "That's very interesting."

"I enjoy making people's fantasies come true," she said.

"How about choking?"

"Choking is a fetish, but that happens more often in lifestyle play because it usually involves sex."

"Lifestyle play?"

"Yes. There's professional play and lifestyle play."

"What's the difference?"

"Professional dominas do sessions for money. They last an hour or two. Lifestyle is more like being in a relationship. Some people live the lifestyle for real. Some of them are hardcore scene players.

They live in the scene 24/7. One person is the master or mistress and the other one is the slave. They usually live together if they do that."

"You don't do that?"

"Oh God no. I'd get sick of babysitting some man all the time. It'd be worse than having a dog."

"How common is lifestyle play?"

"It's more common than you think. In most live-in situations, the woman is the submissive. But most women submissives don't do it full-time. Everybody has their regular life too."

"So it's like a secret life?"

"That's right."

"And choking is sometimes part of that?"

"It can be. If you're interested, there's this lifestyle group that meets every month. I'm friends with the lady who runs it. She does seminars on various aspects of the lifestyle and she organizes parties for people in the scene. She and her husband are lifestyle players. She probably knows more about it than anybody around here."

"You mind giving me her number?"

"Let me check with her first."

"Okay."

Mistress Jasmine excused herself and went into a backroom and made a phone call. When she came out, she said, "She'll meet with you tomorrow. Same rules as with me. You don't repeat her name or tell anyone where you got the information."

"Can I trust her?"

"Yeah. She's a good person. If she can help you, she will. But if you lie to her, she'll track you down and cut your balls off."

CHAPTER TWENTY

THE NEXT MORNING I parked my truck on a tree shaded street in Forest Hills in front of an enormous house that looked like it was built a century ago by a tobacco baron. It had recently been redone and the columns and façade looked newly painted. I knocked on the door and a young woman answered.

She was tall and blonde and wore black pants, a white dress shirt, and black patent leather boots with high stiletto heels and pointed toes. Her blonde hair was pulled back into a ponytail. She said, "Are you Mr. Egan?"

"Yes, ma'am," I said.

"I'm Nicolette," she said. "Please come in."

Nicolette was a very attractive woman. I guessed she was in her mid 30's. She gestured for me to follow her and I followed her down the hallway into a living room and she pointed for me to sit in one of the leather chairs surrounding a large coffee table. The furniture was some classic Victorian style and there were various works of art hanging in ornate frames on the walls.

"May I get you something to drink?" she said.

"No thanks, I'm fine."

She took a seat and said, "I Googled you after we talked. You've had an interesting life."

"Really?" I said. "How so?"

"You solved the Rebecca Munpower murder. You got shot by a crack dealer and lived to tell about it. And of course you killed two people."

"It's not as interesting as it sounds," I said.

"So you're not a detective anymore?"

"Not with the police. No, ma'am."

"Why not? If you don't mind me asking?"

"I had some differences of opinion with my bosses."

"You don't handle authority well, do you?"

"Most people would probably say no."

"Have you ever experimented with domination or submission?"

I laughed. "No," I said. "I didn't know much about it until I started this. . ."

"Investigation?" she said.

I nodded.

"You're looking into the Sheryl Rose murder?"

"You find that on Google?"

"Does it matter where I found it?"

"Yes. To me it does."

"Okay. I found it on Google."

"I feel like I'm being interrogated here," I said.

"I just like to find out what makes people tick," she said.

She took out a cigarette and said, "Do you mind if I smoke?"

"You'd smoke whether I minded or not," I said.

She smiled and lit her cigarette. "This city was built with rivers of tobacco money," she said. "Duke University, Duke Hospital, all built with tobacco money. But today you can't smoke a cigarette anywhere near those places. Ironic, don't you think?"

"Yes," I said.

She crossed her legs. "You don't think that boxer murdered her?" she said.

I leaned forward and looked around the room. "I'm just trying to find out what really happened," I said.

"You'd make an excellent submissive, you know that?" she said.

"Why would you say that?"

"Because I can read people and you're easier to read than most."

"Is that a fact?"

She inhaled and blew out the smoke. "That is a fact," she said. "You don't really understand a person until you know what they're afraid of, and what you are afraid of is losing control."

"Are you a shrink?" I said.

"I have a master's degree in psychology, but I wouldn't need one to make that diagnosis."

She tapped the ash from her cigarette into a large brass ashtray on the coffee table. "A submissive is someone like you who fears control or confinement, but who confronts that fear by submitting and giving someone else control over them. It is a very freeing experience and requires both bravery and honesty with one's self."

"Don't take this the wrong way," I said. "But I don't see anything freeing about being chained up and degraded."

She smiled a mischievous smile. She took another drag on her cigarette. "Have you ever heard the term freedom in slavery?" she said.

I shook my head no. "Sounds Orwellian," I said.

"It's not. It's the freedom you get from relinquishing control and giving yourself over fully to the control of another person. There is an erotic element to it, but there's also a tremendous catharsis. I find that for most people it's very therapeutic."

"How many people are into this stuff?" I said.

"Plenty," she said. "It's like asking how many gay people are out there in the world. It's a percentage of the population, but since most of the statistics come from self-reporting, it's probably larger than we know. Many of the members of our community live their lives in secret."

"Why is that?"

"Shame," she said. "Isn't that a pity?"

"And otherwise normal people do this?"

"Oh yes," she said. "I founded the Triangle group six years ago and we meet once a month at a secret place called La Fortress. It's a wonderful experience. There are dominants and submissives and switches and everyone gets to be who they really are without shame and without judgment. We adhere to two strict principles: anonymity and safe, sane, and consensual play."

"Anybody whose name I'd recognize?"

She gave me a smile that meant yes but she said, "Anonymity is rule number one."

"Sheryl Rose was strangled," I said.

She didn't bat an eyelash. "I know," she said.

"No murder weapon was found, but I'm guessing from the pictures that it was a cord that strangled her. There was no DNA under her fingernails, so she didn't fight back against her attacker. And there were no scratch marks around her throat, which indicates to me that she didn't try to fight to free herself."

"You think she was engaging in consensual play?"

"It's a possibility I considered," I said. "How common is choking as a fetish?"

"Not as common as some of the others but it's on the list."

"Why would someone want to be choked?"

Nicolette tapped the ash from her cigarette again and took another drag. "It's called edge play," she said. "It's very intoxicating but it's very, very dangerous."

"What do you mean intoxicating?"

"It can be used as a form of control. Some find it erotic to have their partner control their breathing. It's most commonly used during sex."

"How so?"

"During intercourse, the blood is pulsing to and from the brain. Placing a restraint around the neck and slowly restricting the airflow makes the person feel lightheaded and puts them into a state of euphoria. Most people who do it try to time their orgasm to the moment of euphoria."

"So you intentionally have someone asphyxiate you for a better orgasm?"

"It is very dangerous," she said. "I teach classes and seminars on various aspects of BDSM and although I have lectured on edge play, it's always been something I have recommended against."

"Have you ever tried it?"

Nicolette crushed out her cigarette. "No," she said. "But I know enough from reading the literature that it's very addictive. The people who try it usually can't stop doing it. It's like a drug."

"Ever heard of anybody dying from it?"

"Yes, I have. That's why I don't recommend it. No matter how much you trust your partner, the danger is just too great. It doesn't take much to strangle a person to death and the very nature of the play takes you right up to the edge of death. That's why it's so exciting and so addictive."

"Do you know any local men who are into that?"

"You know I couldn't divulge that, even if I wanted to."

"I'm trying to solve a murder here."

"If I thought I had information that would help you solve Sheryl Rose's murder, I'd try to help you. But I don't. I'm very sorry she died. When I saw it on the news, I wondered if it could have been related to edge play."

"Why didn't you call the cops?"

"I didn't have any information for them," she said. "Besides, they already had the boyfriend. If this was edge play, I imagine his computer would have quite a bit of information on the subject in its cache."

"I know about the whole anonymity thing," I said. "But can you tell me one thing, yes or no: did you ever see Sheryl Rose at one of your events?"

"No," she said. "I only saw her on television."

"What did you think when you saw her?"

Nicolette smiled. She said, "I thought she'd look lovely in a steel collar naked and kneeling at my feet."

I didn't know what to say to that.

"How about shibari rope bondage?" I said. "You know anything about that?"

"It's an elaborate form of Japanese rope bondage. It takes a very long time to learn to do it properly."

"If a woman was into edge play and shibari rope bondage, is it fair to say that she'd be pretty experienced at this?"

She shrugged. "It's hard to say. Probably so. Either that or she was really curious about it. Either way, she'd have been into the lifestyle for quite a while. She might not be experienced in it, but her fantasies would probably go back to childhood."

"I changed my mind," I said. "I would like a drink."

"What would you like?"

"What do you have?"

"Name it."

"Scotch," I said. "Neat."

"Coming right up," she said. She walked into the kitchen and returned with a full glass of scotch. I drank most of it in two sips.

"This lifestyle," I said. "You said it's something psychological. Something that starts in childhood?"

"Yes. There are arguments over whether you're born with it or whether environmental factors push you into it, but it starts early.

Most people have the fantasies and they feel shame for having the fantasies. They don't truly find themselves until they learn that there are others who have those same fantasies and needs."

"How do they find each other?" I said.

"How does anybody find anybody these days?" she said. "On the Internet."

CHAPTER TWENTY-ONE

I DROVE to Jennifer Coats' house and parked several houses away and waited. Eventually, she pulled into her driveway in a blue Volvo with her two kids. Both of them were toddlers. I watched her unpack them from their car seats and wondered whether she had any idea how close she'd been to a monster. That it could just have easily been her lying there with red ligature marks on her throat and the capillaries in her eyes busted. After awhile, her husband came home in a new green Honda Accord. He walked down to the mailbox and picked up the mail and went inside.

They both looked like normal people. Jennifer was small and thin, with a runner's build. David was maybe five foot ten and weighed about one hundred and sixty pounds. He was wearing a white shirt and yellow tie. I guessed he probably had no idea about his wife's secret Internet life.

I drove back home and made myself some dinner and watched TV for a few hours before going to bed.

The next morning, I followed Jennifer as she took her kids to school and kissed them goodbye. I followed her to a Starbucks and got behind her in line. She ordered coffee and went over to the table where there was cream and sweetener. I ordered a coffee and glanced back at her and saw her take a seat at one of the tables. When I got my coffee, I slid into a seat across from her and startled her.

"We need to talk," I said.

She froze up. "Don't be scared," I said. "I'm a detective investigating a crime. This doesn't involve you, but I think you might have seen something. Give me just a minute or two, will you?"

She looked frightened and asked to see my badge. I took out my private investigator's license and showed that to her.

"You're not a cop?" she said.

"No. Not anymore."

"What's this about?" she said.

"I'm investigating the murder of Sheryl Rose," I said. "I guess you've probably heard about it."

She nodded. "The reporter," she said.

"Yes."

"But I don't. . ."

"Look, Jennifer, I'm going to keep you completely out of this, okay? I give you my word on that. But I know about Kajira11 and I need to know about the guy who calls himself the Pale King."

She looked down at the floor and her hands started shaking.

"Jennifer, calm down," I said. "Nobody but you and I know this and nobody else is going to know about it."

She started crying. She wiped the tears out of her eyes and reached for a napkin and tried to compose herself but couldn't. I reached over and put my hand over hers. "It's going to be okay," I said. "Your husband will never know about this."

She inhaled deeply and looked at me. "I'm just so. . . ashamed," she said.

"Calm down," I said. "It's okay."

"How did you. . .?"

"I do this for a living," I said.

She nodded.

"You met with this guy, didn't you?"

She nodded again. "Right here," she said. "We met for coffee."

"It's none of my business, but how long have you been doing this?" I said.

She looked up at me with a face full of remorse. "I've had fantasies my whole life," she said. "But I just pushed them away."

"Was this your first time meeting somebody from one of those sites in real life?"

She nodded. "I felt so bad about it," she said. "I never did anything with him, but I just feel terrible about it."

"You didn't do anything wrong," I said. "You just met somebody for coffee. I don't even think the Catholic Church is against that."

I saw tears in her eyes again. "I have a family," she said. "I love them so much."

"I know," I said.

"I don't want to lose them."

"Jennifer, I promise you. Nobody has come looking for you until I did. Nobody else will be coming after me."

"How do you know?"

"Because what you did or didn't do doesn't matter," I said. "All that matters is finding the Pale King."

"Do you think he's involved in that murder?"

"I think there's a good chance he is," I said.

"Oh my God."

"Yeah."

"But don't they have somebody else?"

"Yes," I said. "I think they may have the wrong man."

"Why do you think it's him?"

"Lots of reasons," I said. "What I need from you is information about him. Do you know his name?"

"He said his name was Vincent."

"He didn't give you a last name?"

"No," she said. "I told him my name was Emily. I was just so scared the whole time."

"Scared of him or just scared of meeting somebody?"

She took a sip of her coffee. She said, "A little of both, maybe."

"What was he driving?"

"I didn't see his car," she said.

"What did he look like?"

"He just looked. . . I don't know. He looked pretty normal."

"How tall was he?"

"I don't know."

"I saw your husband," I said. "Was he taller or shorter than him?"

"You saw David?"

"Yes. At your house."

"He was taller. He had short black hair and glasses. He had a little bit of beard stubble, like he hadn't shaved in a couple of days."

"What was he wearing?"

"I think he was wearing khakis and a t-shirt. He had a black windbreaker on."

"What did he tell you about himself?"

"He said he designed websites. He said he'd been into the lifestyle for a long time and that he had a lot of experience."

"Were you looking for someone like that?"

"I don't know," she said. "I thought I was, but the reality of it was terrifying to me."

"What did he say about the lifestyle?"

She looked down in shame. "He said he liked to tie girls up, to dominate them. He said that nothing is more beautiful than a slavegirl struggling in ropes. He talked about seeing the helplessness in their eyes."

"Did that creep you out?"

"A little bit, I guess. I mean, I said on the Internet I was into all that stuff too. It just seemed so dirty to hear it in person."

She looked at me and then looked back at her coffee. I could see that her hands were still trembling. "He said one thing that really struck me as weird," she said. "He said something about tasting all the fruit in the garden of earthly delights."

"Did he know you were married?"

She shook her head. "I told him I was single," she said.

She started crying again. This time it was softer and her shoulders just heaved lightly. She looked as fragile as a bird.

"Jennifer," I said. "Look at me. Look here." She looked up at me. I said, "Everybody has secrets. I'm not here to judge you. You're going to be okay. You're going to go home to your husband and your kids and life is going to go on as normal."

"What are you going to do now?" she said.

"I'm going to find this guy and see if I can get a DNA sample from him. I've got one to match it against. The police missed it, but my lab expert didn't."

She wiped the tears out of her eyes again.

"You dodged a bullet here, Jennifer," I said. "Sheryl Rose could have been you. You could have continued to walk into the darkness but you didn't. You walked away from it. You walked back into the light."

"Do you really think he killed her?"

"I won't know for sure until I can get a DNA test. They found fingerprints that didn't match any in the database either. If that's him, he killed her."

She shook her head slowly. "I feel sick," she said, "to know that I was so close to somebody so awful."

"You got a second chance, kiddo," I said. "Make it count."

She tightened her grip on my hand. "Thank you," she said. "I promise."

CHAPTER TWENTY-TWO

S HAKESPEARE WAS GOOD at writing plays. Mozart was good at composing music. I was good at leaking things to the press.

Eric Bain was the chief investigative reporter for the Durham Herald. He had covered the police and court beat for years and knew everybody. When the mob had its torches and pitchforks out for the Duke lacrosse kids, he was the only reporter who didn't rush to join them. He was a fan of mystery novelist James Lee Burke, and I remembered him quoting Burke at the time, saying, "Have you ever seen a mob rush across town to do a good deed?"

I liked Eric and had been an anonymous source in many of his stories over the years. Of course I'd always denied it. What I was about to tell him had technically been sealed by a court order and I was in danger of going to jail for contempt if it ever got traced back to me, but I didn't care. Ray was going on trial for murder and the potential jury pool had been told a story about Sheryl Rose being this innocent little angel who was brutally murdered by a violent black thug. I figured it was time they heard a little more about Sheryl Rose.

I wasn't trying to make her out to be some kinky whore, but I was willing to air her secrets because they were going to come out at trial anyway and by then it would be too late for them to help Ray. I figured it would be better for me to manipulate the timing of their disclosure to help in my search for the truth, even if that was technically illegal.

Eric met me at the Primrose Café, which was a small bohemian coffee shop several blocks down from the courthouse. He was already there when I got there, drinking a tall cup of coffee. He lifted his coffee to me as if offering a toast. I went to the counter and bought a large coffee and then went over to the table beside the register and fixed it up with cream and sugar. I walked over and took a seat across from him. The place was nearly empty and John Coltrane music was playing from the stereo speakers.

He just nodded.

"You look well," I said.

"I'm tired."

"Would a good scoop wake you up?"

"That would do it."

I looked around the room to make sure we were out of earshot of the few people in the front of the café and then I leaned forward and said, "I got something for you."

He looked over my shoulder to make sure no one was close enough to hear. "Let's hear it," he said.

"Same rules as always," I said.

"Same rules."

"What I'm about to show you has been sealed by a court order," I said. "Nobody's supposed to know about it."

I could see the excitement in his face. "Hell fucking yeah," he said.

"You know how Sheryl Rose was this innocent young reporter that was all bright and smiley and shit?"

"Uh huh."

"This was her Internet persona."

I pushed a file folder over to him and watched his eyes as he read through the material. The look on his face was utter astonishment.

"Is this for real?" he said.

"Yes," I said.

"Holy fucking shit."

"Everybody's got secrets," I said.

"So this Pale King guy? This is your guy?"

"I think so."

"Wow," he said, "just wow."

"You can report his name," I said. "And her Internet name. But make sure you say she communicated with multiple men."

"I only see this guy."

"He's the only one I have, but I don't want him knowing that."

He put his hand up over his mouth and balled it into a fist. "This, along with your DNA sample. . ."

"I know," I said.

"Either Ray Marks did it for sure or this guy did."

"That's about how I see it."

"If this city gets caught trying to prosecute another innocent man. . . . Goddamn," he said.

I closed the file and pulled it back to my side of the table and put my cup of coffee on top of it.

"This is going to rock the shit out of WRDU," he said.

"They'll love getting beat on a story about their own reporter, won't they?" I said.

"Oh, man," he said. "I just don't even have the words."

"I'll tell you if I find out anything else."

"Deal."

We both sat back and drank our coffee. Eric's whole demeanor had changed. Watching his face was like watching a Christmas tree lighting.

"Egan," he said. "You are the sneakiest, most calculating son of a bitch I've ever known, you know that?"

"I just want to find out what happened that night," I said. "If I have to skate a roadblock or two, I can live with that."

"This is big," he said. "This is real fucking big."

THE NEXT DAY I picked up a copy of the newspaper. The top headline above the fold said, "Murdered Reporter Had Secret Online Identity."

I read it sitting in my truck in a McDonald's parking lot after getting a cup of coffee from the drive-thru. I felt bad for Sheryl Rose's family. I knew my little stunt would result in their grief being compounded by the public disclosure of her life's most sordid and closely-guarded secrets. I couldn't imagine the pain and the anger and the helplessness they must have been feeling at watching this all play out in public. But at the same time, I looked forward to curling up on the couch with Jill and watching the WRDU news team undertake the humiliating task of repeating a competitor's scoop on a story they'd bragged about owning.

CHAPTER TWENTY-THREE

J UDGE WATSON was super fucking pissed. He had summoned
us all to his courtroom demanding answers about who had de-
fied his order to keep Sheryl Rose's private information under seal.
I sat there in the gallery behind Roth watching the proceedings.
Judge Watson was sitting up high on his bench. He had the flag
of the United States on his left and the flag of the state of North
Carolina on his right. The state seal was on the bench in front of
him and behind him was a large portrait of the late Judge Roscoe
Wilbur Hart, who had been a Durham judge in the 1920's and a
member of the Ku Klux Klan. Stricker was expressing his outrage
and demanding sanctions against the leaker.

"Save it, Mr. Stricker," said the judge. "There's nothing you can
say that will make me madder than I already am. I want answers, I
want names, and I want them now."

Roth stood and straightened his suit jacket. He unbuttoned his
jacket and put his hands in his pockets. He said, "Judge, we were
very aware that this information had been placed under seal and

I can assure you that nobody from our side said a word about this to anyone."

"Bullshit," said the judge.

"Judge, you're placing the burden on me to prove a negative and I can't do that. No one can do that. That is a logical impossibility."

"I'd like some people to be placed under oath," Stricker said.

"So would I," said the judge.

"Judge," Roth said. "As an officer of the court, I already have a duty of candor to this tribunal and I would hope that my word would be enough."

"Fine," the judge said. "You're under oath already. I want to hear from others."

"I'd like to call Mr. Roth's investigator," Stricker said.

"Come up and be sworn."

I stood up and walked around the prosecutor's table and behind the bench and stood in front of the witness chair. The clerk rose and addressed me. "Place your left hand on the Bible and repeat after me," she said.

"Yes ma'am."

"Do you solemnly swear that the testimony you are about to give is the truth, the whole truth, and nothing but the truth, so help you God?" she said.

"I do."

Stricker leaned forward in his chair. He said, "State your name for the record."

"John Egan," I said.

"Mr. Egan, how are you employed?"

"I am a private investigator. I'm currently working for Mr. Stuart Roth, counsel for the defendant."

"Do you know a man named Eric Bain?"

"Yes sir, I do."

"How do you know him?"

"He's a reporter for the paper."

"Have you had occasion to speak with him before?"

"Yes sir, I have."

"When was the last time you spoke with him?"

"I speak with him on a pretty regular basis," I said. "We've been friends since I was on the police force."

"Have you spoken with him recently?"

"I spoke with him the other day."

"Did you discuss this case with him?"

"Yes sir, I did."

"What did you tell him?"

"I just told him what he already knew. That I was working as Mr. Roth's investigator and that we were pursuing all leads."

"Pursuing all leads?" he said.

"I don't know if I said it like that, but yeah."

"Surely, as the Durham Herald's chief investigative reporter, he wanted to know more?"

"Naturally," I said.

"Did you disclose to him anything regarding the information your expert retrieved from Ms. Rose's computer?"

"No, sir."

"You didn't tell him anything about web profiles or Internet search terms or any of that?"

I leaned forward toward the microphone in front of me. "No, sir. That information is under seal."

"Sir, do I need to remind you that you're under oath?"

"No sir. I've testified a bunch of times."

"So if Mr. Bain was to get up here and testify that you provided him with this information, he'd be a liar? Is that right?" Stricker said.

"I'd say he was mistaken," I said. "I don't like to use the word liar."

"Did you tell anyone else about the information that you found?"

"Only the other expert we've retained in this case, Dr. Ellen Page. And of course I sent the information to Detective Fields so that he and other detectives could follow up on it. I didn't think that was prohibited by the court order."

"Just those two?"

"Yes, sir."

The judge glared down at me for a long time. I just sat there. Finally, he said, "Any more questions of this witness, Mr. Stricker?"

Stricker thought about it a minute and then said, "No, your honor."

"The witness may step down."

Stricker next called Ellen Page and Eliot Goodson, who had both been subpoenaed. They both testified that they had not spoken with Eric Bain or disclosed any confidential information to anyone. Stricker then called Eric Bain to the stand. Eric took the stand and put his hand on the Bible and repeated the oath.

"Mr. Bain," said Stricker, holding up a copy of the Durham Herald, with the above the fold headline about Sheryl Rose's secret online identity. "Did you write this story, sir?"

"I did," Eric said.

"And how did you come to learn of this information?"

Eric turned and addressed the judge directly. "Your honor, I respectfully decline to answer that question as it would require me to reveal a confidential source. I don't believe that I have to do so under North Carolina's reporter shield law or the First Amendment."

"I don't want to hear any damn crap about the First Amendment," said the judge.

"If you're asking me to betray a source, I can't do that, your honor."

"Dammit I want a name," said the judge.

Roth rose and addressed the court. "I think we're all disappointed and angered that this information has become public, your honor," he said. "And while I don't represent Mr. Bain or his newspaper, I would point the court to North Carolina General

Statutes Section 8-53.11, which protects a reporter's right to refuse to reveal a source. I recognize that the United States Supreme Court in Branzburg versus Hayes held that a reporter has no such First Amendment right, but I would contend that the court just got that one wrong, your honor. And I'm not the only one who thinks so. Apparently our General Assembly agrees, which is why they passed the reporter shield law."

"I'm aware of the statute, counselor," said the judge.

"I don't mean to lecture the court about the law. The court knows the law better than I do. I'd just like to remind us all that the United States Constitution, at its core, is just one big effort to balance liberty and security. It even says so, right there in the first sentence. It's why we have balancing tests and all that. But when the founding fathers forever enshrined into our enumerated liberties a freedom of the press, surely they meant more than just the right to scribble something down on a piece of paper. Surely they sought to protect the right to gather news without government intrusion."

Roth looked up and lifted his hands like it had just started snowing. "News is the light, it is the disinfectant of our democracy because it acts as an independent check on the powers of the government," he said. "And if the government could just make a reporter name his sources, nobody would talk to reporters. And we wouldn't have any news. Richard Nixon would be remembered as a successful two term president. If that was the case, we'd be just another banana republic and not what we are, judge, the greatest, freest nation this world has ever seen."

"I'm sorry, Mr. Roth," the judge said. "I couldn't hear you over the sounds of The Battle Hymn of the Republic."

"Sacrificing security is never an easy thing, judge. But it is sometimes necessary to protect liberty. Balancing the two interests requires us to make hard choices, consequential choices. But this court doesn't have to make that choice. Our state lawmakers have already made it for us."

The judge silently seethed. He looked at Stricker and then focused his glare on me.

"Besides," Roth said. "The police and the prosecutor's office also had this information. Are we to believe that police officers and prosecutors don't let a little gossip slip out from time to time? Any of us who have ever gone out to lunch with the courthouse crowd would laugh at that."

The judge put his head in his hands.

"Your honor. . ." Stricker said.

The judge motioned for Stricker to sit down. "I know, counselor," he said, "I know. But what the hell can I do? Mr. Bain is protected by a statute that is directly on point. He has a right to refuse to tell us who the rat is, as distasteful, as revolting to us as that may be. If I throw him in jail, his reporter buddies will just make him into a hero and the Court of Appeals will reverse me."

"May I be excused, your honor?" Eric said.

The judge shook his head in disgust. "You may," he said. He looked at Stricker. "Any more witnesses, Mr. Stricker?"

Stricker shuffled his files and closed them and threw his pen at the table. "No, judge," he said.

"Any evidence from the defendant?"

Roth stood up again. "Judge," he said, "I could call a bunch of assistant DA's and detectives and patrolmen and secretaries and grill them with a bunch of questions to try to get answers, but the sad truth is this: what difference would it make now? The damage has been done. Sheryl Rose's secret life is front page news. Nothing we do can undo that harm any more than we could undo the overwhelming prejudice my client has already suffered from the negative pre-trial statements made by officers of the state and members of the media."

The judge nodded resolutely. "The court has no evidence to take any action on this matter at this time," he said. "But hear this. If I find out who did this, I will have your ass."

CHAPTER TWENTY-FOUR

J ILL CALLED ME with news that got my attention immediately. "I've seen this same black car driving down my street several times since I got home," she said.

I told her to lock the doors immediately. "I'm on my way," I said. "I'll talk to you while I drive."

I grabbed my Glock .45 caliber pistol and my snub nose .38 and hurried outside to my truck and got into it and started driving toward Chapel Hill.

"Did you see anybody inside?" I said.

"No. The windows were black."

"What kind of car was it?"

"I think it was a Dodge Charger. It didn't stop but it slowed down in front of my house twice."

"Hang tight," I said. "I'll be there in twenty minutes."

I stayed on the phone with her as I drove and when I pulled into her driveway, I saw her peeking through her blinds at me. I picked up the Glock from the passenger's seat and carried it inside with me.

"What the hell have you got me into?" she said.

"It's probably nothing," I said.

"Sheryl Rose saw a black car right before she died and now there's a black car driving up and down my street," she said. "I didn't sign up for this."

"I'm closing in on him," I said. "You're either going to stay at my place or I'm going to stay here until I've got him. But I'll have him soon. When his DNA matches that second profile, he'll be in jail and there won't be anything to worry about."

"What makes you think he won't try something before that?" she said. "If he knows you're coming for him, he won't have anything to lose."

"He doesn't want any part of me," I said.

"No," she said. "He seems to be more interested in me."

She disappeared into the kitchen. I could tell she was furious at me. "I'll make dinner," I said. "What do you have in there?"

"Go look for yourself," she said.

She walked into the living room and sat down in front of the TV and ignored me. I looked through the refrigerator and pantry and didn't find much. Jill wasn't the type of person who did shopping for the whole week. She liked going to Whole Foods in Carrboro and buying just enough for that night's meal. On the long green lawn across from the store, there was a farmer's market where local farmers sold fresh produce and she loved walking around the various display stands in the late afternoon and buying things from the hippies standing behind them. I found several different types of cheese in the refrigerator. There was a block of cheddar, some gruyere, and a wedge of parmesan. I checked the pantry and found a loaf of bread and several cans of tomato soup.

"How's grilled cheese and tomato soup sound?" I said.

"Whatever," she said.

I went over to her wine rack and poured her a glass of pinot noir. I took it to her in the living room. "Here," I said. "Please drink this and stop being mad at me."

She took the glass and sipped it and went back to ignoring me. I went into the kitchen and made the grilled cheese sandwiches. I poured some olive oil in a skillet and turned on the stove and waited for the oil to start bubbling, then I cut off a slice of butter and watched it melt in the skillet. I cut the cheese up into thin slices and put them on the bread and slowly grilled them on one side and then turned them over with a spatula and grilled them on the other side. I opened a can of tomato soup, poured it into a pot and then filled the can up with milk and poured it into the pot as well. The sandwiches were done and the soup hot, when I took the sandwiches off and cut them in half and poured each of us a bowl of soup and arranged the sandwiches and soup bowls on plates. I put the plates on the dinner table, poured myself a glass of wine, and took the wine bottle back to the table with me.

I walked back into the living room. Jill was staring straight ahead at the TV and ignoring me. I leaned over and kissed her on the top of the head and said, "I'm sorry. I fucked up. I'll make it up to you."

She looked up at me.

"You don't want to miss this grilled cheese sandwich," I said. "It'll change your whole life."

She got up off the couch and came over and sat at the table. I took a seat across from her.

"When are you going to be done with this case?" she said.

"Soon," I said. "I think I might know who this guy is. I'm going to go see him personally to be sure. When I'm sure, I'm going to figure out a way to get a DNA sample from him and get it to Ellen. When she matches it to the profile she found, all of this will be over. He'll be in jail and Ray will be out."

"That could take months," she said.

"No it won't," I said.

"What do you think he's going to do when you go see him? If he's driving by my house, he already knows who you are."

"He'd know that from watching TV," I said. "I've been to court with Roth every time he's gone. He's got to know that the newspaper story came from me."

"What's to stop him from killing you?"

"I don't think he's got that in him. I think he's probably scared to death. But I'll have a gun with me in case he tries anything stupid."

She took a bite of her sandwich and said, "This is good."

"I told you," I said.

"I don't understand why you're going to see him. Can't you just give this stuff to the cops and let them get a DNA sample from him?"

"I could," I said. "But I'd rather do it myself. I don't want them fucking this up and they could fuck up a ham sandwich."

"It seems dangerous to me," she said.

"Monsters don't look like monsters up close," I said. "They look more like scared children."

We finished eating dinner and I cleaned up the plates and then we sat on her couch and watched Marnie. When it was over, Jill got up and went into her bedroom and changed into her pajamas. I guessed I wouldn't be getting lucky, but I was glad that she'd cooled off a little.

"I've got to feed Louie," she said.

"Is he outside?"

"Yeah."

"I'll let him in," I said.

I got up and walked over to the door and opened it and was surprised to see that he wasn't waiting outside. I called his name several times and waited. It was a nice warm night and I figured he was prowling around somewhere looking for birds or squirrels.

"He's not there?" she said.

"He's probably in your neighbor's bushes," I said. "I'll check for him again in a little while."

We got in her bed and turned out the lights and I sat there thinking about Vincent. I was looking forward to seeing him and looking him in the eyes. I was going to pretend to be somebody else but he'd know who I was. I was looking forward to watching him pretend like he didn't recognize me. I was looking forward to watching the reaction of Fields and Jaggers when the DNA sample came back positive. I was looking forward to walking out of the Durham County jail with Ray. I was looking forward to sitting ringside at Ray's next fight. I was looking forward to seeing the joy on Big Ray's face and on Max's. Monster chasing was often a thankless business, but it sure felt good when you got one. It felt even better when you set an innocent man free. I looked forward to Jill and me getting our lives back.

I drifted off and slept until I was startled awake sometime after midnight by a noise outside the window. I got up slowly and climbed out of bed. I picked up the Glock from the bedside table and walked over to the window and listened. I heard something stirring outside in the yard. I peeked out through the blinds and didn't see anything. I walked into the living room and looked out the blinds there. I still didn't see anything but I heard rustling in the bushes behind where my truck was parked in the driveway.

I opened the front door and looked out into the yard. In the darkness, I saw a dark figure climbing over the fence at the edge of the yard. I took off running across the yard. The figure disappeared over the fence and I ran toward the fence and went over it. The figure was almost to the fence on the far side of the neighbor's yard. I sprinted and closed the distance and followed the man over the fence. I pushed my way up on the fence and jumped off of it and tackled the man. We crashed to the ground and rolled over twice and I lost my grip on the gun and lost it in the grass. I tried to grab the man's neck but he rolled his body and struck me in the side of the face with the back of his right hand and knocked me off balance. The man jumped up and I could see that he was wearing

149

gloves and a black mask. I couldn't see his eyes in the darkness. I reached for him and tried to grab him and he pulled away from me and I tried to reach in the grass for the gun but couldn't find it anywhere.

We struggled in the grass and he was stronger than I expected. I brought my right hand up and punched him in the side of the head but I couldn't get much power into the punch because I couldn't put my legs into it. He dropped his head down and grabbed my arms. He released his hands and grabbed my face and tried to push his thumbs into my eyes. I lowered my head and swung at him again and missed and when I reached up to grab him again I felt a sharp stinging pain on the underside of my right forearm. My heart was beating hard now and I looked down at my right arm and saw that it dripping with black blood. The man had pulled himself free and he kicked me in the face and I fell backward into the grass. When I got up, I saw him running around the far side of the house. He disappeared from sight.

I ran after him but when I got around to the front yard of the house, he was already opening the door to a black Dodge Charger parked across the street. When he saw me, he lifted his hand up over the top of the Charger and I instinctively dove into the grass. I saw a flash of gunfire and heard a series of explosions. I saw dirt fly up out of the ground in front of me. When I looked up, I saw the Charger peel away from the curb.

I sat down in the grass and held my right arm in my left hand. I was covered in blood. There was a huge gash on the bottom of my arm and my arm was throbbing with pain now. I walked back over to the fence and searched for the Glock and found it a few feet from where we had struggled. I climbed back over the fence and jogged across the yard and climbed over the other fence into Jill's yard.

I walked back to Jill's house. She opened the door and let me in and said, "Oh my God," when she saw my right arm.

"Get a towel," I said.

She ran to the back and returned with a towel. She wrapped it around my arm and held it tightly against the wound.

"I'll call 911," she said. "Here, hold this on there."

I nodded. She went over and called 911 and told the operator that I had been attacked by an intruder and needed an ambulance. She came back over and looked at the towel. The blood was soaking through.

"I told you," she said. "I fucking told you."

I nodded and winced in pain. I sat up and heard the sound of sirens in the distance. I looked up at her and could tell that she saw something else in my eyes. "It was him," I said.

She nodded.

I took a deep breath and held the towel tightly against my arm. She put her arms around me. When the police and paramedics arrived, they found us both covered in blood.

CHAPTER TWENTY-FIVE

A LOT OF COPS like to brag that they've been on the job for twenty years and have never had to draw their gun. I don't know what kind of neighborhoods they work in, but they sure as hell aren't the ones I've worked. I have drawn my gun and used it on several occasions, and I've never felt much joy or remorse about it.

As the ER doctor stitched up my arm, I thought about how much I would enjoy killing Vincent and watching as the last bit of light left his eyes. Jill had stopped crying and was sitting in the chair next to me. Her eyes were red and she had a blank, defeated look on her face. I knew that telling her how sorry I was wouldn't help anything, so I didn't. Instead, I reminded myself of the old Sicilian proverb about revenge being best served cold and told myself to slow down and do this right.

When I got home, I did an Internet search for website design companies in Durham with the search term Vincent and found two of them. One of them had a picture of the website designer.

He was a middle aged black man. The other was a company called Web Design Solutions. I checked the Secretary of State's corporate registry and saw that it was registered to a man named Vincent Goins. It listed Goins' address as an apartment behind the American Tobacco Campus.

I called the number and a man answered and I told him that my name was Roger Minsky and that I had a landscaping business and was looking to promote it with a website. I said I liked the work I saw on his website and would like to meet with him to discuss setting up a website for my business. He said we could do it over the phone and that I could e-mail him the information and pictures and he'd do the rest, but I said I liked doing business in person. He told me he was available the next afternoon and gave me the address I'd seen on file with the corporate registry.

I drove over to his apartment and parked about half a block down the street and waited. It was a little after six when I saw a man matching the description that Jennifer gave me come out of the apartment building and start walking down the street. I followed him for a couple of blocks, careful to stay at least a block behind him. I studied his build and saw that it was consistent with what I remembered about the man I'd struggled with in the darkness. I watched him walk into a bar and I parked outside on the curb and saw him through the window. He took a seat at the bar and ordered a beer and some food and ate it alone.

I took out my phone and called Roth. "I found him," I said.

"You serious?" he said.

"Yep. I have a meeting with him tomorrow."

"A meeting?"

"Yeah. He does web design. He thinks I'm a landscaper named Roger Minsky."

"Lying is nothing for you, is it?"

"Did a lawyer just say that to me?" I said.

"What are you going to do? He'll probably recognize you from the news."

"I want to look him in the eye," I said. "If he doesn't recognize me, I'll find out what I can find out. See where it takes me."

"Good luck," he said. "Keep me posted."

I hung up and pulled away from the curb. I called Jill and asked if she was up for doing something, but she said she was tired and just wanted to go to bed.

Next I called Ellen. "I got a good candidate for match number two," I said.

"Really?"

"Uh huh."

"How did you find him?"

"It's a long story."

"I'd like to hear it."

"No you wouldn't. Not anymore than I'd want to hear about chromosomes and shit."

"You owe me, Johnny."

"Yes, I do. How's season tickets to the North Carolina Opera sound to you?"

"That sounds good."

"They're doing Il Trovatore. You ever seen that one?"

"No."

"You'll love it. It's like a Tarantino movie with fiddle music."

"That sounds like fun."

"What's the best way for me to get a DNA sample for you?"

"I would need something with blood or saliva or skin cells."

"So if I cut him open with a razor and bleed him out into a bowl, would that do the trick?"

"There's probably a better way," she said. "A glass he drank out of maybe, or a straw. Or if he smokes, a cigarette butt would be perfect."

"He doesn't smoke."

"How do you know?"
"I followed him."
"What do you think you can get?"
"I don't know," I said. "I'll figure something out."

CHAPTER TWENTY-SIX

I LOOKED ONLINE for anything I could find on Vincent Goins and learned that he grew up near Hillsborough and graduated from Orange High School in 1997. He was in the band and the drama and computer clubs. He did a couple of semesters at Durham Tech learning about computers and then worked in retail at several computer stores in Northgate Mall in Durham and Crabtree Valley Mall in Raleigh. He started his own website design company a few years back. From what I could tell, his only hobbies were computers, Renaissance fairs, and sadomasochism. His Facebook profile was full of pictures of him from various visits to the Pennsic War. I had to look that one up.

Apparently the Pennsic War is a giant nerdfest they hold every year in Slippery Rock, Pennsylvania, where Renaissance fair players come and act out their fantasy roles in real life for an entire week. The event climaxes with a huge battle with bow staffs and clubs and maces on a football field and whoever wins gets to be King of the Nerds for a whole year. I had heard of Slippery Rock because I had drank a lot of Rolling Rock beer in my life, and I imagined that the people who made the beer there probably really, really hated the week in August when the Pennsic War crowd descended on their town. The more I learned about Goins, the more embarrassed I was about losing a fight to him.

The Pennsic War thing was useful because it told me something about Goins' psychology. The common thread between the sadomasochism crowd and the Renaissance fair crowd was role playing. People in both of those lifestyles loved to pretend to be people other than who they really were. That's who Goins was. He was a guy who loved to wear a mask. I wanted to rip that mask off and show his face to the world.

The next day I drove to Goins' apartment and knocked on his door. A man opened the door and immediately took a step back. He had a startled look on his face when he saw me.

"Roger Minsky," I said, putting out my hand.

I studied his eyes and I could see the panic unfolding in his mind. He finally put out his hand and said, "Vincent Goins. Thanks for coming."

I shook his hand and he gestured for me to come into the living room and have a seat. I walked in and took a seat at the end of a leather couch facing the fireplace. I watched his hands. If he reached for anything, I was going to draw my gun from under my coat and shoot him to death.

Goins was about six feet tall and heavyset. He had short black hair and a goatee and he wore an untucked short sleeve button down shirt. He had on khaki shorts and tennis shoes and glasses. I remembered the man in the mask being in better shape, but I had only seen him in the dark. I remembered what I'd told Jill about monsters looking like scared children up close. That's what he looked like. He wasn't a menacing figure in a mask anymore. He was just a typical computer nerd who was about to get body slammed on a murder charge. Goins took a seat in a chair across from me and picked up a notebook and a pen from the table beside him.

"So how'd you hear about me?" he said.

"The Internet," I said. "I do most of my shopping on there these days."

He nodded. "So you have a landscaping business, right?" he said.

"Yeah," I said.

He looked at my right arm. He could see the bandage making a bulge in the coat.

"Did something happen to your arm?" he said.

"Yeah," I said. "Funny thing about that."

He nodded and stared at me.

"Oh, you don't want to hear about that," I said.

He was quiet for a moment, then he said, "What kinds of landscaping do you do?"

"All kinds," I said. "I mow, trim hedges, lay mulch. I can fix up your yard to look like the goddamn gardens at the Biltmore Estate."

He started writing something in his notebook.

"Are you looking for pictures or graphics or anything like that?" he said.

"I don't know," I said. "What do you suggest?"

"If you have a logo or something I'd go with that. A picture is always good. You might want a link to some pictures showing off some of your work."

"That's a good idea," I said.

"Do you have a URL yet?"

"What's a URL?" I said.

"A domain name."

"Nope. I don't have one of them."

"You need to get one but I can do that for you. You need a hosting site but that won't run you more than about twenty bucks a year."

"That sounds awesome," I said.

I looked around the room. It was cluttered with papers. There were papers on tables, on the countertops, everywhere. On the wall next to him was a picture of him smiling and standing next to a guy wearing a Darth Vader costume. Over the fireplace was a framed print of The Garden of Earthly Delights. I studied it and looked back at him. He was still writing. When he looked up, I pointed to the print and said, "That's a pretty terrifying painting."

"That's Bosch," he said. "Have you ever seen any of his stuff?"

"No," I said. All I knew about Bosch was what I'd learned from reading Michael Connelly novels.

"He painted triptychs."

"What's a triptych?"

"It's a painting with three panels. It depicts the Garden of Eden on the left," he said. "On the right is the apocalypse. In the middle is the carnival of life."

"It's pretty creepy," I said.

"Most of Bosch's work is like that."

"What's it supposed to mean?"

"It's hard to explain," he said. "Have you thought about a name for your website?"

"Nope," I said. "Any suggestions?"

"You'll have to see what URL's are available. I can make it so your site comes up high in Internet searches, but that'll cost you extra."

He stopped writing and looked at me. I was still looking at the painting.

"You always been into weird art?" I said.

"What do you mean?"

I shook my head. "It's just so stereotypical," I said. "Weirdoes are always into creepy art."

He stopped. "What are you talking about?" he said.

I studied him carefully. "You like watching the news, Vincent?" I said.

He put his pen down and looked at me. Finally, he said, "You're not a landscaper."

"No shit," I said.

"I know who you are."

I smiled at him and stared into his eyes. "I know who you are too," I said.

He pointed to the door. His hand was shaking. "I want you to get out of my house," he said.

I stood up. "Get a good look at me," I said. "You're going to be seeing me again."

"Get out of here," he said again.

I walked to the door and opened it. "Tell me," I said. "What do you think it's like for someone who knows they're living in the last few moments of the world?"

"Get out of my fucking house," he said.

"Goodbye, Vincent," I said.

I walked out and closed the door behind me. When I got to my truck, I took out the phone and called Nikki. She answered on the second ring.

"What's going on, baby?" she said.

"I need you to do me a favor," I said.

CHAPTER TWENTY-SEVEN

THE NEXT DAY, I sat across from Roth going over everything I'd found. He looked it all over and finally said, "Jesus."

"Yeah," I said. "I'll have a DNA sample in a day or two."

"How're you getting that?"

"Don't worry about it," I said.

Roth sat back in his chair and laughed. "This is going to be fucking fun," he said.

"Yes it is," I said.

"After this, Durham is going to need a new museum showcasing all the innocent people it's tried to kill during the years."

"Let other cities be famous for making cars or having palm trees," I said. "We can be famous for prosecuting innocent people."

"I can't wait to tell this story on 60 Minutes," he said. "I'm really going to ham it up good."

When we were done, Roth walked me out and shook my hand and patted me on the shoulder. "You did a hell of a good job on this," he said.

"I'm a one man justice machine," I said. "What can I say?"

I left Roth's office and walked to the parking garage and got into my truck and drove to The Fresh Market. I bought some steaks, some good bread and three bottles of good red wine. I called Jill on my cell and told her it was safe to leave work and come over to my place. I pulled onto the street, got out of my truck, took the groceries out and was carrying them toward my building when it happened.

I don't remember hearing the shot or feeling the bullet hit my body. All I remember is seeing the blood on the pavement in front of me and then being eye-level to the curb. The rest I remember in bits and flashes. Florescent hospital lights on a ceiling, ceiling tiles moving overhead, the sound of wheels on the tile floor, the pneumatic hissing sound of the oxygen mask.

It was nighttime and I was sitting in the unmarked car watching the silhouette of two people in the window. I was listening to their voices on the wire. She was asking him about the girl's murder and he was telling her that they had no choice.

The woman was promising him that she wouldn't say a word to anybody and begging him to be honest with her. He was getting madder and madder, wanting to know why she was asking so many questions, telling her that it was all in the past and that it was none of her business anyway.

She was pleading with him to let her and Ronny go live with her mother in Spartanburg. He was telling her that no one was taking his son away from him and that he would kill her graveyard dead if she ever tried to leave him. She was swearing to God that she would never tell anyone.

I picked up my Glock and chambered a round. I looked up at the light in the bedroom. I saw the silhouettes standing there in the bedroom window. I saw their hands moving. I saw him towering over her, her face upturned in the yellow light. I picked up the radio and pushed the talk button and said I was going in. Stay put, they said.

I punched the dashboard and continued to watch the silhouettes in the window. I heard a scream and saw his giant claw of a right hand come swinging across the window and she disappeared from the light. I heard more screaming. I saw him bend down over her and all I could see was an arm rising up in the window and then disappearing again under the bottom of the window frame. It rose up again and disappeared again.

I got out of the car and ran toward the apartment building. I tried to open the front door to the apartment building but it was locked. I stepped back and kicked it as hard as I could, breaking the doorframe and sending pieces of wood splintering onto the floor. I ran up the stairs. My heart was beating out of my chest.

I heard a tumbling noise coming from inside the apartment. I tried to open the door to the apartment and it was locked too. I stepped back to kick the door in. The lock broke but the door caught on the chain latch above. I stepped back and kicked it again and the door flew open.

When I woke up, several faces were staring down at me. I tried to say something but the faces didn't seem to understand. I closed my eyes again. I saw her there. She was lying on the floor of the bedroom with her eyes open looking at me. Blood was dripping out her mouth and there was blood on the floor all around her. I looked at the wall behind her and it was covered in a spray of blood. I looked at the corner behind the bed and saw more blood and I looked down behind the bed and saw him sitting there upright with his shoulders and head sagging forward like he'd fallen asleep drunk. The knife was on the floor at his feet.

"Egan," somebody said.

My vision came into focus. I saw Jackson standing over me.

"Egan, you there?"

I closed my eyes and opened them again.

"Can you hear me?"

"Where am I?" I said.

"Duke Hospital. Jesus, we didn't think you were going to make it. You lost a hell of a lot of blood."

"Where's Jill?" I said.

"She's downstairs. She'll be back up in a minute."

The nurse pushed Jackson aside and looked me over. "He's coming out of it," she said. "Give him some space."

I closed my eyes again and when I woke up I saw that I was in a hospital room hooked up to a series of machines. Jackson was sitting in a chair in one corner and Jill was standing over me.

"Can you hear me?" she said. "Say something if you can hear me."

"I can hear you," I said.

"Jesus, John," she said. Her eyes were filled with tears. "I thought I was going to lose you."

"Not me," I said. "I'm right as rain."

After awhile the doctor came in. The gauzy layers of anesthesia had slowly fallen away and I was alert enough now to know where I was and a vague sense of what had happened to me. I knew I had been shot. The doctor stood over me holding my chart in his hand.

"You were very lucky, Mr. Egan," the doctor said.

"I feel lucky," I said.

"Do you remember anything?"

"No."

"You were shot in the back. The bullet hit you in the upper right side of your back, right under your shoulder. It tumbled and came out just over the top of your ribs. Two more inches to the left and you'd be paralyzed. Any lower and the cavitation would have taken out your right lung. The whipsaw effect caused heavy trauma to several of your internal organs. But despite suffering such a major trauma, we expect you to survive and make a full recovery."

"How long am I going to be in here?"

"I'll know more when I see how you do in the next few days," the doctor said. "The major risk now is infection."

He scribbled something on the chart. "You were very fortunate. Someone called 911 almost immediately and the paramedics got to you within a few minutes. A few minutes more and you might have bled to death."

"Thank you, doc," I said.

"Rest up," he said. "I'm sure you will have a lot of questions, but there will be time to ask them once you're feeling better."

The doctor patted me on the arm and walked out of the room. Jackson stood up and walked over and looked at me. "You got hit with a .223," he said. "You know what the survival rate for that is?"

"No," I said.

"Fifteen percent," he said. "You're goddamn lucky. They had to give you two blood transfusions."

"Am I going to be able to use my right arm again? It hurts like hell."

"The doctor said yes. They had to put quite a few stitches in you. But you should be good as new once you heal up."

"How long have I been here?"

"Three days."

"I know who shot me."

"Roth told me all about it and I have some news for you on that when you're ready."

I nodded. "Let's hear it," I said.

"Maybe now's not the best time."

"Now's as good a time as any."

"We went to Goins' apartment night before last. Executed a search warrant with SWAT. He didn't answer and we opened the door with a battering ram and threw flash bang grenades. He was gone. Looked like he left in a hurry."

"Son a bitch," I said.

"We found a rifle in his closet. Bushmaster AR-15."

I nodded.

"The crime lab is testing it, but we're assuming the rifling is going to match the bullet fragments they took out of you."

"It's him," I said.

"Yeah," Jackson said. "We figure he was in the bushes across the street. It was still a high velocity round when it hit you, so he couldn't have been far away. We figure he couldn't have been more than fifty, sixty yards back. Any farther back and the bullet might have shattered and ripped you apart."

"He killed Sheryl Rose," I said. "I can't prove they met, but I think they did. He knew I was after him."

"We at least got a DNA sample and we've got a rush order on trying to match it to that profile your expert worked up. He didn't have a record, so he wasn't in the database."

"It'll match," I said.

Jackson nodded. He took my hand and pressed it in his hands. "Looks like you were right," he said.

"What's the department saying?"

"They've been pretty quiet. This is going to be a pretty big black eye for them."

"What about Roth?"

"He's happy as a fucking clam. He says Stricker won't take his calls. But if this matches up, I don't see how they prosecute Ray Marks for the Rose murder. I'm just sorry you had to get shot to bring the truth to light."

I tried to wiggle my body to get comfortable and felt a jolt of searing pain on my right side. "Can you see if they'll get me some morphine or something?" I said.

"I'll go get the nurse."

Jackson disappeared. Jill walked up and put her hand on my cheek. She bent down and kissed me on the forehead. "Rest up, baby," she said. "Stuart will take it from here."

I nodded. "My throat's dry," I said. "Can I have some water?"

She reached over to the bedside table and picked up a cup with a straw in it. "Here's some ginger ale," she said.

I lifted up my head and sipped it and then put my head back down. I looked at her for a long time. "I'm so sorry," I said. "I'm so sorry for all of this."

"Not now," she said. "Just concentrate on getting better. Once the risk of infection goes away, we're going to get you home. You're going to have weeks if not months to lie there and think about things."

"Okay," I said.

The nurse came in and said, "So the pain is biting you pretty good, huh?"

"Yes," I said.

"Here," she said, taking out a syringe and injecting it into the IV that was running into my arm. "This should do the trick."

I smiled at her and then felt the drug hit me all at once. I closed my eyes and drifted away again to some far distant place.

CHAPTER TWENTY-EIGHT

I WAS LYING in my hospital room reading about Jack Stark killing bad guys. The book was getting good now and I wanted to see what happened next: "Roland was a long way away. He was almost out of Stark's range. Almost."

Jill came into my room and kissed me and pulled up a seat next to my bed. "Looks like I was right," I said. "The edge play guy disappeared. He's on the run apparently. They're running the lab work and ballistics, but it's him."

"I know," she said. "I'm just glad this is all over."

"I told you Ray didn't kill that girl."

"I was afraid you were just chasing ghosts."

"I suck at a lot of things," I said. "But detective work ain't one of them."

"I hope they don't take him alive," she said. "I hope he suffers."

"Beggars and choosers," I said.

"We should celebrate."

"We should," I said.

"We will."

"How's work been going?" I said.

"It's been going."

"You should call Ray's dad and tell him the good news, if he hasn't heard already," Jill said. "That'd be a pretty satisfying call."

"Can you hand me the phone?"

She handed it to me and I took it in my left hand and dialed Big Ray's number. When I told him everything, he was quiet and then I could hear him start crying. "Thank you," he said, his voice breaking. "Thank you so much."

"My pleasure," I said. "Now maybe Ray can get back to chasing that middleweight crown."

"I'll never forget this," Big Ray said. "My family will never forget this."

I called Roth next. "When can Ray expect to be out of there?" I said.

"We still need the science, but this gives us motive and shows an intent to cover up his involvement in the crime."

"What do you think Stricker will say?"

"He'll deny reality and offer me voluntary manslaughter and I'll tell him to go fuck himself. In a few months, he'll quietly dismiss the charges. He'll say that in light of recent events, he doesn't have the evidence to get a conviction. He'll never admit that he tried to kill an innocent man."

"Fucking asshole."

"He's actually worse than that."

"Whatever. We won. He lost. Fuck him."

I hung up and talked to Jill for awhile.

WHEN JILL CAME BACK the next day, she told me she had a bottle of Veuve Cliquot waiting for me at home.

"You have any champagne glasses?" she said.

"No. Is it gauche to drink champagne out of wine glasses?"

"It is a super redneck thing to do."

"I don't care," I said.

"Me either."

"We'll say a toast," I said.

"To justice," she said. "I hope that bastard dies painfully."

"I'll drink to that," I said.

"You'll drink to anything."

We kissed each other and laughed.

"So we have our lives back," she said. "What should we do next?"

"I say we go on vacation."

"Let's take a week and go down to St. John," she said.

"I've never been there."

"You would love it."

"What's so great about it?"

"They have this beach there that might be the most beautiful beach in the world. And there's this little cove called Waterlemon Cay where you can snorkel with giant sea turtles and stingrays."

"Fuck that."

"Why?"

"Stingrays?"

"They're harmless."

"Bull fucking shit. One of those things killed the crocodile man. And he fucked with black mambas and charging rhinos and hungry bears."

"That was a freak accident," she said.

"Can we swim with turtles and stay away from the stingrays?"

"I'll protect you. Besides, it's legal to drink and drive there and they drive on the wrong side of the road."

"I'm all in," I said.

"We can rent a villa up on Bordeaux Mountain. Wake up every morning looking out at the ocean. It is absolutely paradise."

"I can't wait. Let's go tomorrow."

"I have to put in for vacation time at work and you have to get better."

"Fuck that noise," I said.

"Don't worry, baby. I've got plenty of days saved up."

CHAPTER TWENTY-NINE

I WENT HOME a few weeks later but I was still too weak to do much besides lay in the bed, listen to opera music, and read Jack Stark novels. In the next few weeks I'd listened to everything ever composed by Puccini, Verdi, and Mozart, and finally got around to listening to Beethoven's only opera, Fidelio, which I decided was overrated. I read the entire Jack Stark series and tried to keep in my head a running count of the people he killed. I had it pegged at about two hundred and eleven, but that included the guy he chased into a parking lot during a thunderstorm where the guy got hit by a bolt of lightning.

Jackson came over from time to time and sat with me. I tried to explain opera to him.

"I don't listen to it to try to sound sophisticated," I said. "It's mostly just violent fairy tales when you get down to it. Plus, it relaxes me."

He nodded.

"Einstein loved Mozart," I said. "He was real skeptical on the question of whether there's a God, but he said that Mozart was the one thing in the world that made him believe there might be. He said Mozart didn't write his music, he discovered it. That it was always there in the fabric of the universe since the beginning of time."

Jackson thought about that for a second.

I played the Chorus of Forgiveness from The Marriage of Figaro for him and then I played the Lacrimosa movement from the Requiem in D Minor. He listened to it carefully. Finally, he just said, "Goddamn."

Jill came over every night and cooked for me or brought me takeout. When I wasn't listening to music or reading crime novels or watching TV, I kept going back to the case.

It all seemed pretty simple now. Sheryl Rose had been living a double life. I'm not sure even she understood who she was or what she wanted. She was a career girl who had grown up in a traditional American family in an All-American town. She'd done the things people expected her to do. She excelled academically, socially, athletically. She went to a good school and learned a profitable and glamorous trade. She'd made a career for herself and had advanced that career at every stop. From Fort Lauderdale to Columbus to Durham.

If she hadn't been murdered, she would probably have gone on to Atlanta, Chicago, Washington, or New York.

But there was something else inside her, something that was probably there since she was a teenager. It was something that probably seemed normal to her but was strange to other people, so she kept it hidden. She suppressed it but she couldn't hold it down forever. Some part of her needed to be dominated, to be controlled, to be sexually humiliated. She probably fought it as long as she could and when she couldn't fight it anymore, she tried to control it.

She knew how dangerous it was to her and to her career, but she couldn't escape it any more than a gay or lesbian person can escape their sexual identity. It began in fantasies and those fantasies grew in things she read about on the Internet. She saw that there was a community of people like her out there. People who were outwardly normal but who had these deviant needs and desires.

Eventually she sought to make contacts to satisfy that aching she'd felt for as long as she could remember. Safely, discreetly. She'd found a website that was a portal to that community and searched for a discreet play partner who could give her the things she couldn't ask for in regular relationships.

I thought back about on what Nicolette had told me and I figured that Sheryl Rose was probably not a newcomer to the sado-masochism scene. I tried to put myself in her mind and imagine the feelings of excitement and terror she must have felt at reaching out into the BDSM community knowing how much she had to lose. I imagined that she would be humiliated beyond belief if she could see the spectacle her death had become.

She was a nice girl, a devoted daughter and hard-working reporter, and she'd worked hard to make the people she cared about proud of her. It hurt me to put myself in her mind, to imagine the shame she would have felt to see herself portrayed publicly in such a sordid, twisted light.

I tried to put myself into the mind of Vincent Goins as well and that was easier. Goins was a guy who barely made it through high school and probably had never had sex with a girl he didn't pay for until he was well into his twenties. He was the only child of a single mother who worked as a waitress and who raised him in a single wide trailer in a trailer park out in the woods near Hillsborough. He grew up with just a few friends. He was never part of the popular crowd.

He was only good at one thing: computers. He was shy by nature but learned to mask that shyness and project an image of confidence. But he wasn't fooling anyone except gullible, sexually confused women he met on the Internet. And based on my conversation with Jennifer Coats, I guessed he didn't fool many of them either.

He knew who he was and unlike Sheryl Rose, he was comfortable with it. He embraced it. He saw the sadomasochism lifestyle as normal and he knew that the larger society which saw it as strange was simply ignorant. He didn't have any need to hide who he was to anyone except potential clients for his website design business. I guessed he'd either attended or tried to attend the parties Nicolette had told me about and that she either didn't remember him or had simply lied to me about not remembering him. It didn't matter.

Goins was just a guy with a need in search of other people with corresponding needs. He might have gotten off on inflicting pain on women, but he never really meant to harm them.

He'd probably been overwhelmed when he made contact with Sheryl Rose. He'd probably lied to her about his experiences in the lifestyle and with women in general. He might not have ever had any real experience with edge play, and maybe that's why he was so bad at it. All that mattered to him was that he had found his submissive and she was more to him than a playmate. She was a trophy that validated his delusional feelings of power and control. She was the triumph over all the shame and degradation he'd suffered from childhood onward.

He tried hard to give her what she wanted. But he went too far. He crossed the line between hurting someone and harming them. That was a distinction I'd learned from Nicolette and it didn't make any sense to me before, but it did now.

I imagined the panic he must have felt when he untangled the cord from her around her neck and desperately pleaded with her to wake up. I imagined the shock and the overwhelming fear he must have felt as he saw her lying there still. The desperation in the days that followed as he waited for a knock on his door. The strange feelings of relief and guilt that must have come from seeing the police and the media label the death a murder and identify Ray Marks as the killer.

With everything I'd learned about Goins through my own investigation and through the information Jackson had given me, I felt like I knew him and understood him to an extent that I could even sympathize with his decision to shoot me. I knew he probably didn't want to do it but that he had no choice.

I was onto him and either he was going to put me down or I was going to destroy his life and drag him kicking and screaming into the light. He'd seen the media circus and he knew what was waiting for him. He knew that he'd be taken and paraded in front of the whole world as a freak before they tried him and convicted him and threw him into general population in Central Prison. He knew a guy like him would never make it there.

And looking at it like that, it was hard for me to blame him for what he'd done. If I'd been him, I'd have probably done the same thing.

What didn't make sense to me was him stalking Jill. That was an act that seemed out of character for the person I understood him to be. His disappearance made complete sense. He was trapped and alone and knew that I had survived his attempt to kill me and that the cops would now come tearing down his door and dragging all his secrets in front of the television cameras.

I tried to imagine what he thought he'd get by attacking me. I had just homed in on him and he knew it. He'd read Eric Bain's story in the paper and he'd seen me on TV with Roth. But following me and stalking my girlfriend weren't going to stop me from coming for him. All it would do was tell him when I was coming for him, and maybe that's all he needed to know. Maybe it was so that he could pick the right time and place to kill me. Or maybe it was just another desperate act by a desperate man who felt the world caving in around him. I wondered if it was just an irrational and useless attempt to hold off the inevitable. I closed my eyes and tried to see what he saw, to feel what he felt, and that still didn't feel right.

I had been home for about three weeks when Jackson called and said, "You're not going to fucking believe this."

"What?" I said.

"The ballistics from the rifle matched," he said. "But the DNA and the prints? They don't."

CHAPTER THIRTY

I WAS FINALLY UP and moving around. I could even lift my right arm, although the right side of my body still hurt like hell every time I did. I was eating Oxycodone pills like Tic-Tacs, then struggling with the nausea the pills gave me. The doctors told me not to drink while taking them, but I ignored that advice and learned that if I took two pills and drank a couple of beers, I got a pretty good buzz and didn't feel any pain for at least a few hours.

I drove to Roth's office and sat in the chair across from his desk. He was sitting in his leather chair wearing a blue Oxford shirt and no tie. He had taken his white gold Rolex off his wrist and placed it in front of him on the desk.

"This is a real goat fuck of a case, you know that?" he said.

I nodded. "I thought we had him nailed down," I said.

"Thought so too."

"We still have her living a double life. We still have the second DNA profile, even if we don't have a definitive match to Goins."

Roth turned his chair sideways and tapped his fingers on his desk. "Stricker will put the SBI analyst on the stand and she'll say the second sample is just background noise. Page will say it's a second contributor. We'll have a battle of the experts. Who the hell knows what a jury will do with that?"

"It's not enough," I said.

"No, probably not."

Roth sat there in silence, turning it over in his mind. Finally he said, "We got a guy who has motive, opportunity, and probably had some sort of relationship with the victim, but we can't prove he was ever inside that house."

"It's strange," I said. "Never seen anything like it."

"Me either," he said.

"What do you think?" I said.

He shrugged. "Arguing reasonable doubt is something you only do in the movies," he said. "That's not good enough for juries. Juries want to hear a competing narrative. Stricker is going to tell them a story about a beautiful young TV reporter whose life was cut short by a roided up thug. I've got to tell them a different story. But if all I have is that she wasn't perfect, that she had some unusual proclivities, they'll convict our client. I'm not even sure Judge Watson will let any of that come in if I can't fit it to an alternative theory of the case. Stricker will have a hell of an argument under the rape shield law to keep it out."

"Who do you believe?" I said. "Ellen Page or the SBI?"

"I don't know. I'm not a scientist."

"I'm not either. But it doesn't make any sense for Goins to shoot me if he didn't kill Sheryl Rose that night, or at least have sex with her."

Roth chewed on his lower lip. "Maybe he got scared," he said.

"He had to know we had the second DNA sample from watching the news and, if he wasn't there, he had to know it wouldn't match him," I said. "What's there to be scared of?"

"Maybe he didn't want to be falsely accused. That's not an irrational fear in this town, you know."

I shook my head. "Doesn't make any sense," I said. "He wouldn't have been scared of being outed."

"Oh yeah? And you know this how?"

I sighed. "I can't explain it," I said. "But I think I understand him. He wasn't ashamed of being in the BDSM lifestyle. Sheryl Rose? She was scared to fucking death of being outed. She probably hated that part of herself and hated the rest of herself for not being able to control it. But him? He thought he was normal and it was the rest of world that was strange."

"So now you don't think it was him who shot you?"

"I don't know. It just doesn't make any sense."

Roth leaned forward. "Well tell me then, Egan. Who the fuck did shoot you?"

I looked down at the ground and then looked back up at him. "If I knew that, I'd know who killed Rose," I said.

Roth put his hands out like he was gripping an invisible basketball. "Let's say there is a third suspect," he said. "Why does he shoot you? He knows you're chasing Rose's Internet hookups and he knows he's not on that list."

"Maybe he didn't want me proving that Goins was innocent," I said. "Maybe he wanted both of us to be right where we are right now: stuck, with nowhere to go."

"Plus," Roth said. "How do you explain the match from the Bushmaster to the bullet that hit you?"

"I don't know," I said.

Roth leaned back again. "Any ideas?" he said.

"The mystery caller," I said. "That's the only clue I can think of that helps us. And we got nowhere to go with that."

CHAPTER THIRTY-ONE

I MET JACKSON at Mangum's when he got off his shift. He was wearing khakis and a green Durham PD knit shirt with a badge sewn onto the front of it. He was wearing his shield on a chain around his neck and his eyes looked very tired.

"Rough day?" I said.

He rubbed his eyes with his hands and said, "Yeah."

I motioned for the waitress. "It's my turn to pay," I said.

He nodded. She came over and I ordered a Blue Moon draft and Jackson ordered a Cruzan dark rum and Coke. The waitress went to get our drinks.

"They've been on our ass to get the murder rate down for years now," he said. "And we finally did it. Hell, I've only caught three homicides so far this year. But the robberies, man, the robberies."

"A bunch of those, huh?"

"Yeah. And the description of the assailant is the same every time. A black man with a gun. About five foot ten and about a hundred eighty five pounds. If I hear that one more time, I'm going to kill myself."

"They say cross racial ID's are the worst," I said.

"The victims are ninety percent black themselves," he said.

"Why no bodies?"

"The gang war's cooled off. Everybody's been quiet. Maybe they finally learned that if they sell drugs without killing each other, we probably won't come looking for them."

"How many murders were there last year?"

"About twenty five, I think."

"Year before last?"

"Probably thirty, thirty five."

"How about this year?"

"Shit, man. Probably not more than eight or nine. And most of those were guys killing their wives. I can probably count the gang murders on one hand."

The waitress brought us our drinks. "You want to pay for these or start a tab?" she said.

"We'll start a tab," I said.

"I'll need a credit card," she said.

I took out my wallet and gave her one.

Jackson kicked one of his legs up onto the seat next to him. He looked at me and waited until I looked back at him. "Fields said to tell you you're welcome," he said.

"Tell him I said fuck you," I said.

Jackson smiled.

"Is he the one who caught the Goins case?" I said.

"Several of us did the raid," he said. "It was me, Fields, Jester, Hunter, and Salinetti. But after the search, it got assigned to Fields and Jester."

"What're they saying about it?"

Jackson took a drink of his rum and Coke and I could tell from the look on his face that it was strong. "Damn that's strong,' he said. "That bartender hooked me up."

He looked back up at me. "Not a whole lot. Supposedly they're looking for him, but I don't know where they're looking. We found a bunch of bondage stuff in Goins' apartment. He had masks and ropes and whips and all kinds of shit. Jester found the Bushmaster in his closet and several boxes of Federal .223 ammo."

I stopped drinking my beer.

"What?" Jackson said.

"Nothing," I said. "Go on."

"You think he'll come back after you?"

"I wouldn't think so," I said. "But maybe I'm reading him all wrong. Maybe he's just crazy. You can't predict what crazy people will do."

Jackson nodded and said, "They took his computer to forensics and they found all the shit you'd expect to find from a guy like Goins."

"No clues on where he might have gone?"

"No," he said. "Some drawers and the closet had been rifled through. He probably threw some shit in a bag and hit the road."

I finished my beer and gestured to the waitress for another one.

"So what you do think happens now?" Jackson said.

"With what?"

"With your boy? Roth's got all kinds of shit to work with."

"I don't know," I said.

Jackson took another sip of his drink. "I don't know what to think about it."

He shook his head and rubbed his eyes again. "I always thought being a defense lawyer would be hard," he said.

"From what I've seen, it is."

"Guess that's why he drives a BMW and I drive a Ford."

"Being a lawyer's no different than being a cop," I said. "People lie to you all day long. At least when you're a cop, you get to kick somebody's ass every once in a while."

"How many innocent, I mean honest to God innocent, people you think are in prison?" Jackson said.

"I don't know," I said. "There's got to be some."

"Has to be," he said.

"Just look at what the Raleigh PD did to the guy they arrested for killing that crack whore in the 90's."

"Greg Taylor?"

"Yeah, him. That poor bastard did seventeen years in prison and was innocent as shit and the Wake County DA still won't admit he's wrong. Even after the state paid out five million bucks."

"That was a terrible case," Jackson said.

"It just goes to show you that the crimes that would put an innocent person in prison are also the ones that carry the most time."

"How you figure?"

"Think about your purely circumstantial murder case, like this one. You and I both know that when you have one coincidence, it might just be a coincidence. But when you have ten coincidences, they're probably not coincidences. Remember the Peterson case?"

"How could I ever forget that one?" I said. "I was in Vice then, but I remember the theory was that he beat his wife to death with a fireplace poker because none of our guys could find the poker. I remember the auction people later found it in the basement covered in about ten years of dust."

"He claimed he found his wife at the bottom of the stairs. And what if she really did just fall down the stairs? She dies accidentally but then he gets his life ripped apart. And when they rip it apart, they find out they weren't happy and he's having an affair. How many people you think have argued with their wives or had affairs?"

He took a drink of his rum and Coke. He said, "Most of them, I would imagine."

"Maybe he was telling the truth."

"If he was telling the truth, he was the unluckiest son of a bitch on earth."

"Maybe he was."

"I never thought about it like that," he said.

"I saw a guy on TV the other night who'd won the Powerball. Luckiest man on earth, right? If there's a luckiest man, there's got to be an unluckiest one."

"I guess there'd have to be."

"And kiddie rape cases," I said. "How many guys have you seen get boxcarred to the fucking sky based on some girl's story. No physical evidence. No corroboration. Just a girl saying the guy touched her. You ever wonder if some of them were lying?"

"I fucking hate those cases," Jackson said. "I hate everything about them."

"Everybody hates pedophiles so there's a natural inclination to want to believe the girl. Because why would she lie?"

"I had one of those where the girl didn't start telling her story until after dad had an affair with mom's best friend," Jackson said. "The kid was six years old and she'd been in mom's custody for several months. The guy was a Marine who'd done tours in Iraq and Afghanistan. Never been in trouble before in his life. He got thirty years and mom got the kid, the house, and all his pension money. I always had doubts about that one."

"How many people have been exonerated since DNA came along?" I said.

"I don't know," he said. "A bunch, probably."

"Can you imagine spending decades in prison for something you didn't do?"

"No. Don't want to. I think I'd rather just die."

"Me too."

"You think you've ever put an innocent man away?" I said.

"God I hope not. I wouldn't be able to live with myself, I don't think."

Jackson took out a pen and began scribbling on a napkin. "You know how many cases come back on appeal every year?" he said.

"I never bothered to look up the numbers," I said.

"Me either. But this egghead I know over in Financial Fraud did. The answer is fifteen percent. Fifteen fucking percent."

Jackson did the math on the napkin. "Say two thousand cases a year go up on appeal. That's three hundred cases where mistakes were made. Three hundred. And that's just legal mistakes. God only knows how many mistakes were made on the facts."

"Yeah," I said. "Makes you scared to live in this world, don't it?"

"How are Big Ray and Barb holding up?" he said.

"They're still in shock," I said.

"Man, I hated hearing it was their kid."

Jackson's eyes wandered and I turned to see what he was looking at. It was a gorgeous young professional woman in a black dress sitting across from a guy who looked like a complete asshole.

"This job," he said. "It'll make you think there's no good left in the world if you don't watch out."

"You glad you became a cop?" I said.

He shrugged. "I wasn't good for nothing else," he said.

"Me either," I said. "And I wasn't even good for that."

Jackson got the waitress' attention and ordered another drink. He said, "I didn't know Big Ray like you did, but I heard stories about him."

"He was one tough ass cop," I said. "I remember him getting into the courthouse elevator with a guy he'd arrested and the guy had his hands cuffed behind his back. When the doors closed, the guy spat in Ray's face. When they opened again, the guy had a broken nose and the floor of the elevator was covered in blood."

"Heard that one too," Jackson said. "I hate how this has all come down on him."

I said: "Sex, race, violence, celebrity. That's a straight flush right there. The trial is going to be a fucking circus."

"What if he really didn't do it?" Jackson said.

"Then he really needs me and Roth."

"Personally, I think it'd be funny as shit if he turns out to be innocent," Jackson said. "Imagine Jaggers and Fields and the rest of them all having to climb down from that. After the lacrosse case, everybody in America already thinks we're a bunch of stupid ass rednecks."

CHAPTER THIRTY-TWO

I KNEW I had to go see Big Ray and Barb to update them on the status of the case, but I didn't know what to say. I'd given them false hope and now I had to tell them that we were back where we started and that the state was still going to try to kill their son.

I had known Big Ray since we were young men sparring against each other at the Bull City Boxing Club. When we were full of dreams of Olympic glory and the professional riches that lay beyond. Both of us loved boxing. I had picked it up in the Navy and he had picked it up when he got caught shoplifting as a teenager and a judge sent him to Max instead of sending him to juvie. Before he quit drinking, we used to get together at my apartment on Saturday nights to watch the fights. He decided to go to the police academy and talked me into following him there and when we got out, we both walked beats in the southeast quadrant and spent all our free time drinking liquor and chasing pussy.

Eventually Ray went into Financial Fraud, met Barb, and became a family man. I went into Vice and just kept getting into trouble. Ray eventually left the force for a private security gig at a big software company in Research Triangle Park. He made good money there and bought a nice house in a leafy cul-de-sac in Cary. His son, Little Ray to everyone who knew them, was their only boy. Their daughter, Vanessa, was a student at N.C. State studying to be a veterinarian.

I parked my pickup in their driveway and knocked on the door. Ray answered it and told me to come inside. I followed him into the hallway and the living room. He gestured for me to take a seat on the couch and I did.

"You want some coffee or something?" he said.

"No, I'm good," I said.

Ray took a seat in a leather chair.

"I never imagined I'd be sitting here with you. Having a conversation like this," he said.

I shook my head.

"Where's Barb?" I said.

"She's upstairs. She can't talk about this stuff. Can't even turn on the TV."

"I know it's been hard on you."

"I thought it was almost over."

"So did I."

"It's like they've convicted him already. And the DA is still talking about the death penalty."

"That's just posturing," I said. "He knows this isn't a death penalty case."

Ray paused for a long time. "You don't look like you got no good news to tell me," he said.

"I wish I did."

"Just tell me."

I took a deep breath. "The DNA and fingerprints didn't match Goins," I said.

"What?"

"Yeah."

"How is that possible?"

"I don't know. I was sure they would."

Ray put his head in his hands. He looked like a man trying to wake up from a nightmare.

"You think my boy killed that girl?"

"No, but we don't have an alternative suspect. We have the second DNA sample, the mystery prints, and the mystery caller. But we don't have a person to match them to."

Ray shook his head. "My boy didn't do this," he said. "That means somebody out there is walking on this."

"I've tried everything I know to get a name and a face," I said. "I don't know what else to do."

I paused. "Roth thinks Ray's best play might be to take the stand and say it was kinky sex that got out of hand. He thinks that might get us down to involuntary."

"Involuntary?"

"Yeah."

"That still means he'd be admitting to something he didn't do."

"I know."

"He's not going to do that," Ray said.

"I didn't think so."

"Why would he kill her? I mean, they seemed like they liked each other and all, but he wasn't crazy in love or nothing like that. I only met her one time and that was when she came to interview him for that TV piece. And this kinky sex thing? That don't sound like Ray to me. He's a normal kid."

"Had they had any arguments that you know of?"

"No."

"He say she had an ex-boyfriend or current boyfriend or anything?"

"No. You ask him?"

"Yeah. But you know how it is with people facing charges. They clam up on you even if you're trying to help them. They won't tell you what you need to know even when it's in their best interest to tell you. They act like you're one of the cops looking to nail them."

"Seems like it'd be different, though. He knows you."

"That makes it even more unlikely he'd be completely honest with me," I said. "Let's say there's something he's embarrassed about. You and I would probably be the last people to hear about it from him."

"I told him to do whatever you and Roth tell him to do, but I can't tell him to say he did something he didn't do."

"It might be his only chance to avoid a murder conviction."

Ray stood up and crossed his arms and stared at the wall. "I can't believe this," he said. "I can't believe any of this."

"I still think there's somebody else," I said. "Maybe we're overlooking something."

"When you go see him, how do you think he's doing?"

"I don't think it's sunk in yet. He doesn't have that look in his eyes. You know the look I'm talking about."

Ray nodded. "He's still asking me about Biloxi," he said. "I'm worrying about the needle and he's worrying about a fight that's never going to happen."

"He's just in denial," I said. "Dreams are all he's got left right now."

"Denial's a powerful defensive mechanism," he said.

"He always was a master of defense."

"I taught him that from day one," he said. "Me and Max. I didn't want my boy to be no banger. Get his head beat in and all his money took. Hell with all that. How many fighters you see washed up, brain damaged, broke?"

"Most of them," I said. "Boxing and pornography have a lot in common. They seem glamorous at first. But you usually end up toothless living under a bridge."

Ray gave a gesture with his arm indicating something he couldn't put into words. "What happens next?" he said.

"They've set a calendar date for the trial," I said. "Roth will be filing more motions. Then they'll set a date to hear them and the judge will rule on them. Then, depending on what happens, the DA will probably make a plea offer. Roth can tell you better than I can. This is not a normal case. If the victim was a drug dealer or gangbanger, they'd already be coming down off murder one. But you know how it is. When a case hits the media, the DA gets stuck and won't offer shit. He'd rather try it and lose it than take the political hit for pleading it down. This one, for obvious reasons, is about as bad as it gets."

"So we're definitely looking at a trial?"

"Probably so."

"When will that happen?"

"Maybe six months, maybe more, depending."

Ray wiped his face with his hand.

"Don't know how Barb is going to handle something like that," he said. "I want to fall to pieces myself but I can't cause I got to be there for her."

He sat down and put his head in his hands and then sat up and put his palms on his knees. "When we were working the streets, cracking heads with the pimps and the pushers, all I used to worry about was getting hurt," he said. "About not coming home. I never even thought to worry about something like this. Seems like the truly awful events in life are the ones you never see coming."

I thought about that for a minute. "Yeah," I said.

"I just wish there was something I could do," Ray said. "That's the hardest part. All I can do is sit here and worry. Ain't a damn thing I can do to help my son."

"I'm not going to stop looking for John Doe," I said. "If I find anything, anything at all, I'll let you know."

CHAPTER THIRTY-THREE

I DROVE OVER to Durham-Chapel Hill Boulevard and met Jill at the Guglhupf Restaurant. It was one of those new artisan cafes that started to spring up when the New York and New Jersey crowd started to migrate to the Triangle. For all the bitching we did about the yankee invasion, and we did a lot of it, you had to admit they had improved the restaurant and arts scene considerably. When Durham was just a tobacco town, the best meal you could get was chopped pork barbecue and hushpuppies with sweet tea and the only entertainment was college basketball and country music concerts. Now we had German restaurants and opera performances.

The hostess took me upstairs where Jill was waiting for me at a table amid the globe lamps with pastel shades. The restaurant had a warm, orange glow to it, and Jill was already halfway into a glass of Chilean pinot noir. She had ordered a cheese plate and was eating some sort of melted brie on a sesame cracker. I ordered a half liter of Schneider Weisse and made myself a cheese cracker with parmesan cheese and plum sauce.

"How was work?" I said.

"Lovely," she said.

"Any exciting breakthroughs?"

"Yes. We discovered that cat piss cures cancer."

"I always suspected that. So when's the Nobel ceremony?"

"Next month."

"I can't make it," I said. "I'm still wanted by Interpol."

"Shame," she said. "I have such a lovely speech prepared."

"You're going to thank me for making it all possible, I hope."

"No. I'm going to have an affair with a fellow laureate."

"Why's that?"

"Have you ever fucked a Nobel prize winner?" she said.

"No."

"Me either. And it's on my bucket list."

I laughed and was happy to get a smile in return.

"I'm on my second glass of wine," she said. "You going to make me drink this whole bottle by myself?"

"When I went to AA meetings, they called that a red flag," I said. "You should consider that you might have a problem."

"You still go to AA meetings."

"When I went to them for real, I mean."

"I don't think I could have dated you then," she said.

"No?"

"Who can tolerate that kind of shit?"

"Not me. That's why I stopped going."

"So tell me about your day."

"I went to a park," I said. "Read some poetry. Did a little bit of yoga. Meditated for awhile on the teachings of the Buddha."

"Did you come up with anything profound?"

"I realized that life is ridiculous."

"I saw your boxer friend on the late news last night. Channel 5 is still having a field day."

"They're short a reporter," I said. "They can't cover everything."

"That's a horrible thing to say."

"I know. I shouldn't have said it."

I took the bottle of wine and poured some into my glass. "Was it at least funny?"

"No."

I took a sip of the wine and enjoyed the peppery taste of it. I decided that I preferred Chilean pinot noir over Australian shiraz. The thinness of its texture had previously caused me to lean the other way but my palate had evolved.

"I'm in a hell of a spot," I said.

"Yes you are."

"I've got Ellen's testimony, but the state's expert will say she's wrong. I've got the mystery number, but that leads nowhere. I've got the possible affair with Goins, but I can't prove that and the judge might not allow it in anyway."

"Why not?"

"The rape shield law."

"For what it's worth, I don't think Ellen's wrong," Jill said.

"Me either. But who knows what a jury will think. They're going to hear from a certified SBI analyst with a badge and they might choose to believe her over Ellen, especially since we don't have a face to put on the second profile."

"That's a damn shame," she said.

I drank some more wine and reached for another cracker. This time I mixed the parmesan cheese with some slightly melted brie. I bit into it and decided that it was a weird combination and that those two cheeses probably didn't belong together on the same cracker.

"Why can't anything ever just work out?" I said.

Jill shook her head. "Because life just sucks sometimes," she said.

She took a drink of her wine and I saw tears in the corners of her eyes.

"What is it?" I said.

"I can't stop thinking about seeing you lying there unconscious. I knew you were going to die."

"I always try to promise low and deliver high," I said. "That makes a good impression on people."

She didn't laugh or smile or look even the slightest bit amused.

"I'm sorry," I said. "What can I do?"

"You can drop this case."

"No, I can't."

"If you die, you don't just throw away your own life, you know?" she said. "It'll ruin my life too, and what hurts the most is that you don't seem to give even a little bit of a shit about that."

The waiter came over and brought my beer and asked if we had decided on dinner yet. We ordered some wiener schnitzel and pan roasted chicken breast with spatzle, kale, and shitake mushrooms with lemon garlic pan jus. The waiter took down our order and headed back into the kitchen.

"When I was out, who did you talk to about the case?" I said.

"Just your friend."

"Jackson?"

"Yeah."

"Fields never came by?"

"No. He probably figured I wouldn't talk to him."

"Anybody else?"

"No."

"What did Jackson say?"

Jill shook her head. "Not much. He just asked me again about the fight you had with Vincent at my house."

"What'd you say?"

"I don't remember."

"I've been thinking about that too," I said.

"Why?" she said.

"What do you think he was up to that night?"

She stopped and put her wine down. "I think he was there to kill us," she said. "Or at least to scare us."

"I don't know," I said. "Guy seemed like a pussy to me."

"You don't think it was him?"

"I don't know what I think," I said. "If it wasn't him, whoever it was sure knew what I was up to. Nobody but you, Roth, Eliot, and Ellen even knew I was zeroing in on him."

"That's why it was him," she said. "I mean, some mind-reading serial killer didn't do it."

She sat there in silence looking at me and I looked right back at her. Something about what she said unlocked something in my brain. I looked down at my phone and it hit me like a sledgehammer.

"Son of a fucking bitch," I said.

AFTER DINNER, we went out into the parking lot and walked over to my truck. I opened the glove compartment and took out a flashlight. I got down under the back of the truck and used the light to scan around the edges of the underside of the truck bed. It was right where I expected it to be. Right where I would have put it. I pulled off the magnetized tracking device.

I sat up and held it up for her.

"What is that?" she said.

"It's a GPS tracking device," I said. "Private detectives use them. So do the cops, although the cops need a warrant to put one on your car."

She looked puzzled.

"That's what he was doing at your house," I said.

"Why would Vincent want to track you?"

"Who said Vincent put it there?"

She stared straight ahead and let herself absorb what I was saying. When her eyes met mine, I couldn't tell whether I was looking at fear or anger.

CHAPTER THIRTY-FOUR

W E LEFT Guglhupf and drove back to my apartment. I put
on La Traviata and turned it down low and we sat next to
each other on the couch.

"We need to think about this," I said.

"I don't know what to say," she said.

"We can't talk candidly on the phones anymore," I said. "We
have to assume that the cops have an illegal wiretap and are listening to us."

"You really think the cops would do this?"

"Who else could tap a phone?" I said.

"But why?"

"I don't know why. But why is there a tracking device on my
truck?"

She shook her head. "I don't know," she said.

"Let's assume they've been listening to my conversations and
to yours. They would have heard everything we've talked about."

"Okay."

"They would have known I was zeroing in on Goins."

"Why would they care?"

"Maybe because they liked what they heard and decided that it gave them the perfect chance to take me out and blame Vincent for it."

She just pointed in the direction of the kitchen without looking back at it.

"I don't like this, John," she said. "I don't like any of this."

"I don't like it either," I said.

I stood up and went into the kitchen and poured us each a glass of wine. I took a seat on the couch next to Jill. "Tell me more about the black car?" I said.

She sat up and thought about it. "It was just a black Dodge Charger," she said. "It drove by slowly several times. The windows were black. I couldn't see who was inside."

"Did you notice any unusual markings?"

"No," she said. "You really don't think it was Goins?"

"That's what I used to think," I said.

"What do you think now?"

I took a deep breath. "Let's say they have a wiretap. They've been listening to us. We talked about all this on the phone. They would have known I'd gone to see Goins."

She set her wine glass down on the coffee table. "Are you saying they're behind the reporter's murder?"

"It doesn't make any sense," I said. "Why are they tracking me? Why are they listening in on my phone conversations?"

"Why couldn't it have been Goins?" she said.

"It could have been. Maybe he got scared and thought he was about to get dragged into the Sheryl Rose murder. Given the media attention, that'd scare the shit out of anybody. But then again, what if he didn't have anything to hide? Why would he shoot me if he's innocent? The more I learn about him, the more unlikely that seems to me."

"What's the alternative?" she said.

"That Bushmaster didn't get in his apartment by accident."

"Who do you think put it there?"

"Who are the only people that could have put it there?"

Jill put her hands up over her mouth. Her fingers started shaking. She sat there silently.

"Jackson was with the team that went in," I said. "That's what confuses me and scares me the most. But it wouldn't be hard for them to plant it without him seeing them do it. They all had AR-15's when they executed the warrant. They could have easily put it there and in the chaos of the search, Jackson wouldn't have noticed any difference. Once a target has been cleared, most cops put up their rifles and focus on searching the residence. But what if Goins didn't just go missing? It'd be a smart move to put Jackson on the raid team because it would make it much less likely for me to suspect that the whole thing was a setup. Those guys know Jackson's a good friend of mine."

"I don't even want to think about what that means," she said.

"Me either," I said. "But we have to."

Jill gave me an angry look. Her eyes were wet and her upper lip was trembling. "John," she said. "I told you I couldn't go through the darkness with you again. And I wasn't even thinking about anything this bad."

"I know," I said. "I never meant to get you into something like this. But we're in it."

She wiped her eyes. Her voice was shaking. "We have to be very, very careful," she said.

"Yes we do."

"What do we do now?"

I sat there for a minute and thought about it.

"When I call you on the phone, don't say anything about any of this," I said. "Just follow my lead. If they're listening, they don't know we know they're listening. What they'll be listening for now is what I'm going to do next. I say we use their own wiretap against them. If they're following us, we can lead them into a brick wall. Can you do that?"

She nodded.

"You sure?" I said. "It's got to be convincing. If they suspect we're on to them, we'll be in even more danger."

"Maybe if they think you're not focusing on them, it'll at least buy us some time," she said.

"That's my girl," I said.

Jill turned up her wine glass and drained it and then held it out to me. I went back to the kitchen and refilled it and handed it to her and she drank that one too.

"What are you going to do?" she said.

"I don't know," I said.

I picked up my phone. "Here," I said. "I'm going to go into the bedroom and call you and you answer and pretend like you're home."

"What if they're watching us?"

"They're not watching us," I said. "If they're listening to us in secret, there's no need for them to follow us because they know where we're going before we get there."

She nodded and took out her phone and put it on the table. I walked into my bedroom and dialed her number. She answered on the second ring.

"Just wanted to make sure you made it home okay," I said.

"I'm here," she said.

"You going to bed?"

"Yeah. It's been a long day."

"Look," I said. "I'm really sorry about all this. But it'll be over soon. I've just got to run down one or two loose ends and then I'm done. So make those reservations for St. John. I'll buy a Hawaiian shirt and a straw hat and start practice drinking rum."

"What kind of loose ends?"

"I'm going to get Ellen to take another look at the DNA evidence. And I'm going to go talk to some of Goins' old acquaintances in

Hillsborough to see if anybody might know where he'd go. But for me, this case is pretty much over. It's all about reasonable doubt now, and that's Roth's job."

"You owe me after all this."

"I know.," I said. "But it's in Roth's hands now. He's got Ellen and he's got the mystery caller. Even if he can't get the Goins stuff into evidence, that ought to be enough to at least hang the jury. Either way, I've done everything I can do."

"Good," she said. "It'll be nice to have our lives back."

"Yes it will," I said. "You get a good night's sleep. I'll talk to you tomorrow."

I walked back into the den. She gave me an angry look. "Why didn't you just say you were fucking done and it's over?" she said. "Fuck this loose ends bullshit."

"I don't want them trying to kill me again," I said. "But I don't want them to stop listening either."

CHAPTER THIRTY-FIVE

I WAS NOW truly stuck. With everything that had happened, I believed now more than ever that Ray was innocent of Sheryl Rose's murder. But I also didn't believe Vincent Goins had anything to do with it or that he had ever even met her. I believed more than ever that the mystery caller was her killer. But I couldn't connect that number in any way to Ray or to Vincent Goins.

The police hadn't closed the investigation into Goins' disappearance because they didn't have any good leads to follow. They had closed the investigation into my shooting and named Goins the shooter. But I didn't believe that Goins shot me or that he disappeared. I figured he was dead and buried in a hole somewhere.

As a student of human nature, I always had to remind myself that when something appears improbable, it's usually because that thing is untrue. That's the first thing you learn in detective school and you learn it again and again in the streets. One coincidence is not suspicious. But when coincidences stacked up like cordwood, you have to go back and look at the patterns objectively. When

I looked at the patterns and considered the rough probabilities, what I saw was a picture that was truly disturbing to me.

Why would Goins put a tracking device on my truck? Why would he shoot me? Why would Ray strangle Sheryl Rose? Why would my phone be tapped? The answers to those questions all pointed to only one conclusion. That conclusion was implausible on its face and standing alone, but in light of the objective evidence, it made the most sense.

Somebody with a badge shot me. Somebody with a badge made Goins disappear and planted the Bushmaster in his closet. If those things were true, that meant somebody with a badge murdered Sheryl Rose or was covering up for somebody who did.

I went back and looked at the phone logs and searched the Internet for news stories around what I now believed to be the relevant timeframe: the time right before the calls from the mystery caller started. In those days, I noticed that Sheryl had talked to her mother every day. She had talked to her producer every day. And she had talked to the Durham mayor and police chief every day.

I learned that she had interviewed Jaggers and the mayor during an event promoting the Special Olympics during the week the calls began. I knew from her dealings with Ray that she called her subjects for background information before she interviewed them. I knew from him that she wasn't shy about quickly forming sexual relationships with her subjects. And I knew that she was insecure and reckless and probably at least a little bit disturbed.

It made sense to me that the mayor or Jaggers would welcome her advances. She was young and beautiful and famous, at least locally. And they were as vain and amoral as most politicians. I knew from years of watching them rise through the ranks of the bureaucracy that their only real concern was themselves. That was a trait common to most humans. Politicians just had a little bit more of it in them.

It made sense to me that if Jaggers or the mayor had started screwing Rose, they would be smart enough to stop talking to her on their personal cell phone and start using a number that couldn't be traced back to them.

I knew that the mayor was tight with Jaggers and that Jaggers was tight with Fields and with several of the other incompetent toadies he had cherry picked from the ranks and placed into senior roles in the Major Crimes unit. Guys like Brian Hampton, Mark Jester, and Richie Hunter. That was a scary thought to me, because Jackson was tight with those guys too.

If this was a police murder and a police cover up, I couldn't be sure that Jackson wasn't also somehow involved. That went against everything I had ever known about him, but I knew enough about people to know that you never really know everything about a person. And Jackson was there when they found the rifle, which meant that if they planted it there, he either knew about it or they did it behind his back. Doing it behind his back would have been easy, because people are going in and out constantly during searches, carrying evidence out to the cars and inventorying it. Maybe they used him as a decoy. Maybe they thought I'd never suspect them if he was there during the raid.

None of it made any sense, but it made more sense than any other theory of the crime I'd considered. Still, it was hard to believe that Jaggers would cover up a murder for the mayor or that Fields and his crew would cover up a murder for Jaggers. The idea that Jackson could be involved was incomprehensible to me, but I couldn't completely rule it out.

After you saw enough dead bodies, they became something less than human to you if you weren't careful. It became easy to see them as numbers and statistics. To see a dead face and look at it as just another poor bastard who was in the wrong place at the wrong time. To tell yourself that you were just glad it wasn't you or someone you loved.

But I had a hard time believing that even a guy like Fields could become so jaded as to help a murderer go free, or to go so far as to kill innocent people to make sure that it happened. Mayors and police chiefs were like toilet paper. When you got shit on one square, you just flushed it and got a clean one.

Nailing the mayor for murder would make Jaggers a hero. And nailing Jaggers for a murder would make Fields a hero. It might even make him chief of police. Covering up a murder for the mayor or for Jaggers risked destroying not just Fields' career, but his entire life. And that was a risk I couldn't see Fields taking unless he had to. Which meant that either Fields was personally involved somehow or that he was covering for the mayor or the chief because he had no other choice.

I logged onto my computer and did an Internet search for property tax records and learned some interesting things. Jaggers made $88,000 a year as police chief, but he paid property taxes on homes in Durham and on a new beach house in Duck, North Carolina, which had some of the most expensive real estate in the Outer Banks. He paid property taxes on a boat he kept down there as well. Fields also had a new boat and a new house on Emerald Isle. Brian Hampton, Mark Jester, and Richie Hunter were also living above their means. Jackson still owned no property and the only vehicle registered to him was his eight year old Ford truck.

I knew what those guys made as cops, and according to the state property records, they were all living like hedge fund managers. It was possible that one or two of them had family money, but that didn't seem likely. I'd never known a cop who was a trust funder and I'd never known one who married into money. I did searches for the other detectives in Major Crimes and Vice and found nothing but cops living on cops' salaries.

I went back to what I'd heard on the street. Guys from Major Crimes robbing illegals. Bernard Little living like a king. Those things had seemed interesting but unconnected at the time, but now I figured that maybe there was some connection to those things and the newfound wealth of my old friends and that somehow all of those things were connected to the death of Sheryl Rose. Maybe Rose's death was a murder. Maybe it was an accident. Either way, it threatened to expose them, and that was something they couldn't let happen.

Looking at the evidence in that light, I came to suspect that Durham police officers killed Sheryl Rose or covered up her murder. They murdered Vincent Goins, got rid of his body, and faked his disappearance. And they tried to murder me to bury the whole damn thing. If that was true, it was also true that they wouldn't hesitate to try again.

So I had two choices: I could walk away with my body and my relationship with Jill intact. Or I could try to take them all down and risk losing everything. Unfortunately, I didn't have the walking away gene in me. My Scots-Irish bastard fathers who wandered from the bogs of the Celtic Sea to the mountains of North Carolina in generations long past had bred that gene away.

The mystery phone was a dead end. I knew that. It was rotting in a landfill somewhere and I'd never find it. But the science didn't lie. And there was one secret none of them could hide if I was careful enough to get to it: their DNA. Those particular combinations of human molecules that separated one person from the next and which no man could disclaim would speak the truth.

The key was the second DNA profile Ellen had discovered. If I was right, that profile would match either Jaggers or the mayor. If it did, it meant that Durham's mayor or police chief was a murderer and that his accomplices were running the Major Crimes unit. It meant that the parade of police and prosecutor scandals that had made Durham something like an amusement park of corruption and injustice were nothing but a prelude, and that we were now a city entirely ruled by human predators.

So I decided to keep it simple. I knew they were listening to my phone calls and probably to Jill's. So I would lie on the phone to manipulate them just like I leaked the story to Eric Bain and then lied about it on the stand. There was a certain irony to it all that you had to admire. You sometimes had to tell lies and commit crimes to expose even bigger lies and bigger crimes. And in a city of liars, thieves, junkies, race hustlers, scam artists, drug dealers, and other assorted felons, the very worst people of all were the politicians and police officers who were supposed to be protecting us from all of them.

If the regular people had any idea what kind of city they were living in, they would run from it like fugitives from a burning house. But the regular people weren't my problem right now. My problem was my colleagues in the crime business. We were all liars, me included. But lies were things with relative values, and all that mattered now was uncovering one single truth: who killed Sheryl Rose? As I sat there, I worked out a plan. It was very dangerous. It could work or it could get me killed. Even worse, it could get Jill killed.

Walking away was the smart thing to do. It was the safe thing to do. If Ray ended up getting railroaded, that would be a tragedy, but he wouldn't be the first or the last innocent man to go to prison. And I'd already kept my word to Big Ray. I'd given Roth some things to work with, and maybe it was time to let the justice system do its job.

I sat there in silence thinking it all over and weighing my options. I knew I should just walk away. But I couldn't force myself to make that decision. I told myself that I was being selfish, stubborn, prideful, and that I was taking this case personally when in reality it had nothing to do with me. My stubbornness had already cost me my career as a Major Crimes detective. Why should I let it rob me of the only things I had left?

I meditated on that for a while and eventually realized that it wasn't really a hard decision. If I walked away, I would never respect myself again, and a man who can't respect himself has no reason to go on living. When I looked at it that way, I realized that I was risking death either way. If I went after them, there was a good chance they'd kill me. But if I didn't, I'd be letting them kill whatever was left of me that mattered to me.

If I really hated injustice and cruelty, if I really believed in standing up to bullies, if I really believed in fighting against the evil to protect the weak – and these were all things I'd always told myself that I believed in – I wouldn't pack it in just because the bullies were a lot stronger than me. And in that respect, I realized that this case was about me. It was about whether I really believed in those things or if I was just a bullshitting coward.

I made my decision and felt at peace with it. Jill had it right, though. Doing the right thing isn't what's hard. What's hard is living with the consequences afterward. I didn't know what that those consequences might be, but I wasn't going to quit. Not on Ray, not on myself, and not on the possibility of justice finding a pinhole of light in the darkness. I had what I needed. I had the target and the strategy and the will to see it through to the end.

CHAPTER THIRTY-SIX

MY PLAN involved lies, manipulation, criminal activities, misdirection, and violence. In other words, it was perfectly tailored to my personal skill set.

It was just after noon and I was driving through Little Mexico. I saw beaten up trailers lined up and down through improvised roads in scablands of gravel and weeds and people with coppery skin wearing weary, beaten looks on their faces. I pulled into a strip mall where a Blockbuster Video store and a Sam Goody record store used to be. Those stores were now gone and in their place was a Mexican restaurant named Ciudad Toro. There was only one other vehicle in the parking lot when I pulled my truck into a space in front of the restaurant.

I walked in and took off my sunglasses. The place was empty but they were playing Mexican pop music on the stereo system and the TV screens were turned to a European League soccer match. I took a seat in a booth next to the window looking out onto the road.

A man came out of the kitchen and greeted me with a wave and said, "Hola, amigo."

"Buenos dias," I said.

"Igualmente. Habla Espanol?"

"Hell no," I said.

The man laughed. He was wearing jeans and a western style work shirt which was buttoned up halfway. He had a white t-shirt on underneath it. He had on snakeskin boots and a large gold belt buckle. He had short black hair and a finely trimmed goatee and he looked like an extra from a Sam Peckinpah movie.

"Can I get you something to drink?" he said.

"I'll have the biggest, baddest beer you got," I said.

He smiled. "How about a thirty six ounce Dos Equis?" he said.

"You don't have anything bigger than that?" I said.

"You could order another one after you drink it."

I nodded.

"Chips and salsa?" he said.

"Sure," I said.

I looked around the restaurant. There were various soccer posters, a Mexican flag, and a large sombrero mounted on the wall. On the far wall was a mural painted by a talentless artist that I guessed was supposed to depict the Mayan pyramids. Or it could have been the Aztecs. I didn't know. I could never keep those two straight. All I remembered about them from history class was that they used to play soccer against each other and the winners got to decapitate the losers. The man returned with a giant glass of beer with a lime wedge attached to the rim of the glass. The glass had been frozen in the freezer and the beer was so cold that the foam had flakes of ice in it. I squeezed some lime juice into the beer and then set the lime wedge aside and took a drink of the beer.

"You ready to order or you need a minute or two?" the man said.

"I may need a minute or two," I said.

"Take your time."

"You the only one here today?"

He shrugged. "Waitress called in sick," he said.

"You own this place?"

He nodded. "With my brothers," he said.

"What's your name?" I said.

"Tino," he said.

He put his hand out and I shook it. "Egan," I said. "How long you been here, Tino?"

He thought about it for a second. "About six, almost seven years now."

"Where you from?"

"Atemajac. It's a town in Jalisco. Near Guadalajara."

"Jalico?"

"Yes. Jalisco."

"I hear it's nice down there. You've got the beach and the mountains. Kind of like North Carolina," I said.

"Yes," he said. "Jalisco is the heart of Mexico. We invented mariachi and tequila."

"That's something to be proud of," I said.

"Very much, my friend," he said.

"I hope you don't take offense to me asking, but how's business around here these days?" I said.

"Business is good," he said.

I gave him a suspicious look. "Doesn't look too good," I said.

"You know how it goes. Sometimes we are busy, sometimes not so much."

"How long you been speaking English?" I said.

"Since I came here," he said. "For me, to learn English, it was nothing."

I took a drink of my beer and leaned my back against the window and propped my legs up on the booth and reclined. "It's amazing," I said. "You guys cross the Rio Grande and you're speaking English in no time. I had four years of Spanish in high school and the only Spanish words I can remember are hola, amigo, cerveza, and adios."

He laughed. "I guess you do what you have to do," he said.

"Tell me," I said. "You get any of that cartel violence down in Jalisco?"

"In Jalisco?"

"Yeah. All the shit you see on the news with the beheadings and the kidnappings," I said.

"There are some places you should not go," he said.

"Jalisco's not one of them?"

"No. Jalisco is nice."

"No cartel down there?"

He smiled a little and shook his head. "Cartel is wherever cartel wants to be," he said.

"Of course," I said. "They're businessmen. They go wherever there's business. Which is why they've come here."

He looked at me for a long moment and said, "You police?"

I shook my head. "I'm the opposite of police," I said.

"You ask a lot of questions for someone who is not police."

"I'm a student of human nature," I said.

"That is not a job," he said.

"It ought to be."

I took another long drink of beer. "I like to talk in hypotheticals," I said. "You know what hypotheticals are?"

"Yes," he said.

"Suppose a businessman sets up a business in a place where he knows there's a steady demand for his product and he needs someone to make sure everything stays quiet and runs smoothly, that'd be a smart thing to do, wouldn't you say?"

"I would say that would be a very smart thing to do," he said. "A smart businessman wants things to be predictable. He wants things to work in a logical way."

"Exactly," I said. "When these become unpredictable, business gets interrupted, everything gets all fucked up, and that's no good, right?"

"That is true."

"In your country, how does the cartel deal with the police?"

"In my country?"

"Yes."

"They pay them money or they kill them. They kill them until the police becomes somebody who will take their money."

"And competitors?"

"That's where you have the wars, my friend."

"Because there can only be one cartel, right?" I said.

"For a short time, maybe two. But for a long time, there can be only one."

"You know what cartel means?" I said.

He looked at me like I'd asked him to solve a riddle.

"A cartel is a syndicate," I said. "It's like a trust or a partnership. It's a group of men coming together and sharing one common cause. In our hypothetical, that cause is to make money."

"Yes," he said. "That is why things need to be reliable."

"I take it you're in pretty good with folks around here?" I said.

"What do you mean?"

"You're friends with a lot of the local Mexicans, aren't you?"

"Yes," he said.

"What do you know about police breaking into people's houses and robbing them?"

He took a step back. "I thought you said you were not police."

"I'm not," I said.

"Then why are you asking about that?"

I put my hand up and said, "I get it. It seems strange to you, me asking these questions like this?"

He nodded.

"You want to know what I want?" I said.

"Yes," he said. "You know a man better if you know what he wants and what the value of that thing is."

"What kind of value would you put on revenge?" I said.

"Revenge?"

"Yes. Revenge."

"Revenge is not a thing with a value," he said. "Revenge is a thing outside of things which have value."

"So what's it worth?"

"Revenge is worth nothing if it is something you are trying to buy or sell because it has no value to other people. But to the person seeking it, it is worth everything."

"Exactly," I said. "So what do you know about cops robbing illegals?"

He looked around the parking lot and then slid into the booth across from me. He put his elbows up on the table and laced his hands together. "What does a sheep want out of life?" he said.

"A sheep?" I said.

"Yes. A sheep."

"A sheep wants to eat grass and get fat and be happy," I said.

"Yes. That is all a sheep wants," he said. "But there is a price for everything. And the price a sheep pays to live in a world with grass and happiness is to know that there is also a thing called a wolf. And a wolf will sometimes come out of the forest and eat a sheep. What can the sheep do except for try to not be eaten by the wolf?"

I nodded and drank some more beer. The beer was cold and smooth and I wasn't even halfway through my glass and already I felt a nice warm buzz seeping through my body.

"That wolf wouldn't mess with a bigger wolf, would he?" I said.

"Not if he was a smart wolf."

"So in our hypothetical world here, have you heard of any wolves visiting any sheep with friends that are bigger than the wolf?"

He grinned and shook his head no. "Everybody think he is a badass," he said. "Until the real badass arrives."

"The wolf would have to know who the sheep's friends are to be sure, wouldn't he?" I said.

"Yes. Or he would have to be very lucky," he said. "But a wolf has no luck. That is why he is a wolf."

"So they're just hitting poor guys who work for cash?" I said.

He nodded.

"And guys who think they're wolves but are really just sheep?"

He nodded again.

"Where is there to complain?" he said.

"You know a guy named Bernard Little?" I said.

He smiled and gave me a knowing look. "You are a smart man," he said. "So I will not insult you. But some things are beyond discussions between men such as us, even if those discussions happen entirely in a hypothetical world that bears no resemblance to our own."

"I understand," I said.

We sat there in silence for a moment and then he turned his body sideways in the booth and looked up at the TV.

"You a futbol fan?" I said.

"Yes," he said. "Futbol and boxing."

"Boxing, huh?"

"Yes. Boxing is very popular in Mexico."

"You must know about Canelo Alvarez," I said. "He's from Jalisco."

He smiled. "I know about him very much," he said.

"You ever hear about Ray Marks?"

"Oh yes. The Bull City Wrecking Ball."

"You seen him fight?"

"Yes. Several times. I was hoping to see him fight Eduardo Hernandez. He is from Guadalajara too."

"You heard about the murder?"

"Yes. Very sad. She seemed like a very nice girl."

"Very sad," I said.

He looked at my glass, which was almost empty now. "Would you like another beer?" he said.

"Mas cerveza, por favor," I said.

CHAPTER THIRTY-SEVEN

I FOUND Eric Bain sitting in the back left corner of the Pinhook drinking a draft beer. He raised his glass to me when he saw me. I gestured to the bartender and pointed to Eric's drink and he nodded and poured me one and gave it to the waitress to bring over to me.

"I thought you were a dead man," Eric said.

"I'm unkillable," I said.

Eric was wearing a blue dress shirt and he had his sleeves rolled up and had unbuttoned the top button of his shirt and wore his tie loose around his neck.

"At least the guy who shot you did the right thing and skipped town," he said.

"Can you keep a secret?" I said.

He looked at me like I'd just insulted him. "What do you think, motherfucker?" he said.

"I'm not so sure it was him."

"What do you mean?"

I leaned forward. "I know you know what off the record means," I said. "But what I'm about to tell you is way, way, way off the fucking record."

Eric's eyes got big. He just said, "Fuck."

"I got some questions for you and I got some information," I said. "But I don't want anybody to know I'm asking you these questions or telling you any of this shit until I know more about it."

Eric finished his beer and rubbed his eyes. "Go ahead," he said. "And don't worry. I'm used to knowing shit and not being able to write about it by now."

I took a drink of my beer and pushed my chair closer. He saw me wince in pain and said, "You okay?"

"I'm okay," I said.

"Your boss could probably sue Bushmaster. Get you some money for that. Lawsuits against gun manufacturers are all the rage these days."

"I'm not the litigious type," I said.

Eric looked over my shoulder to make sure no one was close enough to hear our conversation. "I feel guilty sitting here with you," he said.

"Why?"

"I still feel like it's my fault you got fired."

"I'm a grown ass man," I said. "I'm responsible for my own decisions."

"Still."

"Well here's your chance to make it up to me then."

"What do you need?"

"I figured you have everybody's number."

"I don't know anybody's number," he said. "But I got a bunch of them saved in here." He took out his cell phone.

I reached into my coat pocket and took out a piece of paper and unfolded it. "Try this one," I said, pointing to a number in the call log.

He started punching the numbers into his phone. "This is a joke, right?" he said.

"No joke," I said.

"That's the mayor's personal cell number."

"I know. You talk to him much?"

"I talk to him whenever I need to talk to him."

"Is that what I think it is?" he said.

"Yeah."

"So she got calls from him?"

"That's what it looks like."

"How many times did he call her?"

"Several."

"That doesn't strike me as that unusual."

"How about this number?"

He dialed it into his phone. "That's Jaggers' personal cell," he said.

"How about this one?" I showed him the mystery number.

"Nope. Don't have that one," he said.

"That one's a burner," I said. "It's a pre-paid phone that somebody bought with cash. They paid cash for cards to add minutes to it too. But look here. She talks to the mayor and the police chief several times. In Jaggers' case, it's more than several. Then the calls suddenly stop. Then this number starts calling her. And it starts calling her more and more. It calls her at 8:06 on the night she died."

"You think it might be one of them?"

"I think it's an odd coincidence."

"Have you tried calling that number?"

"Goes straight to voicemail. No voice on the voicemail. It's probably in a landfill by now."

"Was she working on any City Hall stories? I know you've already checked into that."

"Not that I can tell. She'd done a story on the fire over in Crown Point and a feature on a Southern Durham classroom that was doing project based learning. According to her boss, she was supposed to be working on a piece about a new development near the DPAC."

He nodded and said, "Anything else?"

"She was also pushing her bosses to do a feature series on the influx of illegals. She was calling it Living in the Shadows."

"They spiked it?"

"Said there was no local news hook."

"I hear things from over there that might be newsworthy, but I don't have anything good on that shit either," Eric said.

"You hear anything about the cops doing warrantless searches of Mexicans and robbing them?"

"I've heard those rumors, but that's all they are at this point," he said. "Nobody will go on the record. But you know how it goes. Rumors don't come from nowhere."

"You think there's anything to it?"

"Yes," he said.

"What makes you say that?"

"I've gone down there and talked to some of them. I can't print any of this, but I think there's a detective unit busting into their homes and stealing cash and possibly drugs."

"You got any names?"

"What do you think?

"Let's hear them."

"You didn't hear any of this shit from me."

"Of course not."

"I've heard Fields and Hampton mostly. I've also heard Mark Jester's name and Richie Hunter's name come up. Jaggers should never have made those guys detectives."

"You find any paper trail?"

"Nothing. I've talked to people who say their houses were raided and their money taken, but there's no search warrants in any file I can find. And none of those people want their names in print. I even heard they found a couple kilos of coke on this guy, but there's no arrest record and no court date in the system."

"How much money do you think there'd be in that racket?"

"I don't know," Eric said. "These Mexicans, they work for cash. They don't have driver's licenses or bank accounts. Even the honest ones probably have ten, twenty grand under their mattresses. The ones dealing dope probably have ten times that."

"So you're hearing the names of four guys in Major Crimes? Any other guys from Major Crimes or Vice?"

"I don't have to tell you how it works over there," he said. "It's hard to tell who knows what because nobody will talk on anybody else. Now that you're gone, anyway. Besides, I haven't asked them. I don't have enough to go over there and ask questions that they would take as serious fucking accusations."

He took a drink of his beer.

"They hate your ass, by the way," he said.

"Yeah," I said. "You hear them say anything about me lately?"

"Just that you're an asshole."

"So," he said. "How many times did your mystery man and Rose call each other?"

"Sixty two times."

Eric looked stunned. "Sixty two times?"

"That's what the logs show."

"What times, typically?"

"Early morning. Late afternoon. Evenings when she wasn't on the air."

"Jesus," he said. "What if it was Goolsby or Jaggers?"

"That'd be interesting, wouldn't it?" I said. "The calls from their cell phones can be explained. They were just returning a reporter's calls. Being good public servants and all that. But it would be hard to explain calling somebody twice a day when she's not interviewing you on TV. Be hard to explain to your wife if she went through your phone."

"Did she do any stories on them when the calls started coming from their cells?"

"They were at the same event for the Special Olympics that week. She had them both on air saying that the Triangle would be a good place to host the Special Olympics."

"But nothing after that?"

"No."

"But the other calls started after that?" Eric said.

"Yes. And here's the thing. She went out of her way to fuck Ray. She came back to the gym after she interviewed him and asked him out and they fucked on the second date. So we know she's not above being sexually aggressive and she's not above fucking somebody from one of her stories."

"She fucked him on the second date?"

"Yes."

"The mayor or the chief probably could have fucked her on the first date then."

"I don't know that it would have taken them that long," I said. "They're professional creeps. They probably could have fucked her in the parking lot of the Special Olympics thing."

"You talk to her friends at the station?"

"Apparently she didn't have any."

"She's been here almost two years now. She's got to be friends with somebody."

"She was cordial to the anchors but none of them so much as had a drink with her."

"That strikes me as weird."

"Her cameraman said she could be a bitch. He also said she was weirded out by a black car that was parked across the street from her townhouse when she came home from jogging one day. Said it had black windows but that she got the feeling somebody was inside watching her. That was about a week before she died. About the same time she was knocking on doors in Little Mexico."

"That could be nothing."

"It could be," I said. "But Jill saw a car matching that same description driving by her house several times right before I got shot. And the guy who cut me fled in a black Charger."

"Jesus Christ," he said.

"Yeah."

He sat back in his seat. "You know who drives black Chargers?" he said.

"Yeah."

"Fuck," Eric said. "Just fuck."

I drank some more of my beer.

"If this is what it's starting to look like, you might want to think about getting out of town," Eric said.

"I'm not going anywhere," I said. "If these assholes shot me and killed that boy to frame Ray to cover up for Goolsby or Jaggers, I'm going to bury every last fucking one of them."

"You're going down a dangerous path, my friend."

"I know," I said.

"So you've got an escalating pattern of calls that could be from the mayor or the chief," he said. "You've got the cops possibly watching Sheryl Rose and your girlfriend. You've got somebody trying to kill you. And you've got a missing pervert."

"All this started right after you printed the story about Sheryl Rose's secret Internet life and right before I talked to Goins. And here's the thing. Fields knew about it. He knew everything about it. But there's no way he could know about it unless he's listening in on my calls."

"Are you sure?"

"Sure."

"And you think the Mexican stuff is connected?"

"I think it might be," I said. "I go asking about it, I get blow-back. Sheryl Rose tries to do a story about it, she ends up dead. There's rampant rumors out there about Fields and his buddies robbing illegals. So much so that you and I have both heard them. If I was doing that, I'd sure want to stop somebody from finding out about it."

"How'd you hear about the Mexican stuff?" he said.

"I asked around," I said. "I still have some reliable snitches who will talk to me."

Eric said, "I always thought the term 'reliable snitch' was funny."

"Why's that?"

"Because cops never believe anything criminals say," he said. "Except when they're telling on other criminals."

"You'd love federal court then. You know what ghost dope is?"

"Yeah. If the public had any idea how bad it really is in there, they'd march on Washington."

"No they wouldn't."

"Why not?"

"Because everybody hates criminals," I said.

"You hear anything else?" he said.

"I hear Bernard Little has consolidated control over the co-caine and heroin trafficking business in Durham County."

"I heard that too," he said.

"If you and I both know that, you know Jaggers and Major Crimes knows it."

"Maybe somebody's protecting Bernard," Eric said. "Maybe all this is somehow connected."

"It would help explain the sudden drop in the murder rate, wouldn't it?"

I finished my beer. "None of it makes sense if you look at any one piece of it. But you put it together and it sure as hell looks like something really, really dirty is going on at City Hall. And Goins' shooting me and vanishing into thin air? Pretty unlikely, don't you think? And how convenient that they find the same Bushmaster that shot me in his closet?"

"Tell me then," he said. "What exactly do you think happened in Sheryl Rose's townhouse that night?"

"I don't know," I said.

"Give me your best guess."

"I don't think Sheryl Rose was dead when Ray left that apartment," I said. "I think somebody came by after he was gone. I think that somebody indulged her edge play fantasies and she ended up dead."

"What about Stricker?"

"I don't know enough to say one way or another. But nothing surprises me in this town anymore."

"Lot's of cops have AR-15's," he said.

"Yes they do. And any cop who would try to use one in a murder sure as hell wouldn't hesitate to dump it to frame a dead man."

"You make any other enemies lately?"

"I've asked around about Bernard."

"You think it could have been him?" Eric said. "If he's got a stranglehold on the drug trade and the cops are protecting him, he could be fronting for a cartel."

"You ever heard of Los Pelones?" I said.

"No."

"They're a gang of Mexican assassins who work for the Sinaloa cartel. They shave their heads. Their name means The Bald Ones."

"You think that's who Bernard's hooked up with?" Eric said.

"Could be," I said. "Look, fuck appearances. Bernard's small time. He thinks he's a big swinging dick but that's just what his suppliers want him to think. He's a goddamn idiot and he's too stupid to know it."

Eric nodded and sipped his beer.

"They need a front man," I said. "It's a layer of insulation for them. Behind every flashy drug dealer wearing gold chains and diamond earrings is a Mexican guy living in a single wide and driving an old Ford truck. And he's the guy who knows the guy."

"What happens if Bernard gets pinched and gives that guy up?"

"Then that guy knows what the deal is. Either he keeps his mouth shut and takes life in federal prison and the cartel looks after his family or he talks and they kill his whole family and everybody he ever said hi to in Mexico."

"Is that really how it works?" Eric said.

"That's how it works," I said.

"Damn."

"You ever go into one of those Mexican restaurants on the south side?" I said.

"Maybe once or twice."

"Go over there sometime. Get a Dos Equis and sit there and look around. If you go in at lunchtime, they're empty. If you go in at dinner time, they're empty. On a good day, there's maybe two or three booths with people in them."

"You think they're money laundering operations?"

"Got to be," I said.

"You think Sinaloa is behind it?"

"Either them or the Zetas. They're the ones fighting the war over the smuggling routes. But last I heard, Sinaloa runs the traffic up this way."

"You don't think they shot you?" he said.

"I doubt it. I'd be dead right now if it was them. All of those dead bodies down in Juarez? They've had a lot of practice killing people. They've gotten pretty damn good at it by now."

"If it wasn't them and it wasn't Vincent Goins and it wasn't Bernard Little, it had to be somebody on the force," Eric said.

"My thoughts exactly."

"Doesn't it concern you that they might try again?"

"The thought has crossed my mind," I said.

"Damn, Egan," he said. "Just fucking damn."

"So what's next?"

"I got a plan," I said.

"Tell me about it."

"I can't right now. I'll tell you when I can."

"Fuck. See? This is what kills me. Nothing sucks more than knowing something and not being able to write a goddamn thing about it."

"When I can, I'll give you an exclusive. How's that? Until then, don't say shit to nobody. Deal?"

"You know me," he said. "Deal."

CHAPTER THIRTY-EIGHT

I WAS BACK at the Pinhook at two o'clock the next day meeting Judge Jackie Privette. She was wearing a red dress and her brown hair was hanging neatly around her shoulders. She looked fantastic. She was a certified rising star in the Democratic Party. She had graduated with high honors from Duke Law School, prosecuted drug dealers and murderers as an assistant DA, and had made a name for herself in private practice at a prestigious downtown firm before getting herself elected to the District Court bench all before her thirty third birthday.

But Jackie and I shared a secret. During her undergrad years at Duke, she had worked as a high class call girl for an escort service that catered to wealthy individuals. She had traveled all over the country to meet rich men and tend to their needs, so to speak. I was in Vice then and I caught her in a sting at the Marriott in which I pretended to be a wealthy cardiologist.

She was a smart girl, though, and she knew how to protect herself and her ambitions. She told me about the operation and offered to cooperate before I could even put her name in the system.

Since the operation spanned multiple states, I ended up taking it to the FBI and they set up multiple stings in multiple cities. Jackie never even had to testify and was never charged with any crime, while the people who ran the escort service got ten years each for conspiracy to commit human trafficking.

I never told anybody about it and Jackie and I had been friends ever since. I never had anything against working girls. George Carlin once said that selling is legal and fucking is legal and that therefore selling fucking should be legal. And I agreed with that. I had seen girls mistreated and extorted by pimps and almost all of them were forced into it because they couldn't do anything else or because they had addictions to feed. But I never saw how locking them up and stigmatizing them helped them out much.

I was drinking a Blue Moon when Jackie walked in and took a seat across from me at the table. She ordered a sweet tea and a Reuben sandwich.

"You done with court for the day?" I said.

"All done," she said.

"God, you District Court judges have it tough," I said. "A hundred and twenty five grand a year to do, what, twenty hours of thankless work every week?"

She laughed. "Beats practicing law," she said.

"You have any good ones today?"

"Had a couple DWI trials. Did a felony plea on possession with intent to sell or deliver marijuana."

"That's a shame," I said.

"I don't make the laws," she said. "I wish I did."

"You probably will someday."

She smiled. "A girl can hope," she said.

"Seriously, what's next for you?"

She sipped her tea through a straw and used the straw to stir the crushed ice in the glass.

"There's a rumor that Judge Watson might retire when his term is up in two years," she said.

"Superior Court," I said. "That's logical. I'd rather see you as the next DA. The one we got now sucks."

"We can't seem to keep them for very long," she said. "They indict innocent people and make us a national laughingstock. Then they go nuts and accuse judges of having, what was it, oh yeah, 'The reprobate mind of a monarch,' and have to be removed from office."

"I always liked that line," I said. "The reprobate mind of a monarch. Who puts that shit in a court pleading?"

"A crazy person, that's who," she said.

"That's why we need you," I said. "But I know you got your mind on things bigger than Durham."

"You never know."

"You still go to a lot of the Democratic functions, don't you?" I said.

"Oh yeah. You have to pay your dues."

I leaned in. "I need a favor," I said. "And I need it done very discreetly."

"Oh, for Christ's sake, Egan," she said.

"You know I wouldn't ask you if I could do it any other way."

"What is it?"

"You see the mayor at those functions?"

She nodded. "Usually."

"He still smoke Winstons?"

"Yes, but not in public."

"None of y'all do anything in public, do you?"

"I'd be drinking with you right now if we did," she said. "That's one of the things that sucks about being a judge. I can't have somebody I just put on probation for DWI coming in here and seeing me drinking a martini."

"He still smokes them in private though, doesn't he?"

"Oh yeah. Still smokes. Still cusses. Still drinks like a fish."

"I need you to get me one of his cigarette butts," I said.

She looked at me like I was crazy.

"What are you up to?" she said.

"I can't tell you," I said. "But trust me when I say it's important."

"I don't like the sound of this."

"Your name will stay out of it. Nobody will ever know you did it."

"You promise me?"

"I promise you."

"A cigarette butt?'

"Yeah. I need it preserved in a plastic bag. You could just sneak one out of the ashtray when the opportunity presents itself. A straw from a drink would work too."

"You gotta tell me what's going on."

"I don't know what's going on," I said. "I'm working a couple of angles on something and I just need it to rule some things out. That's all I can tell you right now. Can you do that for me?"

"You better not burn me on this," she said.

"Have I ever burned you before?"

"No."

"You'll do it then?"

"I'll see what I can do."

"All you'd have to do is pick up a cigarette butt or a straw."

"That sounds easy enough."

"Just don't let anybody see you."

"I'll be careful," she said.

"Thank you," I said. "I'll be in touch."

I got up to leave.

"You be good," she said. "I don't want to read your obituary in the paper."

CHAPTER THIRTY-NINE

JILL GOT to my apartment a little after seven. She was wearing jeans and a black t-shirt. She had her hair pulled back in a ponytail. I went to kiss her and she stopped me.

"Ellen called me on my way over here and told me to tell you to call her."

"Why?"

"I don't know. She just said to call."

I picked up the phone and called her and she answered on the third ring.

"Ellen?" I said.

"Yeah, John, it's me."

"Jill said. . ."

"I'm sorry, John," she said. "I've got some bad news for you."

"What kind of bad news?" I said.

"In preparing for my testimony, I ran the tests again. I still think there's a second profile, but I'm not sure. The second allele wasn't as pronounced as I thought."

"What does that mean?" I said.

"It means the SBI may well be right. We might be looking at a single contributor."

"Fuck," I said.

"I'm sorry, John."

I sighed. "I appreciate all your help," I said.

I went into the bedroom and got my Glock and clipped it onto the left side of my belt in a paddle holster and tucked the .38 snub nose into the small of my back and put on my coat to hide the guns. I looked at Jill. "Come on," I said.

"Where are we going?"

"Just come on."

She had a scared look on her face. "Please," I said. "Please. Trust me, just come on."

I reached out and took her hand and she followed me out to my truck. We got in and I drove out on Fayetteville Road and doubled back to 98 to make sure nobody was following me, then I turned around and took a back road to I-40 and drove to the sprawling campus that housed BioSolutions. The parking lot was empty except for a few cars. I parked right in front of the main entrance and texted Ellen: "What was the name of that Chinese restaurant again? Me and Jill were thinking of going there for dinner."

Two minutes later, Ellen appeared at the door and unlocked it and let us in. She had a nervous look on her face. "Were you followed?" she said.

"No," I said.

"You sure?"

"Pretty sure."

"What do you got for me?" I said.

"I got a match," she said.

I closed my eyes and opened them and said: "A match?"

"All the protein ladders line up," she said. "It's him."

"Jesus fucking Christ," I said.

"Follow me," she said.

We followed her back to her lab and she nervously rifled through the slides. "Look at this," she said. She held two printouts showing a series of DNA markers. "This is the source sample," she said. "This is sample number one. No match."

I looked at it and could see that the protein ladders were white and gray and black in different places. She put down sample one and picked up sample two. "See," she said. "No match." "Sample three, no match." "Sample four, no match."

"But," she said, "look at this one."

She put the sheet showing the source code down on the table and placed a sheet next to it showing sample number five. All the markers lined up perfectly. The DNA from both samples came from the same person.

Ellen looked up at me. "You want to tell me who this guy is?" she said.

"I don't have time right now," I said.

I picked up the phone and called Nikki. "Hey girl," I said.

"How you doing, baby?" she said.

"Missing you," I said.

"I'm missing on you too," she said.

"I thought maybe we could maybe get together tonight if you're not busy," I said.

She laughed. "The girlfriend working late in the lab?"

"Yeah," I said. "What she don't know won't hurt her."

"Same place?" she said.

"Same place," I said. "How close are you to the Econo Lodge?"

"Bout fifteen minutes," she said. "I'm just getting my hair done."

"I'll see you when you get there," I said. "Call me and I'll give you the room number. You want me to stop by the liquor store?"

"You know it, baby."

"Absolut?"

"Absolut anything, baby."

"You got it."

I hung up. "Come on," I said. "Both of you."
I looked at Ellen. "Bring that shit with you," I said.
"How much of it?"
"All of it," I said.
She went over to another table and picked up a box and started putting her research materials into it. I could see that her hands were shaking.

When we got to the door, I took out my Glock and held it in both hands and scanned the parking lot. "The truck's unlocked," I said. "Both of you get in. Hurry."

I watched them and continued to scan the parking lot. I ran to the truck behind them and got behind the wheel and put the gun on the dash and pulled the truck out of the parking lot and turned out of the research campus and drove up to the stoplight and turned left and followed the road until it merged onto I-40 east toward Raleigh.

I looked over at Jill and Ellen. Their faces were frozen with fear. "We're going to Garner," I said. "I've got a room for both of you there. It's in somebody else's name. You'll be safe there."

Jill was breathing heavily like she was about to have a panic attack. Finally, she said: "What the fuck is going on?"

"Sample number one is a cop named Greg Fields," I said. "You know about him. He hates my guts. Sample two is his partner. Guy named Brian Hampton. Sample three is the mayor. Sample four is me."

"Who is sample five?" Ellen said. "Jesus, what did you get me into?"

"Sample five is the police chief," I said.

Both women gasped. Jill put her head in her hands.

"There's this girl," I said. "She's the girl I just talked to on the phone. I know her from my time in Vice. She's a street girl. She helps me out sometimes. She knows about the phones. That Northgate thing was misdirection. She's getting us a room at the

Days Inn in Garner under her name. Tomorrow, I'm sending both of you away from here until I can find a way to finish this."

I looked at Jill. She was crying. She said, "But how did you. . .?"

"The chief eats lunch with all the guys from Major Crimes at least once a week over at Clyde Sill's Barbecue on Dawson Street," I said. "They've been going there for years. I used to go there with them. Nikki got a job there waitressing. When she cleaned up their glasses and straws, she put them in plastic bags and numbered them and brought them back to me. She called in sick the next day and never went back."

"My God," Jill said.

"What about the mayor?"

"I can't tell you how I got that," I said. "I made a promise to somebody. But you can believe it's the real deal."

"You're positive number five is the chief?" Ellen said.

"Yes," I said. "How sure are you on the match?"

She took a deep breath and breathed out slowly. "The science doesn't lie," she said.

"Any chance you're wrong?"

"Yes," she said. "There's about a one in four quadrillion chance I'm wrong."

CHAPTER FORTY

THE NEXT DAY, I took Jill and Ellen to get bagels and coffee and we sat there in the restaurant and ate without saying much of anything. Then I drove them to Enterprise and rented them a car. They got inside and I told them to get out of the state of North Carolina and wait for my call. Jill said they could go stay with her sister in Brooklyn for a few days. I stood outside the car and spoke to them through the open window on the driver's side. I tried to lean in to kiss Jill but she pulled away and just stared straight ahead. I just stood there and nodded.

"Stay off your cell phones," I said. "Call your sister from a disposable phone or a pay phone. Don't tell anybody about any of this."

Jill nodded sadly. "We don't even have any clothes to change into," she said. "Do you have any idea what you're doing to us?"

"I'm sorry," I said.

"That's it?" she said. "You're sorry?"

"I don't know what else to say. It's not safe for you right now."

"What are you going to do?"

"I'm going to put this stuff together and take it to the Feds," I said.

"You think they'll take the case?"

"I sure hope so."

Jill shook her head. "I told you I wouldn't do this again," she said.

"I know," I said.

Jill sat there behind the wheel staring at the cars going past on the road. Finally, she said, "If I call you, should I pretend I'm still in town?"

"Yes," I said.

She nodded.

Ellen leaned forward and looked at me from the passenger's seat. "What do I tell the lab?" she said.

"Tell them you have the flu," I said. "Tell them it might be three or four days before you're back."

"Okay," she said.

They said goodbye and pulled out of the Enterprise lot and headed north toward I-40 east and I got back in my truck and took I-40 west toward Durham. I decided to make a little detour and passed the Durham exit and drove to Chapel Hill. I got off on the 15-501 exit and drove past the Dean Dome and took the Columbia Street exit toward the UNC campus.

I pulled into the gravel parking lot of Merritt's Country Store, which was a charmingly quaint little place famous for having the best BLT's east of the Mississippi, and decided to get a sandwich. There was a long line but it was worth the wait. I got a double BLT with pesto on toasted sourdough bread and a six pack of Shotgun Betty ale. I sat in my truck in the parking lot behind the store eating the sandwich and drinking the beer.

I thought about Jill. I could tell from the way we left it that she was probably done with me and I didn't blame her. My stubbornness had almost got me killed and put her life in serious danger.

She was a girl from a good family who had done all the right things in life. Made good grades in school, went to college and grad school, got a good job. It wasn't supposed to be like this for her.

Maybe she thought there would be some adventure in dating a guy like me, but she never imagined she'd have to deal with something like this. There was nothing I could say or do to change any of it now so it didn't matter, but I knew I'd never forgive myself if something bad happened to her.

I turned on the radio and found a station playing old Hank Williams music. I sat there and listened to the music and looked out at the woods beyond the gravel lot. I thought about the case. There were still some loose ends, but I'd done what I set out to do. I knew who killed Sheryl Rose and I knew who tried to cover it up.

I thought back to my days in the Navy. I had seen too many bad things in my life to doubt the existence of evil in the world, but I had also seen too much indifference toward those things to have much hope in there being a God. But I remembered the Bible verse we used to say before battle. It meant something to me then and it meant something to me now.

Detective work was a lonely business and it often required you to go down the dark roads that most normal people would just avoid. And you were tempted to avoid them yourself, but you knew if you didn't go, nobody would. I thought about my life coming to an end, dying for nothing, and I wondered, in that moment, whether any of this would mean anything. I said the verse to myself, and then I backed the truck out of the parking lot and turned left onto Columbia Street. I took the ramp onto 15-501 and headed back to Durham.

It had been a long time since I said the words and I thought about their meaning for the first time in years: "Then I heard the voice of the Lord saying, Whom shall I send? And who will go for us? And I said, Here am I. Send me."

CHAPTER FORTY-ONE

W HEN NIKKI got to my apartment, I let her in and told her to take a seat on the chair across from the coffee table. She looked at the couch and just said, "Shit."

On the couch I had two Colt M4 LE 6920's, a large cache of ammunition in an evidence bag, several handguns, and a stack of envelopes addressed to various places.

"Baby, whatever you're getting ready to do, I'd say don't do it," she said.

"I don't have a choice," I said.

She shook her head. "Baby, you can't be going and dying on me."

"I don't want to," I said.

She nodded and took out a cigarette and lit it. "You got an ash-tray?" she said.

I went into the kitchen and opened the cabinet and took out a plastic cup I'd saved from a UNC football game. "Here, use this," I said.

She put it on the table in front of her. "Who are those packages for?" she said.

"They're for you," I said.

"How you figure?"

"Can you do me one last favor?" I said.

"I don't got to touch none of those guns, do I?"

"No."

"Okay."

"These packages all have the same thing in them. One's addressed to the Feds. The others are going to The New York Times, The News & Observer, WRDU, The Charlotte Observer, The Washington Post, the Atlanta Journal-Constitution, the Miami Herald, the Associated Press, Fox News, and CNN. I need you to take them to the post office and mail them. Make sure you send them so they get there overnight. It'll be more expensive, but here's two hundred bucks to cover it. You can keep the change."

I gave her the money. She took it and put it in her pocket. "I can do that," she said.

I picked up one of the packets and showed it to her. Across the front I had written the word Urgent in big letters with a black magic marker. "This one doesn't go in the mail," I said. "I need you to personally deliver this to Eric Bain at The Durham Herald. You know where their office is?"

"No, but I can put it in my GPS."

"Good. Don't leave it with a receptionist. Make sure you put it in Eric's hands. Tell them it's very important. If they give you any shit, call him on his cell phone. The number's on there. He absolutely has to have it today. Make sure you tell him it's from me and that he should open it right away."

"Okay."

"Here," I said. I picked up a plastic shopping bag and put the packages inside. I left the one for Eric out and put it in Nikki's hand. I looked her in the eyes and smiled. "Thanks for all your help," I said. "I couldn't have done it without you."

"I'm worried about you, baby," she said.

"I'm worried about me too," I said.

"Maybe you shouldn't go out there."

"I shouldn't but I have to."

"I'll say a prayer for you," she said.

"That can't hurt," I said.

She kissed me on the cheek and took the packages. She opened the door and then stopped and looked back at me. "I really hope I see you again, baby. Hope we can laugh about all this over a drink someday."

"I hope so too," I said.

She closed the door behind her.

I picked up the phone and called Jill. "What are you up to?" I said.

"Just working," she said. "What's up?"

"I got them," I said.

"What?"

"Yeah. Got them cold."

"Got who?"

"Jaggers killed Sheryl Rose and I can prove it. Fields, Hampton, Jester, and Hunter are all in on it. They murdered Goins and disposed of his body. They're the ones who tried to kill me."

"Are you sure?"

"A hundred fucking percent," I said. "I can prove it too."

"Jesus Christ. What are you going to do?"

"I'm calling Jackson right now. I'm going to get him to meet me and show him what I've got. Then I'm taking him with me and we're going to the Feds. Jaggers and the rest of those sons of bitches are going to be lifting weights in Leavenworth when I'm done with them."

"Oh, Johnny," she said. "Please be careful."

"I will. Once I get this stuff to the Feds, there's not a damn thing they can do to us."

"Call me," she said. "I'm going to be worried sick until I hear back from you."

"I will," I said.

I picked up the phone and called Jackson. He answered on the second ring. "What's going on?" he said.

"Meet me at the top of the parking garage on West Main Street in twenty minutes," I said. "Can you get there?"

"I can get there. What's up?"

"I'll tell you when you get there. It's very important. You're not going to fucking believe this. We're going to have to take this to the Feds."

"Tell me now," he said.

"I don't have time. I'm still putting stuff together to bring to you. Just be there," I said.

"I'll be there," he said.

I hung up the phone and checked both the rifles and the handguns. Okay, I said to myself. Time to go make some music.

CHAPTER FORTY-TWO

WHEN I GOT to the parking garage, I drove in circles going from one level to the next until I got to the roof. The
cars thinned out the higher I went and when I got to the roof, the
deck was empty except for Jackson's truck, which was backed into a
space against the concrete barrier at the far end of the parking lot.
Jackson was leaning against the side of his truck. He was dressed
in jeans and tennis shoes and he had a Glock .40 caliber pistol in a
holster on his right side.

I backed my truck in next to his, leaving an empty space between us. I looked around and got out. I left the door to the truck
opened. I walked over to Jackson.

"Have you talked to Dever?" Jackson said

"I talked to him."

"Is he coming?"

"He'll be here."

"You want to tell me what the fuck is going on?"

I looked into the dark cave of the tunnel to see if any cars were
coming up. "You're the only cop in this city I can trust right now,"
I said.

"Whatever it is, it can't be that bad," he said.

"Roth is in hiding," I said. "So is Jill."

Jackson looked down and shook his head. "If I got shot with an AR, I wouldn't be taking any chances either," he said.

"Jaggers killed Sheryl Rose and Major Crimes is covering it up for him."

"Are you fucking crazy?"

"The second DNA sample belongs to Jaggers. Look, I don't have time to lay out the whole case right now, but I called you about this on my cell phone. I know they have an illegal wiretap on that. If I'm right, Fields and the rest of them are coming here to kill us right now. I say we kill anybody who shows up."

"Fuck," Jackson said.

I walked back to my truck and took out one of the Colts and handed it to Jackson. He pulled back the charging handle and clicked off the safety and opened the passenger door to his truck and took a position behind it, steadying the muzzle of the carbine in the jam of the door. I picked up the other M4 and chambered a round and got in the same position behind the driver's side door of my truck.

Jackson turned his head and looked at me. "How many are coming?"

"Probably Fields, Hampton, Jester, and Hunter. You know Jaggers doesn't have the balls to."

"Why the fuck are they covering for him?"

"I think it involves them robbing illegals and probably some payoff thing with Bernard Little," I said. "Those are the only things that make sense."

"What about the reporter?"

"I'm guessing that was an accident. She was into dangerous sex. Jaggers probably just went too far. But they're covering for him. So there has to be something they're protecting."

Jackson looked around. Our backs were to the concrete barrier with only our trucks to hide behind. In front of us was the descending tunnel of the parking garage and above that was a government building across the street from the parking deck that was several stories higher than the deck. It cast a shadow across half of the empty lot. Jackson said, "Could you have picked a worse spot?"

"That thing is loaded with armor piercing bullets," I said.

Jackson's eyes moved back and forth across the horizon. When he was satisfied that the periphery was clear, he stared directly into the darkness of the tunnel in front of us.

"Where are Dever and the Feds?" he said.

"They're not coming."

"Fuck," Jackson said. "Why the fuck didn't you call him?"

"I don't want to arrest these guys," I said. "I want to kill them. After all this shit, do you really want to leave it up to the courts? In this city?"

He shook his head in anger.

"I should fucking kill you," he said.

"You could do that," I said. "They'd love to have you on board. You could have your own beach house and your own fishing boat."

He took a deep breath and exhaled. He said, "How do you think they'll come at us?"

"Straight ahead," I said. "Pin us against the wall and overwhelm us with numbers."

"Why the fuck did you call me?"

"I have a plan," I said.

"Goddamn it."

We waited.

"Where did you get armor piercing bullets?" he said.

"They're from that house we searched after the SWAT team shot the crack dealer," I said. "They were already in my car. The guy was dead. I just said fuck it."

"Fuck it?" he said. "Of course you said fuck it."

"We have to shoot first," I said. "Whoever comes deserves to get it."

"That's our only chance anyway."

Jackson wiped the sweat off his forehead and leaned against the door of his truck. "I hate this city," he said. "Two crooked DA's in a row. The evidence room shit. Now the chief of fucking police."

"The regular people are still good," I said. "Some of the criminals are too."

"Yeah," he said.

"It's going to be okay," I said.

"Yeah. You got a plan."

"I do."

Jackson just shook his head.

"I took an oath to this city," he said. "To protect and to serve. Some fucking oath."

"Now is your chance to prove it," I said.

"Sons of bitches," he said. "Goddamn sons of fucking bitches."

"Work left to right," I said. "I'll work right to left. But don't worry about Fields. I got him covered."

We heard the purr of a car engine coming from one of the decks below us. It was quiet at first but grew louder and louder as it came closer. The sun was shining down on us and we looked into the tunnel across the empty parking lot. We saw a black Dodge Charger come driving slowly up the ramp and out of the tunnel. The car slowly pulled to the right side. It stopped at the far edge of the parking deck, then slowly circled around to where it was facing us from about thirty yards away.

"Come on, show yourselves," Jackson said.

Another black Charger came up the ramp and pulled around to the other side. The cars blocked both the lanes feeding the tunnel. The driver's side door on the car to the right opened and then the passenger door opened as well. The doors on the other car did the same. Fields got out of the driver's side of the car to the right and Mark Jester got out of the passenger side. Brian Hampton and Richie Hunter got out of the car to the left. All four of them were wearing Kevlar vests emblazoned with the word Police and they all had department issued M4's that they held at the low ready position. They stood behind the doors of their cars, using the doors as shields. We did the same. We stared at each other across the empty space of the parking deck. The sun was high overhead.

"Put those guns down," Fields shouted.

"I kicked your ass good in that fight," I shouted back.

"Rodney, what he's telling you is bullshit."

Jackson didn't move. Fields shouted: "Goddamn it, Rodney. Don't make us do this."

"How much money was it?" Jackson shouted.

"Rodney, it's bullshit."

"If it's bullshit, what are you doing here?"

"You guys are outnumbered," Fields shouted. "Put em down."

"No thanks," I shouted back.

I could hear Jackson breathing across the distance of the parking space between us.

"I mean it," Fields shouted. "This is your last chance."

"I mean it too," I shouted back.

Fields' head exploded and his body slammed against the door and ricocheted backward and hit the deck of the parking garage. All that remained of his thoughts and his memories, all that he knew and loved and had ever dreamed of doing evaporated in one instant into a bloody cloud and disappeared forever. His mangled body lay motionless on the concrete and blood poured out of him. The rest of them jerked their heads back to look in the direction of the explosion behind them. It was perfect. It was just like I planned.

Fields thought he had us outnumbered and cornered. It never occurred to him that he was standing right where I wanted him or that Big Ray was watching the back of his head through the scope

of a .300 Winchester Magnum from the roof of the building behind him. Big Ray would never kill a cop. But he had no problem
killing a man who was trying to frame his son for murder. And
that second principle was a little firmer than the first one. Big Ray
was right. The truly awful events in life are the ones you never see
coming.

Now Fields was dead and the game was three on three and we
had a shooter in their blind spot. Panic was an awful place to be in
a fight, but it was even worse when you were trapped in a crossfire
and your enemy had the initiative. I think Sun Tzu said that.

I sent a line of bullets tearing through Mark Jester as he turned
his head back toward us and he fell dead on the pavement. Jackson
fired on Hunter and killed him the same way. Hampton hesitated
and then ducked behind the car door. He didn't even get a shot
off. He hid behind the door of the Charger. With the windows
smashed and smoke rising from the fresh bullet holes in the doors
and the grill and the hood, it now looked like Bonnie and Clyde's
car. I could see Hampton's feet moving frantically under the door.
He had no idea where the third shooter was.

"These are armor piercing bullets and I have no idea when that
other guy might start shooting again," I shouted to him.

We waited to see what he was going to do. He really had no
choice. He dropped his rifle. "Don't kill me," he shouted to us.

Jackson came out from behind the door of his truck and started walking slowly in a crouch toward him. He had his rifle pointed
at the door of the Charger and he moved to his left to get a shot
line clear of the car door. I came out from behind the door of my
truck and followed him, moving to the right to further triangulate
the shot lines.

"Any funny shit and I'm killing you just for the hell of it," I
shouted.

Hampton shouted back: "Don't shoot me. I'm unarmed."

It was perfect for it to end like this. Fields and Jester and Hunter lying dead on the deck and Hampton hiding behind the door of a police car and begging for his life.

"Show us your hands," Jackson said.

Hampton's hands crept up slowly over the top of the car door.

"Step out from behind there," Jackson shouted.

Hampton stepped out slowly. Jackson shouted, "Walk backwards. Hands behind your head. Come toward me. Stop. Kneel. Cross your legs."

Jackson looked over at me and then took his right hand off the handguard rail of the rifle and reached for his handcuffs. He set the rifle down and walked to Hampton and cuffed his hands behind his back. He took Hampton's Glock off his belt on the right side and put it on the ground and kicked it in my direction and then patted Hampton down.

I walked up and made sure both cars were clear then walked back and stood next to Jackson. "Why did you do it?" I said.

"I'm not saying another word," he said.

"I don't see what the harm is now," I said.

"Everybody had everybody by the balls," he said.

"What was it? The Mexicans or Bernard or both?"

He just shook his head. "I want a lawyer," he said.

Jackson got on the radio and called dispatch and told them to tell Patrol that they would be getting a call about shots fired in the downtown parking garage and that he had the scene secured. I was curious to see how Patrol would respond to a crime scene with three dead cops, another cop in handcuffs, and another cop standing over them all with an assault rifle. Especially when all of those guys were Major Crimes detectives. That was a situation they never even thought to teach at the academy.

I took out my cell phone and called Special Agent Dever at the FBI. I told him what happened and told him to bring every federal law enforcement officer in area code 919 to the top of the parking deck on West Main Street.

"Tell them not to shoot us from a helicopter or anything," I said.

Jackson turned back and looked at me. He said, "Who the fuck shot Fields?"

"It was probably a drive-by shooting," I said.

"Seriously. Who was your sniper?"

"All I saw was a black man with a gun," I said. "He was about five foot ten and he weighed about a hundred and eighty five pounds."

CHAPTER FORTY-THREE

I TOOK OUT my phone and called Jill. It went straight to voice-mail. I told her I loved her and I missed her and to come back home to me.

She called me back later that afternoon and said she was sorry for missing my call, that they had gone with her sister to the movies and that her phone had been on silent.

"Tell me about it," she said.

"There's a lot to tell," I said.

"I want to hear it all."

"Just come back, okay?"

I could hear her crying on the other end. "Are you sure it's safe?" she said.

"I'm sure."

"Did the Feds take it?"

"They didn't have a choice."

"What happened? Please tell me."

"Watch the news tonight," I said.

"I'm in New York City."

"Watch it anyway."

"Really?"

"Yeah. The police chief is looking at murder and racketeering charges."

"And you're okay?"

"I've never been better."

"What about Ray?"

"Roth shouldn't have any problem getting the charges dropped now."

"So your call earlier was just to set them up?"

"Yes," I said. "And they walked right into the murder trap."

I had a bottle of Liberty Ale in my hand and I took a sip of it.

She was silent for a moment and then she said, "Did you hurt anybody?"

"We killed three cops," I said.

"You killed them?"

"Yes," I said. "They had it coming."

"Are you in trouble?"

"I don't know yet," I said. "I doubt it though."

"How are you not in trouble?"

"The right to defend yourself is the oldest right there is," I said. "When somebody tries to kill you, you have every right to plant your feet on the ground and kill them first. A murderer with a badge is still just a murderer."

"I was so scared," she said.

"I was scared too," I said.

We sat there in silence for what felt like a long time. Finally, she said, "We'll head back tomorrow."

"I'll be waiting for you when you get here," I said.

She was quiet again, and then she said, "I'm going to miss you, John. I'm really going to miss you."

"I'm going to miss you too," I said.

"We had some really good times together, didn't we?"

"Yes," I said. "We really did."

CHAPTER FORTY-FOUR

T HE NEXT TIME I saw Hampton was at the federal courthouse. He was in an interrogation room with his lawyer and
I was with Jackson and Special Agent Edmunds on the other side
of the two way mirror. Agents Dever and Glaseck were asking him
questions.

"When did this start?" Dever said.

Hampton sat there with his arms crossed and his head down.

"About a year ago," he said.

"Was that when it started or when you became involved in it?"

"When it started."

"Who in Major Crimes was involved?"

"Greg Fields. Mark Jester. Richie Hunter."

"Whose idea was it?"

"Greg said it would be easy money. He said the Mexicans
couldn't go to the cops and the deal with Bernard would bring
down the homicide rate and make us all look good. He said the
drugs would find their way into the projects one way or another

and we might as well get a cut of it. He was going to buy a boat and retire early to Florida."

"Why do you think they involved you?"

"Greg was my best friend."

"What did they tell you?"

"Greg said it'd be easy. Said the chief would come on board if we cut him in."

"Did you?"

"Yes."

"And these raids on illegals? These were all warrantless searches?"

"Yes."

"How many times did you do this?"

"I don't remember."

"Think hard."

"Dozens of times, I guess."

"What else?"

"We picked up payments from Bernard Little every few weeks. He gave us information about his competitors and we took them down. I figured we were just stopping a war from happening and making some money on the side."

"Was this so that he could be the exclusive supplier of cocaine and heroin in Durham?"

"Yes."

"How much money did Bernard Little give you?"

"I don't know. Greg always made the pickup and then gave us our share. It was a lot."

"And he directed you to his competitors?"

"He told us what they were up to and where we could find them."

"Tell me about Sheryl Rose," Dever said.

Hampton squirmed in his seat. He said, "Greg called me that night. He said the chief had been having sex with her and there was an accident and she died. He said we had to help him or he might not protect us. He said we all had to hang together or else we'd hang separately."

"How about Vincent Goins?"

"Greg and Mark did that. They killed him and weighted his body down in the Haw River. When we searched his house, Mark Jester planted the rifle there to make it look like he shot Egan."

"And you had an illegal wiretap on Egan's phone?"

Hampton nodded. "Egan, Stuart Roth, Egan's girlfriend. We got scared when they found that second DNA sample. We knew if it came back to Jaggers, we'd all be in deep shit."

Agent Dever stood up. "I've got to take a piss," he said. "You want a Coke or anything while I'm out there?"

"Yes, please."

"I'll be back in a minute."

Dever straightened his tie, pulled his pants up over his waist, and walked out of the interrogation room and into the room where we were standing.

"Nice business model," he said.

"Yes it was," I said. "Robbing illegal Mexicans. Cutting down the murder rate. Getting rich in the process."

"The shame of it is that a lot of the money they took from the Mexicans probably wasn't even drug money," Dever said. "A lot of those folks don't use banks. They work under the table for cash and they hoard it so they can send it back to their families in Mexico."

"And there's no paper trail," Jackson said. "Ever."

"Human greed is something else," I said.

"How much money you think they made?" Jackson said.

"Who knows?" Dever said. "Hundreds of thousands, I'd guess."

"Bet you'll try to put a figure on it when sentencing day comes," Jackson said.

Dever smiled. "We'll do the best we can," he said.

Jackson looked at me. "Talk about bad luck," he said. "All over one girl's sexual fantasies."

Meanwhile, Glaseck kept questioning Hampton.

"Did you ever see the chief himself take any of this money?"

"Yeah. Sometimes I was with Greg when he delivered it to him."

"Did he ever admit personal involvement in the cocaine dealings?"

"We all talked about it."

"Where did these conversations occur?"

"In his office."

"In his office?"

"Yes."

"In the police chief's office?"

"Yes."

Glaseck shook his head. He'd seen a lot of sordid things in his life, but you could tell he was struggling to wrap his mind around this.

"Did Jaggers ever say anything in your presence about the murder of Sheryl Rose?"

"No."

"What about the murder of Vincent Goins?"

"No," Hampton said. "But Greg wouldn't have done it without talking to him."

Dever patted me on the back. "I better go get that boy's Coca Cola," he said. "Where he's going, I don't know if they have Coca Cola."

I nodded.

Before he made it to the door I stopped him.

"So what now?" I said.

"Now we bring the weight of the United States government down on Jaggers," he said. "We've got him on the conspiracy and racketeering and corruption and trafficking charges. But he's got other problems besides us. The state has him on the murder charges. One way or another, he's looking at life without parole."

"So he's looking at state and federal cases?" I said.

"I expect there will be parallel prosecutions."

"The state gets him on the murder charges and you go after him on the rest?"

Dever nodded. "A police chief's head makes for a nice trophy on your wall," he said.

"What about Hampton?"

Dever shrugged. "He's got some leverage. The other three conspirators can't talk because you guys killed them. He gives us Jaggers and cooperates in the state's prosecution. That plus the DNA and fingerprints ought to be enough."

"What's Hampton get?"

"A sentence cut, probably. They'll work that out later with the U.S. Attorney. He's already said he's going to plead in and cooperate. And that's his only play here. But cooperating with us is like having sex with a gorilla. You don't decide when it's over. The gorilla does."

"What's your best guess?" I said.

"Twenty, twenty five years probably."

"How about the state charges?" Jackson said.

"The state agreed not to indict him on those if he took a plea with us."

"So they're not going to prosecute him for the murders or for shooting Egan?" Jackson said.

"They can't prove he had anything to do with the murders. As for Egan, well, sorry Egan. Cost of doing business."

"That's okay," I said.

"Okay?" Jackson said. "They tried to kill you."

"That's why I called Dever after we killed them," I said, "and not before."

I pointed to Hampton. "Besides, look at him. A crooked cop doing twenty years in the federal pen? That's going to suck big time. I almost feel sorry for him."

"I don't."

"He's like the guy in his village who was only a Nazi because everybody else was, but who got killed by the Russians just the same."

"How's that make you feel that he'll never have to face you in court? That would piss me off."

Dever looked at me for a reaction.

"I'm fine with it," I said. "If cutting a deal with him gets Ray out of jail and nails Jaggers and changes Goins' disappearance to a murder, I can live with that. Life is nothing if not a series of compromises."

"That's a very mature attitude," Dever said.

"My mama raised me right," I said.

Dever smiled and closed the door behind him.

Jackson and I stood there for a few minutes watching the interview. After awhile, I said, "What do the boys on the force think about you getting mixed up in this mess?"

Jackson put his hands in his pockets. "Most of them have been supportive," he said. "Jaggers wasn't exactly the most popular chief we ever had, you know? And the rest? Fuck em."

"What happens now?"

Jackson scratched an itch on the back of his neck. He crossed his arms and took a deep breath. He said, "There'll be a reshuffling. Various internal investigations into the who's and what's and when's. The Feds and the SBI will be up in everybody's shit. New people will be appointed. There'll be press conferences and promises of reform. All that shit. Everything will settle back down to normal eventually and life will go on."

"How about for you?"

"I'm staying in Major Crimes, man. Keep living the dream."

I walked over to the window and took a good hard look at Hampton. He seemed to sense that someone was there behind the mirror and he looked right up at the mirror, like he could see me there watching him. His eyes were the eyes of a broken man. His friends were dead and he had nothing to look forward to but suffering and fear.

"You got dinner plans tonight?" I said.

"Nope," Jackson said.

"Why don't you come have dinner at my place. It's supposed to a nice night. I was thinking about putting some steaks on the grill. Doing some sautéed spinach. Maybe making some appetizers and pulling a cork or two."

Jackson looked at me and smiled. He nodded his head. "I'd like that," he said. "I'd like that a lot. You sure your girl won't mind?"

"I'm sure," I said.

CHAPTER FORTY-FIVE

W HEN I WALKED into the Bull City Boxing Club, Max had his back to me. He was shouting instructions to Ray who was sparring with a larger fighter who I guessed was at least a super middleweight if not a light heavyweight. The man was fighting in a southpaw stance and they were wearing headgear and sixteen ounce gloves.

The opponent was crouching and moving and Ray was pawing at him and measuring him with the left jab. I watched Ray's footwork. It was amazing. His balance was perfect and no matter how the angle changed, he kept his attack funneled right at the center of his opponent's chest.

"That's it, kid," Max was yelling. "Cut off the ring. Circle to his right. Keep that left foot outside of his right foot. Straight right lead over the jab. Keep that chin tucked. Feign that right then wipe his nose with the hook."

"Shaking off the ring rust?" I said.

Max turned around.

"He's had a long layoff," he said. "Takes a while to get back into fighting shape. Give the kid some time, for fuck's sake."

"You're going to have yourself an honest to God world champion before you die, Max. A prophet told me so in a dream."

"Shove it up your Irish potato eating ass, fuck face."

"I mean it. The boy's just like his old man."

"His old man wasn't this good on his best day."

Ray circled to his opponent's right and his opponent turned, putting him in a corner. Ray covered up and bent his body forward into the man. He hooked his right elbow over the outside of his opponent's right elbow which was bent under a peek-a-boo guard. Ray pulled his arm back and the momentum spun the other fighter around and the two fighters switched places, this time with Ray on the outside trapping his opponent in the corner. It was an old veteran's trick and Ray executed it flawlessly, effortlessly.

He feigned a right to his opponent's body and threw a short left hook that landed flush and wobbled the man. Ray took a step backwards, faked like he was going to circle to the man's right, and then shot a straight right lead that connected over his opponent's jab. He used his momentum to fall into his the man, hitting him with his fist and his head at the same time and tying him up with his right arm while leaving his left arm free to fight. Ray shot two uppercuts into the man's jaw. The man fell to his knees on the canvas.

Max turned and looked back at me and said, "Remember how I said he wasn't mean enough?"

"Yeah," I said.

"We ain't got that problem no more."

ACKNOWLEDGEMENTS

I would like to thank Wendy Sherman and Clyde Edgerton for their belief in me, for their time and advice, and for connecting me with people who could help me. I would like to thank Jane Rosenman, an editor of extraordinary talent, for her friendship, encouragement, criticism, and advice. I would like to thank my Dad and the rest of my family for their patience and love and support. I would like to thank Chris Munz and Van Alston, two of the best friends a guy could ever have, for their insight and feedback and advice. Most of all, I'd like to thank Marjorie Braman for editing this novel and for sharing with me so much of her time and wisdom. Elmore Leonard once said that she was the best editor he ever had. Having worked with her, I can't imagine he'd have said anything different.

ABOUT THE AUTHOR

Ryan McKaig is a former journalist and criminal defense attorney. He lives in Raleigh, North Carolina.

Made in the USA
Lexington, KY
01 August 2016